Edgy, erotic, irresistible—
drink in this thrilling collection of vampire
fiction from some of today's hottest
African American writers.

Dark Thirst

"These sensual vampire stories should not be read alone.
Read them quickly and watch your pulse!
Dark Thirst packs quite a bite."

—Sheree Renée Thomas, award-winning editor and creator of the
Dark Matter series

"With stories ranging from the erotic to the ironic
to the outright disturbing, *Dark Thirst*
will satisfy vampire familiars everywhere."

—Tananarive Due, author of *The Living Blood* and *The Good House*

"A dark, disturbing, hauntingly unique compilation
of stories told in multiple, talented voices.
Sip slowly and savor!"

—L. A. Banks, author of the *Vampire Huntress Legend* series

Dark Thirst

THE URBAN GRIOT

DONNA HILL

MONICA JACKSON

LINDA ADDISON

KEVIN S. BROCKENBROUGH

ANGELA C. ALLEN

Edited by Angela C. Allen

POCKET BOOKS
New York London Toronto Sydney

POCKET BOOKS, a division of Simon & Schuster, Inc.
1230 Avenue of the Americas, New York, NY 10020

Library of Congress Cataloging-in-Publication Data
Dark thirst / edited by Angela C. Allen— 1st Pocket Books trade pbk. ed.
p. cm.
Contents: Introduction—The ultimate diet / Monica Jackson—Vamp noir /
Angela C. Allen—Human heat: the confessions of an addicted vampire /
The Urban Griot—Whispers during still moments / Linda Addison—The touch /
Donna Hill—The family business / Kevin S. Brockenbrough.
1. Vampires—Fiction. 2. Horror tales, American. 3. African Americans—
Fiction. 4. Short stories, American—African American authors.
I. Allen, Angela C.

PS648.V35D376 2004
813'.0873808375—dc22   2004053382

ISBN: 0-7434-9666-3

First Pocket Books trade paperback edition October 2004

1 3 5 7 9 10 8 6 4 2

POCKET BOOKS and colophon are registered trademarks
of Simon & Schuster, Inc.

Manufactured in the United States of America

For information about special discounts for bulk purchases,
please contact Simon & Schuster Special Sales at
1-800-456-6798 or business@simonandschuster.com.

Contents

Contents

Introduction

In 1865, as African American slaves were getting their first taste of freedom following the Civil War and being granted the legal right to read and write, French author Alexandre Dumas was creating a five-act play entitled *Le Vampire*. This grandson of a Haitian slave and a French aristocrat was the first black writer to pen a version of the vampire myth and, some might argue, was also the father of black horror. The play was set in Spain and predictably peopled mainly by whites—but, interestingly enough, Dumas did introduce the first dark-skinned character to appear in a vampire story, a woman he described as "Moorish" and cast in the role of a pagan witch.

The myth of the vampire had been around for centuries in as many forms as there were foreign languages, embodied in tales of fanged demons like Kali in India, stories of the shape-shifting and bloodsucking *tlahuelpuchi* of Mexico and the legends of soul-stealing witches among the Hausa tribe in Niger. In pre-colonial Africa, among the polygamous Yoruba in Nigeria, the vampire tale took the form of witch-wives. These women were described as jealous witches who secretly sucked the blood of their husbands and of the children of their other wives. The local folklore even said women could be turned into bloodsucking witches against their will if they were tricked into eating human flesh or drinking human blood.

But the vampire myth didn't take on literary life until it traveled beyond the remote villages of Transylvania in Eastern Europe and into Western Europe, where it was reborn in the deliciously decadent novels of early English horror writers, who added dark twists and turns to the supernatural legend of an undead being who haunted the living and stole their very blood.

In 1897, Bram Stoker's *Dracula* burst onto the literary scene. It was not the first vampire book, but it was to become the most well known, setting the standard for later efforts and spawning a new genre so vivid and so enthralling that other writers would follow his lead for centuries to come.

It would not be until one hundred years after Dumas that black hands would again take up the vampire torch. African American writers were diving into speculative fiction with authors like W. E. B. DuBois and George S. Schuyler giving us race-based science fiction stories like "The Comet" (1920) and "Black No More" (1931), but the field of horror seemed strangely off-limits, a segregated social club populated solely by whites. One of the first black writers to integrate the genre was Octavia E. Butler. This literary diva gave birth to "Doro," the compelling Nubian immortal and star of her Patternist series that debuted in 1976. This vampirelike character was a departure from the evil-incarnate vampire fiends created by early European authors. Instead of physical force Doro used his telepathic powers to suck his victims dry before taking over their empty bodies.

It was during the 1970s that the vampire was to undergo a renaissance, with its eerie blend of death and eroticism capturing the imagination of a new generation, thanks to creations like the Marvel Comics character "Blade," an African American superhero who was half-human and half-vampire. This period also saw the birth of Anne Rice's prolific Vampire Chronicles series and Stephen King's *Salem's Lot.* But, again, horror writers of color working in this popular genre were still out of the ordinary. Ironically, it was Hollywood, with its voracious appetite for profit, that unwittingly served as the evolutionary catalyst that transformed the traditionally pale-skinned vampire into a dark-skinned African prince. In the 1972 blaxploitation movie *Blacula,* the late actor William Marshall brought new fans to the vampire genre with his stunningly powerful portrayal of the tortured dark prince. Critics could only watch in wonder as he stole the show by bringing an unmistakable grace to every scene, breaking our hearts at the climactic end when he perishes under the glare of a red-hot sun.

A black man would not play the role of the vampire again with such commanding charisma for nearly thirty years, until Wesley Snipes slashed his way onto the big screen in 1998 as "Blade." His rippling muscles under smooth chocolate skin mesmerized audiences, while his dazzling martial arts moves brought the popular Marvel Comics hero to life and propelled the film to blockbuster status. Snipes gave the ancient Eastern European myth of the bloodthirsty vampire yet another face and gifted it with the cachet of cool.

The 1990s also brought an end to the long literary drought as groundbreaking writers of color like Jewelle Gomez gifted us with unconventional story lines that for the first time presented the vampire from an African American viewpoint. The 1991 *Gilda Stories,* about a runaway slave girl from the Mississippi Delta of the 1850s who turns vampire, once again flipped the script on the original Stoker creation. In its wake has come a rush of talented writers like Tananarive Due, Jemiah Jefferson and L. A. Banks, whose vivid imaginations gave us books like *The Living Blood, Voice of the Blood* and the übercool vampire huntress Damali Richards, bringing the vampire into the new millennium with an edgy, urban energy.

Dark Thirst aims to push the envelope still further and shatter stereotypes about the face of contemporary horror. Three of today's most popular black writers, Omar Tyree, Donna Hill and Monica Jackson, along with a few noteworthy newcomers, have stepped outside their usual genres and entered the dark world of the vampire. As you will soon see, there are few rules and no taboos. The vampires in these pages range from the traditional image of a demonic, fanged-tooth monster to the leather-wearing icon of urban cool, a sexy, fallen hero or a seductive temptress able to lure her prey with a single steamy glance.

Each of these artists has dared to enter the world of the vampire not as pale imitations of themselves, stripped of all cultural identity and reduced to cheap caricatures, but as strong African American writers who bring a new dimension to an old story, taking it above and beyond the accepted norm. In doing so, they change the definition of vampire forever.

Angela C. Allen
New York City, 2004

Dark Thirst

The Ultimate Diet

MONICA JACKSON

Desire

It was almost midnight. I wrapped my mouth around the pizza, the doughy crust mingling with the tart sauce and the salty melted cheese sliding over my tongue. Then the roof of my mouth hit the spicy pepperoni, the tangy sausage and the meaty hamburger and I rolled it all over my taste buds, my teeth working the gooey goodness.

It was something like sex, the sensation building to the point where you can't let it go . . . *Oh, don't stop, baby.* I stuffed another bite in my mouth before I swallowed the first one. My cheeks pudged out and my eyes closed. I was in pizza hog heaven. This was as close to nirvana as I got.

Shoving it in fast, I covetously counted the pieces in case my girl Angelica, or Jelly, like everybody calls her, got ahead of me and copped some of my share. Jelly jams as good as I do when it comes to food. I feel downright petite next to her. I weigh two hundred and twenty-five pounds. I know Angelica tops three hundred.

Jelly and I go way back. I met her in high school when we

3

were picked out of the projects for a math enrichment program, of all things. Nobody had ever given a shit about potential mathematical Negroes before. But some bleeding hearts had this idea to test tons of black kids and apparently Jelly and I were among the cream of the crop. They said we had high IQs and big potential. We both were surprised because you couldn't have guessed our smarts by our grades. We were run-of-the-mill fat black girls newly promoted into would-be math nerds.

We liked it because they took us all on fancy field trips and bought us stuff. We got big-time perks. It was the only reason we hung in there because the whole thing was a social drawback. It was definitely not down in an inner-city black school to be stylin' like some sort of nerd.

But Jelly and I often discussed that if it wasn't for that program, we'd probably still be in the projects with ten kids between us and less than ten dollars left out of our welfare checks each month once we'd spent for the necessities.

Now we were both computer programmers with nice homes and healthy incomes. But when you think about it, success is all relative. If we were back in the projects, we'd be getting fucked, maybe by low-life, no-working, dependent losers, but we'd at least be getting some. We'd get high when we could and we'd party when we could. We'd have friends and family and kids and we wouldn't worry too much about shit.

All we had now was each other and our jobs. We worked together in a big company, you've probably heard of it, with a bunch of white folks. White folks don't think much of fat black women. Surprise, surprise.

One thing I've noticed about white nerdy men, they worship bony white women with big tits. It ain't natural. But I don't envy white women, because most of them don't look like that.

Jelly pulled me away from my thoughts when she snorted, turned the lights off, and pulled open the window blinds. I was irritated. What could be going on outside that was important enough to interrupt my pizza groove?

"Keeshia, check out those Mexicans heaving that heavy shit like it was nothing. They're moving fast too. Where were they when I moved from my house and had to deal with those niggas leaning upside their truck and holding it upright while I was getting billed by the hour?" she demanded.

I sighed and moved to the window. Short, stocky men were unloading a moving van. I guess Jelly decided that they were Mexicans because of their small size and height. But they seemed uncommonly strong as I watched one handle a seven-foot sofa as if it were made of Styrofoam.

A classic silver VW Beetle pulled beside the van and Jelly and I both drew in a breath when we saw the woman who stepped out of it. She stood under the streetlight as if she were voguing for a magazine shoot. The light threw her ebony marble features into relief. Her hair and skin blended, both the color of black patent leather.

She turned slowly, surveying our quiet tree-lined suburban neighborhood like she owned it. She had fine, chiseled features and huge eyes, the whites standing out against the black skin like they were opals. Her hair fell almost to her waist in waves like black ocean water.

Her outfit matched her attitude. She was decked out in head-to-toe bloodred leather. To top it off, she was tiny, one of those skinny little hos with big tits and a round African ass that filled me with envy.

Suddenly, she looked straight at us. Jelly and I shrank back from the window. Her lips parted and her teeth reflected the light like pearls. I shivered.

I wondered why she was moving in at midnight. What did it

feel like to be a skinny bitch like her? Not that I was the envious type or anything. I just wondered. I stared at her through the window as she went in the house and pointed out to the movers where her heavy and expensive furniture was to go.

I suddenly felt empty, despite the sodden mass of pizza lying at the pit of my stomach. If only I could . . . I stuffed another slice of pizza in my mouth rather than finish the thought.

"There's sauce on your chin," Jelly said, holding two slices of pizza at once. I wiped at my chin.

"You still starting that Paradise Resort diet Monday with me?" I asked.

What if I could get little like that skinny heifer moving in across the way? My life would be perfect. Everything would be easy. Everyone would admire me. I wouldn't have to deal with my goddamn job and my asshole boss. . . . I'd have the man of my dreams, fuck, I'd have a man, period. Satisfaction of the sexual sort consisted only of my fantasies and the fingers of my right hand.

"Keeshia!" Jelly was saying. "I was asking you about walking."

"Walking? I walk every day, otherwise I wouldn't get from point A to point B."

Jelly sighed. "You know what I mean. Around the block, a couple of miles a day."

"That's not going to lose me any weight. I'm going to blast out on the Paradise Resort diet on Monday. Are you with me?"

"You always starting some diet, girl, and they never stick. I'm giving up on the diets. I'm going to walk and cut out the sugar and fast food. That pizza was it, I'm cooking at home from here on out," Jelly pronounced, trying to fold her arms over her girth.

I raised an eyebrow. So my obese partner in dietary trauma was giving up on me. "I ain't never going to give up," I said softly. "Whatever it takes." I meant every word.

I admit I was hungry as fuck the next week. I'd get off my job and cook up my diet crap and go into the living room and open my blinds, eating my nasty food in the dark while I watched that skinny ho eat. Every evening, a little after dark, she sat right in front of the window and *grubbed.* I do not exaggerate the word. The bitch ate full-course meals with wine, soup and the works. She ate steak one night, rare. Slurped up lasagna the next. Ate what looked like veal on Wednesday, tender and babyish, covered with cheese. Then she munched on leg of lamb with new potatoes. Friday, she sat down to crispy fried catfish.

I had enough. I pushed my plate of rabbit food and tasteless dry chicken breast away and marched my fat ass to her apartment. I carried a cup and fork like they were weapons. I do admit that I sincerely wanted to stick the fork in her small, shapely, overeating ass. It wasn't fair.

I punched at her doorbell with a stiff finger. She opened the door fast, like she was standing on the other side waiting for me. I jumped back and blinked. Then I noticed that the skinny bitch looked better close up than she did far away. It wasn't fair.

"Can I help you?" she asked.

She had some sort of strange accent.

"Hi, I'm Keeshia and I live over there." I gestured to my apartment across the parking lot. "Welcome to the neighborhood." I handed her the fork. She stared at it. "It's a collector's item," I said.

"Oh," she said.

Then I held out the cup. "I wondered if I could borrow some sugar."

"I'm sorry, but I have none. I'm not much into baking or

sweet things." She had this cute crooked smile with gleaming white perfect teeth. Then, without an ounce of shame, she dropped the fork in the trash can. I had said it was a collector's item!

"Won't you come in?" she asked.

The hell with the fork. I didn't hesitate to step inside her apartment. The door closed behind me with a swish and a thud. I noticed the sound because the coreless doors of my apartment don't close with such finality.

My thoughts turned again to her skinny body. Maybe she was on some exotic diet I hadn't heard about yet. Something like that grub-down-at-dinner-only diet. But I'd tried that one with the ever-burning hope that it would be different. I'd gained weight on it.

I settled down on her overstuffed couch. She pulled the drapes to her big picture window and sank down next to me. I studied the table, still filled with mounds of golden catfish and fried potatoes exquisitely sliced to thin crispy perfection. The coleslaw looked as if it were confetti and gleamed with mayonnaise. My mouth watered.

"Would you like to eat?" she asked.

I averted my eyes, realizing that I'd been staring. I mumbled no, the word almost unintelligible.

"Maybe later," she said.

I noticed her scent. It unsettled me, made me feel strange. It smelled better than the aroma from her table. I leaned toward her and caught myself almost reaching for her. I jerked back as if I'd touched hot coals. Shit, I was going to . . . touch her. Wanted to touch her. Like she was a man. And there wasn't a thing male about her. It was crazy. I curled my fingers and stuck my hands in my pockets, not a graceful move since I was sitting. I sucked in a breath.

"My name is Sofia," she said, her voice breaking the silence like cream pouring into coffee.

"Where are you from?" I asked, relieved to have a distraction from my confusing reaction to her.

"Originally from eastern Africa," she replied.

"Kenya?"

"No, I'm from a kingdom closer to what is now Ethiopia."

Kingdom? I didn't know of any kingdoms in present-day Africa, but I let it ride. My brain oozed slow-motion-style around my chaotic emotions, but my mouth kept running. "I'm trying to lose weight and I noticed how you're in great shape," I nattered, all perky like a white girl in a TV commercial. "I wondered if you'd let me in on your secret."

She smiled at me and leaned closer. My mouth went dry. "You want to know my secret?" she whispered.

I tried to focus my suddenly fuzzy vision on her ruby lips, bloodred. Juicy. I felt the beginnings of moisture between my legs, a hot sweetness tingling and spreading.

Her sexy smile widened, her white teeth gleaming in the golden lamplight.

She moved closer and I felt my nipples harden. When I realized that her face was moving toward mine like she was going to kiss me, a rush of excitement mixed with astonishment flooded through me.

Now realize that my sexual fantasies have always centered around the concept of a big, hard cock. I loved the idea of a hot dick shoving up into me, pounding my pussy. This lesbian shit was tripping me out.

"Keesh, girl, you in there?" I heard Jelly's voice yell through the door and I swear I almost cried in relief.

"Yeah, I'm coming," I yelled, and I was off that sofa and to the door before you could say jackshit on a cat. I didn't look back. I was afraid to.

"How did you know I was in there?" I asked her as I shut the door behind me, panting slightly.

"You left your door open, your food half-eaten on the table

and the house was dark, the window open. Not to mention I could see you two sitting there from your living room window. You've been going on and on about how that woman eats, so it wasn't hard to figure out where you could be. So what's she like?"

I swallowed hard. "Garden-variety skinny bitch," I said, but I was lying. I just didn't want Jelly to talk about her anymore. Because then I'd have to wonder why I wanted to go back and find out how her lips would feel against mine.

After Jelly left, I couldn't stop thinking about Sofia and, worse, I couldn't stop watching her. The next night this fly white boy went to her apartment. They ate a bloody rare steak together, and he touched her constantly. I imagined the outline of his hard dick through his jeans. I know he wanted her. How could he help it? Then she pulled the blinds, but there was this small sliver of golden light trickling through.

I couldn't help myself. I put on black sweatpants and a black sweatshirt and I crept outside, easing into the bushes outside her apartment. I crept along the walls, the shrubs tearing at my skin. I rubbed my hand across wetness trickling down my cheek. I thought it was sweat and I was surprised to see my hand come away red with blood.

When I finally peeked through the opening of her heavy drapes, I saw Sofia naked on the sofa, splayed out. Perfect, she was perfect, every inch of her gleaming black skin flawless. Her breasts round and firm with hard, black nipples, the black areolas blending into the darkness of her skin. Her muscles flexed under her skin like a panther, and her glossy black pussy hairs were neatly trimmed.

The white boy was worshipping her body. He'd taken off his shirt and I could see the sweat trickling down his back. His pink tongue trailed down her taut belly to her pussy. His eyes were closed. He knew what he was doing, his tongue holding a rhythmic dancing beat, right next to her clit. Her head was thrown back in ecstasy, her neck and back arched.

My fingers crept inside my sweatpants and under my panties to work in rhythm with his tongue. I was close to coming when he suddenly stood up and pulled off his jeans. His dick sprang free, pink and engorged. He moved on top of her in one motion and drove his dick deep into her pussy. I came in hard jolts when I saw her mouth move with the cry of her pleasure as he shoved his hard, pink dick in and out of her slick pink cunt edged in blackness.

When I looked up again, she was burying her face against his neck. I gasped as I saw redness seep from around her lips. Then she opened her eyes and looked straight at me. I dropped down into the bushes and scrambled away, barely getting my sweatpants back up over my ass.

Back in my apartment, I stared at my hand. Blood, blood? White boy blood oozing from under Sofia's lips. Her knowing glance up at me. Fuck, I was more scared than a lobster staring down at a boiling pot. I locked all the doors and checked the windows.

I never thought much about weird shit like monsters or ghosts. Horror flicks had never been my thing because the black guy usually dies first. When black folks started getting some play in scary movies as the big-bad, I knew we'd arrived and my interest picked up a touch. But I never dreamed that shit could be for real.

Maybe the blood on Sofia's lips was my overactive imagination. But I remembered her hypnotic hot attraction. Her too-white teeth. And I wasn't the imaginative type.

I suppressed a shudder.

But being scared for too long isn't my style. I rummaged in the kitchen and found some macaroni stuck in the back of a cabinet, boiled it up and made some from-scratch mac-and-cheese. Then I booted up my computer and signed on to the Internet while I chowed down straight from the pot. The diet was history. What was important was what the fuck did I know about vampires? Not bloody much.

Idea

"She bit him on the neck, I swear," I told Jelly the following evening. For some reason I really needed her to understand. The shit was getting to me. Jelly always had my back and I needed her now. In many ways, Jelly was the sister I never had.

Jelly sighed and rearranged her bulk. "Maybe it was some kinky sex thing. This vampire stuff . . . it's not like you. You're trippin', girl. That Paradise Resort diet must be getting to you."

I didn't want to admit the diet was history. "It's not the diet." I tore a napkin to shreds on the end table until it was tiny pieces of white confetti, and then cursed when I sneezed and they drifted to the floor. "I'm afraid to leave my house after dark," I near-whispered.

Jelly's right eyebrow raised. "All because of that heifer that moved in across the street?"

I nodded. "She knows."

"Knows what? That you're too big to be crawling around the bushes like a cat burglar? If she has the balls to fuck somebody in front of an open window, she probably doesn't give a shit."

Jelly was right. What was I afraid of? Then I thought about that studly white boy, her mouth on his neck, and the blood seeping between them. Yeah, I didn't have a damn thing to be afraid of, other than getting killed and eaten.

"What if I'm right?" I asked Jelly. "What if she is a vampire? I'm probably high on her menu. Think of how juicy I am," I said, patting my belly.

Jelly laughed, "Yeah, you're mighty juicy."

"But vampires are limited," I reminded myself. "They only operate at night and you have to be out then and allow yourself to be isolated."

"I know of several ladies who mainly operate at night in the style you describe, and they're not vampires," Jelly said. She shook her head. "There ain't nothing scary about a ho, unless you're spending money on her skanky ass."

Jelly wasn't going to believe me easily, so I dropped the subject. Something in me felt abandoned and a little hurt. Maybe a little angry. Jelly cooked, since she wasn't into fast food or eating out anymore. We ate baked chicken with a decent taste to it, baked potatoes and green beans seasoned with ham and watched TV until darkness fell. I looked out for her as she went to her car. Jelly was juicier than me and the only friend I had.

But I couldn't stop watching Sofia. She had visitors, several a week. Young, beautiful people, both men and women of all races. The interesting thing was that when they went in, few of them came back out. I was too scared to crawl back and peek through her window. But I knew what she was doing, fucking and eating, and fucking and eating some more.

I decided to do some more research and check out the missing-person list online. I checked the stats and it was no longer the usual. People disappear all the time. My eyes scanned the photographs and I didn't even gasp when I saw the white boy's picture. I knew it would be there.

"Why you keep talking about that ho?" Jelly said to me the next night when I went over to her place. She had a touch of her namesake spread over a slice of high-protein bread instead of her customary jelly doughnut. But I wasn't worried about her losing weight and becoming thinner than me. She wasn't going about it right. Everybody knew you had to diet to lose weight and Jelly refused to diet. She kept up with walking around for no good purpose and she didn't eat the sweets she used to, unless it was a small dessert.

"That woman hasn't done anything to you. You're just jealous," Jelly accused.

I started to say that I wasn't jealous, but I pulled up. It wasn't true. I was slime-green jealous of that fine bitch with her dog-in-heat scent and all the rich food, hard dick and hot pussy she could handle.

I always thought I was one hundred percent straight, but lately my dreams had the scent of women in them, along with a certain soft wetness. I'd wake up with my fingers in my own pussy, my fingers working fast and hard as I came.

Did she get to stay alive forever, looking fine as hell, fucking and eating with abandon and without consequences? What did she do to deserve such bliss?

Oh yeah, she was a goddamn vampire.

"You ever saw a fat vampire, Jelly?"

"Bitch, I ain't ever seen a vampire, period," Jelly snapped back. I could tell she was getting a little tired of hearing about vampires.

Frankly, I was getting a little tired of her skepticism. "You want me to prove it?"

Jelly looked at me as if I'd lost my marbles.

"Twenty bucks," I said.

Jelly liked to spend money and she knew my word was gold on a bet. She heaved herself off her sofa. "Let's go, sucker," she said.

We both crept through the bushes. I had a wooden ruler I'd carved to a point with a kitchen knife, and a large silver cross around my neck, though I doubted either really worked. If she came from ancient Africa, her gods predated ours, and assuming I could pound that ruler with enough force through bone at the right place, she probably wouldn't stand still long enough to let me get through the procedure.

I'd put enough garlic on my hamburger to asphyxiate her with my breath if what they said about vampires not liking the stuff was true.

Sofia's drapes were pulled shut, so the eating was over and the fucking had commenced. The golden light shone through exactly at the same spot. I gestured to Jelly to look.

She stood on her tiptoes and peeked through the opening. "Who's she fucking?" I whispered. Jelly gestured at me to be silent, her eyes wide. I settled down to wait.

Jelly's breath quickened and I knew she was feeling it too. I imagined Sofia naked, her legs wide. I wondered who was sticking it to her this time. Some big black buck? Another white boy?

It was a while before Jelly dropped to the ground like her legs had lost their bones. She started moving quicker and more silently to her car than I would have imagined. I followed and got into the passenger seat.

She turned on the motor and I started to question her, but she held up a hand. "Later," she said and put the car in gear.

Jelly drove up to a brightly lit convenience store. I followed her in, not about to be left alone in the dark.

She gave me my twenty from the bet, then bought a six-pack

of beer and went back to the car. She opened a beer and, driving with one hand, gulped it down, then opened another.

I reached for a beer and cussed when I saw it was low-carb. What would they fuck up next? I popped the top anyway and sipped. It wasn't too bad, after all.

"So who did she do?" I asked conversationally. Jelly shook her head.

"A woman. A sister." Her voice was hoarse, choked.

I felt a tingling between my legs. I wished I could have seen it.

"She killed her," Jelly said. "I saw it, she killed her." Jelly opened another beer. Tears were flowing down her fat cheeks.

She pulled up in front of her apartment and parked. We didn't move. Nobody wanted to open the door to enter the dark night first.

"She knew we were there," Jelly said.

"I know," I answered. "She let us see."

We sat in Jelly's apartment with every blind tightly drawn, every light in the place blazing. "We have to do something," said Jelly.

"What do you propose we do? Offer ourselves up as an alternate menu selection? From what I've seen of her choice of entrées, we run a little high fat for her."

Jelly turned to me and met my eyes for the first time. "You need to be serious. This is serious. People are dying and I can't believe all you've talked about is how good she looks and how many folks she gets to fuck."

"She gets to eat all she wants, too. Just think of it. Everything you ever wanted to eat and never gain an ounce. Have you ever heard of a fat vampire?"

Jelly's eyes narrowed. "Didn't you feel the evil? She's an abomination, a monster and a sin against the Lord. What is this shit about fat vampires? She needs to be destroyed."

The thought of Sofia's perfect flesh being destroyed touched me like a cold finger in the middle of my spine. How can you destroy beauty? Obliterate power and pleasure?

"How do you propose to do that? I doubt if the mythical bullshit like a stake in the heart works. I'm not going to bet my life on it, anyway."

"Evil can always be vanquished."

"Vanquished? What are you talking about? You ain't Buffy. You can close your eyes and dream all you want, but you're not waking up bony and blonde."

"Your problem is that it all comes down to the superficial to you. That's why you're so obsessed with weight and looks. You need to realize that looks mean nothing."

Something flared inside me. "Yeah, looks don't matter," I said, my tone dripping sarcasm. "That's why you didn't get that promotion you deserved. That's why people stare through you as if you're invisible. That's why I know you get disrespected every day in subtle ways just like I do. You got no man, have had no man and never will have a man unless you feel like supporting some sorry-ass piece of one in return for the little bit of dick he throws you. You're lonely, ugly and as worthless in the eyes of the world as I am. And you know why? Because you're fat and that's all that matters."

Somewhere in my speech, the sarcasm turned to pain. I wiped my eyes with my arm, and my face felt hot. Jelly stared at me, silent.

I met her eyes. "If I have the chance to be fine like that woman and have what she has, I'll grab it," I said, "because that's what I want. That's what I need." My voice broke and I shamed myself by sobbing. I sank in a chair and Jelly handed me a box of tissues. It took a while to pull myself together.

"We need what she has and I'm going to figure out how to get it," I said. "That's all that matters."

Jelly looked like she was going to cry also. "You have it wrong. That's not all that matters. That's not what matters at all."

Jelly took me home and watched until I got into my apartment. I never was afraid of anything waiting for me there, because I had a feeling that one thing that I had read about vampires was correct. Something like vampires had to be invited before they entered your home. *Or your heart.*

I'd had it with hoping and wishing. Jelly was the one who was wrong. She was misguided in the sappy way the weak often are. I was going to get what I wanted. What I wanted most in the world was to be like that vampire slut, Sofia.

Plan

I don't want to die. Yeah, I know that vampires are undead, but that's my point. I want to stay conscious and not visit the hereafter. My heaven is going to be here and now, fucking, sucking and gorging for eternity.

But how was I to accomplish my goal and get Sofia to bite me and transform me into a vampire when she had this nasty habit of killing her victims? Nobody walked in her lair alone and came back out. So my odds of continuing to breathe if I directly approached her were woefully low.

I tried to find some other vamp and I couldn't. I'd know it if I spotted one. They'd have Sofia's preternatural air, her supernatural beauty and top-of-the-fucking-food-chain attitude.

I learned on the Internet that vampires are solitary creatures with large territories. They rarely sire whelps because that would be competition. The world can't support too many vampires. Historically, when their population gets too high, humans rebel and fight back. Prey becomes scarce.

Sofia lived and hunted alone, but the woman fucked too

much to be lonely. She went out and partied almost every night. One night I cruised behind her silver Beetle in my beat-up Ford and parked outside the club to watch and wait.

Sometimes Sofia brought two or three folks home at once. I liked that because it meant more sex and less blood. It was also nice to know she had a weakness. She couldn't take on more than one person at a time. Sofia's guests only died if they entered her place by themselves.

Last night Sofia went down on this little Asian guy with a huge joint, licking it like a Popsicle, and then opening her mouth wide until he disappeared inside. She worked that dick, sucking it, pulling on his balls until he arched and screamed in ecstasy, gobs of white gizm oozing out of her mouth. Then his screams changed and I saw the blood. Ouch.

Best of all was a few weeks ago when three women did her at once. One was blonde, one black and the other Hispanic. My hands drifted downward as I remembered. I'd almost fallen out of the bushes, I had gotten so hot. I watched the blonde girl frantically rub her light pussy hairs against Sofia's black crispness, cream oozing out of both of their pink crevices. The black girl's tongue danced around one of Sofia's hard, black nipples, and the Hispanic girl's rosebud mouth worked on the other. Their fingers danced in and out of each other's pink cunts, covered with juices while they licked and tongued on pussy round robin. Fish-o-rama buffet, sushi style. I came so hard I thought I was going to suffocate.

I wasn't her type if I went by the fine, fit and young folk she fucked. I was young enough, but that was the only qualification I met. So how was I supposed to get close enough to her to make her turn me into a goddamned vampire without killing me?

I had lots of time for research because— Did I mention that I'd been fired? The late nights spying on the vampire next door jacked me up. I came into work late half the time and called in sick the rest. When I was there, I didn't do that great either. I was tired, and sitting in front of a computer coding can be boring as hell. Fat, black chicks don't get cut the slack white folks do. We can get away with being a little evil, but that's about it. I'd seen white boys drag their asses for months on end when they went through some shit and get no more than a referral to the employee assistance program and some time off, usually paid. But after two weeks of my tripping over the vampire out of four years of near-perfect service, they told me to pack my shit and not to bother to show up the next day.

I didn't really give a fuck, because it gave me more time to concentrate on what really mattered. Pretty soon I wouldn't need a job. I never heard of a nerdish vampire who coded computer software. Maybe a vampire with a glamorous career, like a supermodel or a rock star, but not a vamp doing some shitty software coding. What would be the point?

I was still able to pay my rent and figured I had about six months' living expenses. That would be more than enough time.

Jelly tripped when I got fired, and rushed over to my apartment with some goddamn fruit. Can you believe it? Fruit! In times of angst, she used to have enough sense to break out the chocolate, at the very least. I moaned and groaned and whined and told her I needed space because I was depressed.

Do you know what she said? She said she'd pray for me. Jelly is way off the deep end and she ain't pulling me down with her. I'm getting what I've always deserved. For the first time in my life I'm going to be accepted and admired. I'm going to get me a life, even if I die trying.

Nope, Jelly wouldn't approve. Spooked by Sofia, she no longer came over to my place, but she used to corner me at work and go on and on about killing the vampire. Get this, I finally said to her, the vampire is already freaking dead.

Then she went off on another tangent, bitching and moaning about evil.

What's evil? I asked. Did she really know? Is it evil to bomb children into bloody little bits for economic reasons and power? Is it evil to benefit the wealthy and screw the poor? Is it evil to ruin the earth for profit? A lot of these gray dickheads around here think that so-called evil shit is better than sex and chocolate. So what the fuck is evil? Let the cream rise, the strong prosper and the economy grow. Fuck all that whiny crap like caring for the downtrodden, helping the weak and protecting the poor. Grab all you got coming to you. Evil is relative, my fat girl Jelly, and I'm changing my politics.

Jelly stared at me, eyes wide, and her sorry bleeding heart didn't have a word to say.

I was talking loud and those crackers at the company about had a stroke. The boss called me into his office and told me politics weren't an appropriate subject for the job. That's probably another reason they fired my ass so fast.

Fuck Jelly. She'd regret not being there for me when I got the payoff and she was still a beached brown whale working her ass off in a sea of white folks who turned their noses up and eyes away when she passed.

But Jelly would come to her senses once she saw how good I had it and then I'd help her get it too. But in the meantime, I needed to keep things on the down-low, so I avoided Jelly. I told her Sofia had moved and I was depressed and job hunting and needed some time to myself. I didn't think she'd try to storm Sofia's apartment with a wooden stake or something, but I didn't need the complications of having to watch out for Jelly's silly ass on top of everything else.

Because the only way to get what I wanted was to use magic—dark magic. Once I admitted the shadows existed, I saw them more clearly. Vampires existed, and more. Much more.

Magic was a science. A science of the mind that took skill and study. But I had the brains and I had the time. Most important, I had the will.

I started practicing spell casting and disciplining my mind with meditation and other practices. I worked quickly through the disciplines. I fasted at least once a week to prepare my body and get in the proper frame of mind.

Whoever said that fat chicks have no willpower had no clue. I hear skinny bitches whining and moaning about how they can't do some easy shit all the time. Try to diet for months on end, bitches. Starve your naturally skinny asses. They can't do it unless they're off the deep end like those crazy anorectic freaks. I quit a pack-a-day habit in a week. That was nothing in comparison.

Yeah, I had the will; all I needed to perfect was the way. My will was powerful enough to stay on the beet, bacon and orange-rind diet for a whole three days, so I knew it was powerful enough to enlist the assistance of something more powerful than me. Something more powerful than Sofia.

That would be a demon.

Demons were some scary sons of bitches, but for creatures that supposedly served the Lord of Chaos they sure seemed to have a lot of rules to follow. Like everything else, they were under the ultimate control of Order.

I needed a demon of the big-daddy caliber to force Sofia to turn me into a vampire. But demons were touchy creatures. If you let him, he'd figuratively screw your ass. Technically, demons were "its" instead of "hes" since they got no real dicks, po' things. *Wanting* to screw your ass was all they could do. There ain't no fucking in hell. No eating, either. Shit, no wonder they had a rep for being grumpy. I'd be pissed too. I guess that's why they call it hell.

Some of the stuff I read seemed to make demon summoning easy. Rustle yourself up a denizen of hell in ten easy steps, some of these grimoires instructed.

Wipe a little chalk on the floor, scribble some drawings, mutter a few words and maybe scatter a bit of incense and blood about, and that's it, you get McDemon ready to carry out your every whim in twenty minutes or less.

Also, supposedly if I drew a circle right, stood in it and did everything correct, I could summon up the biggest, baddest, mack-daddy demon and he wouldn't fuck with me. After I summoned him, he'd run around doing errands until I decided to let him go.

Ain't that some bullshit?

I was born and bred in the projects, a place where hell reigns on earth most of the time. I know a thing or two about badass motherfuckers. There ain't enough chalk and words and silly rituals in the world to make a badass motherfucker not kill your ass if he can.

You got to give him a reason not to do it. The best reason would be that he could use you to get what he wants. Bottom line, you better want what he wants or your ass is his. The demons I read about all seemed to be gaming folks, like a cat that plays with a mouse before it attacks.

The magicians who wrote those demon-in-ten-steps grimoires were probably the usual run-of-the-mill arrogant, privileged white folks, disrespectful and delusional. In this day and age they got it like that. But once they start fooling with demons, I'd bet money that they ended up some unpleasantly dead white folks. Disrespect a badass motherfucker and pain will be all you have to look forward to between your next breath and your last. Demons are the baddest motherfuckers of them all.

Did I mention the problem of payment? One rule is that everything had a price, and a demon's price was high. If you want something from a badass, you don't get to tell him what you're going to pay. He gets to tell you what he wants.

But I thought I could handle it. I had the will and I seriously doubt that the depths of hell could compare with the agonies of the Mayonnaise Clinic Diet that I stuck to for two whole months. A demon would quail before that fucking horror, pain and degradation. No, my problem was I couldn't keep up the effort for months on end, so I needed to get this shit over with.

I had to be certain to pick the right demon, a simpatico one with goals aligned with my own. Then I had to control myself well enough so as not to come under its control.

The final key was making the effort worth its while. That wasn't too difficult because I was going to give up my blood and my soul, hefty tender for any hellacious creature. The biggest payoff was Sofia, a tasty morsel of a vampire. It would be a win-win deal for the right demon. You know the saying: why not kill two birds with one stone?

Action

The demon was one jacked-up motherfucker. He had horns, wings and a tail and was in serious need of some attention to his feet. That son of a bitch's feet seriously stank, with the longest, fungiest yellow nails you could imagine and gobs of black toe jam stuck between his toe cracks.

He was naked, which didn't help his overall appearance one bit. It did prove that I was wrong about demons not having dicks. His dick matched his crooked-up, scaly, little charcoal-gray body. His little dick must have not worked worth a fuck either, because he sure looked like an irritable asshole.

"What do you want?" he roared, shaking my whole apartment, with crap flying off the walls and out of the cabinets. Pissed me off big-time, because I knew he wasn't going to stick around and clean up any of the mess.

But I do admit I admired his special effects and how he got to the point. So I got to the point also. "I want to be a vampire," I answered.

I think I surprised him. The shit whirling around in the air settled to the floor.

"Vampire? Can't do it," he growled.

I knew he was getting ready to split, and probably kill me as a side diversion, so I said quickly, "I need you to force Sofia to do it."

He paused. I could tell he was interested. I'd named her so I might as well have shone a spotlight on her and pointed her out on a map to him. But I needed to get him to act fast, before he got bored and decided to rip my guts out for fun. "Pain, death and spilled blood," I said. It doesn't do to be long-winded with a demon.

He eased down on his haunches and I knew I had him. Bingo.

Then I blinked and I was in Sofia's apartment. That demon truly didn't believe in conversation or wasting time. My stomach was in knots and I was freezing. I looked down. The SOB had stripped me naked! I started to protest, but the words faded when I saw the vampire. Sofia was headed for me, teeth bared, eyes blazing, not bothering to put on her façade of humanity. She was beautiful, but terrible. A predator. I about pissed myself. The concept of being undead and all was cool, but when actually faced with dying, well, let me tell you, if at that moment I could have changed my mind, I would have.

I ran like hell, but that bitch was fast. She'd almost grabbed me when a gray whirling fog enveloped us and Sofia screamed.

I would have screamed too if I could have breathed. It was like being squeezed by the wind. Cold damp wind. Quite unpleasant.

"Sire her," the demon's voice rasped.

"Noooo," Sofia screamed.

Then this nasty brown shit started seeping through her skin and leaking from her eyes. I took a second look and saw it was blood. Old, congealed, stinking blood. I couldn't fully appreciate the smell, not being able to breathe too well and all, but the tiny whiff I got made demon's feet smell like spring flowers.

Sofia hit the floor, writhing, gasping and moaning. The demon giggled. "Sire her," he repeated. He wasn't one to be wordy.

Sofia struggled to her feet and reached for me. Her bicuspids had grown long, snakelike fangs and her eyes matched—slitted and red. I tried to get away, but the solid winds were like heavy rope, crushing my body, holding me into place.

And despite my terror, when she pressed her body against my naked skin, the heat of arousal rose from my pussy. She must have sensed it, because she thrust her fingers in my pussy as her fangs pierced my neck.

The demon screeched with glee. Her fingers worked over and around my wet clit as she sucked my blood. My breath came in gasps, accompanied by pain, dizziness and the feeling of molten lava flowing through my veins.

Sofia's fingers were without mercy. My thighs opened as wide as they could go, my hips rotated. I was on the knife edge of pleasure and agony. Hurting, fearing and aching to come, but she wouldn't let me. My world had narrowed to the beat of my heart, the throb of my pussy and her moving fingers. Nothing else mattered. My heart was fading, going fast and faint. Something like a light flared under my eyelids and I exploded, convulsing in agony and ecstasy. She rubbed my clit past the ecstasy to pain and I sobbed.

With my cry, my mouth filled with fetid death, tepid, decaying, metallic. She'd opened her vein and filled my mouth with her blood. I could no longer choke, feeling the foul liquid run unchecked into my lungs and stomach. When she was finished, she let me drop to the floor.

Blackness fell as I felt my heart flutter with the last dregs of my blood. I knew I was dying.

Where was the demon? We had a bargain. Had he lied? They have a habit of that. Had I miscalculated? I whispered his true name in anguish. My last conscious human memory was the small sound of triumph that Sofia made.

When I opened my eyes, I was on the floor of my own apartment. I lay there naked, like so much meat. There was no more pain. I tried to move and my body betrayed me. It no longer transmitted pleasure, pain or anything else. I can't communicate the pure terror I experienced when I realized my chest no longer rose and fell with my respirations; my pulse no longer beat a familiar low rhythm in my ears.

My body lay there like the dead thing it was, stinking and putrefying. I was a prisoner in my dead flesh. Maggots, juices, bloating, the works. You know, when someone tells you that you're full of shit, they're right? The shit worked through my guts first, then rotted the rest of my flesh. But you probably don't want to hear about that. Most of you human motherfuckers are squeamish about the details, like your ass ain't one hundred percent guaranteed to rot eventually. If you're lucky, you won't have to smell yourself. You better believe I was relieved when my olfactory sensors finally went.

After about seven days, I must have hit critical rot, because the pain hit. Blazing fire, it was fucking excruciating. I couldn't scream or move; I just had to lie there and fry. Shit, I thought maybe that demon had finally come and dragged my ass down to hell. I finally lost consciousness.

When I came to, I tingled with sensation. I moved air in and out of what had to be newly grown lungs. I stood in a fluid motion and stared at the bones of my hands covered with familiar brown skin. I rushed to a full-length mirror. It was too good to be true. I had to be dreaming. Beyoncé and Halle Berry stand back, there's a new bitch in town. My, oh my, I was fine. Better than I thought I'd be. I was as slim as I'd imagined. I ran my bony hands down my sides and felt my ribs. No tits, but I'd fix that within a week with some implants. I'd get my ass fixed up good too. That's what all the real skinny bitches had to do. It wasn't all bad, though. I had long, shapely legs, and I must have been all of a size six. Maybe even a four or a two. I was all bone and gristle, a white man's dream girl.

The hair was best. It had reverted to its natural dark brown color and kinky texture. But it had grown crazy long, flowing down my back almost to my waist. It was wonderful, a deep chocolate froth over my butter pecan skin. I'd need to braid it at night, but that would be it.

I was hot, wild, everything I wanted to be. Exultation filled me. I'd done it! I'd pulled off the biggest damn project of all. It was the ultimate fucking diet.

Then I noticed things looked different. The air looked like it moved, or things moved through it. I could perceive waves and thick mists. Nothing was clear anymore. Things blurred and flowed and shadows were everywhere.

But screw things I could do nothing about. I was hungry as hell. And for the first time in my life I could eat whatever the fuck I wanted and not get fat.

I picked up the phone and ordered two pizzas with the works, a Coke with the sugar in it and cinnamon rolls on the side.

While I waited, I thought about calling Jelly. Where was she? It was strange that I hadn't seen anything of her. More depressing was that I'd been dead all week and nobody even bothered to find my stinking ass.

Granted, I'd been deep into my own project and had been avoiding Jelly. When I called her a while back, she'd mumbled something about working on something too. Probably another scheme to lose weight. She'd shit when she saw me.

The doorbell rang and I rushed to the door, my mouth watering. The delivery boy wrinkled his nose when I pulled open the door. I must have gotten accustomed to the smell of my rotted flesh and forgotten to air out the house. I was going to have to replace the living room carpet. Rotting is hell on floors.

When he held out the pizza, I was almost dizzy from the aroma—from him, not the food. He smelled salty. I stared at the tiny pulse on his wrist and it looked delicious. Before I knew it, I'd pulled him by the arm and dragged him inside.

He struggled a little, but calmed down quick when I let my dress fall to the floor and kissed him, working my tongue in and out of his mouth like it was a little dick.

I grasped his hard bulge. "I need it bad. It won't take much of your time," I said, my voice soft and silky. His adolescent cock was rock hard. I couldn't wait to taste it.

He wanted to fuck me right away. The silly human tossed me on the couch and dived in without stopping to pull on a condom. He came in two strokes.

Then he ate out my pussy. He tried, but it was nothing like the orgasms I used to have easily. Maybe the smell of his blood and the beat of his heart distracted me. Anyway, it was the seed he shot into me that I craved, and the sweet human lusts and energies.

I sucked and licked dick, my tongue working the crown and traveling each vein as it refilled with blood. I was so hungry, and it looked so good, I just couldn't wait.

I nipped one of the swollen veins and the blood flowed. He made such a racket. My strength was such I could hold him down with one hand.

I lapped up the blood running down his cock and bit off one of his balls and chewed. He writhed and gurgled, and I reached up to hold him still by the neck. He tasted better than chocolate. My appetite whetted, I opened the artery at his groin with an arc of my teeth. The blood gushed out and I drank it, hot and steaming, in great gulps.

His life was in the blood, filled with vitality and strength. I was high as fuck. This was like the best meal I ever ate, along with the best drug you can take.

Too soon it was gone. I needed more. All I had was meat on my couch and I was all sticky. I frowned at the body. What did Sofia do with the leftovers? I looked around the strange twilight atmosphere of my home and I suddenly got it. She didn't do a damn thing with them. She probably had them stacked up in the astral level of a back bedroom or something. I just hoped the smell didn't leak.

When I studied the magical arts, I learned about the astral realm. It overlaid and mirrored the human world in many ways, but at a lower vibration. Humans visited it in dreams at times. It was home to many rather unsavory creatures, vampires included.

I heaved a sigh, and squinted my eyes so I could see the *other* place clearly and dragged the pizza fucker's meat to the astral level. I felt a commotion as what I gathered to be carrion eaters fell upon it.

I took a shower, trimmed my pussy hairs and pondered what I could possibly wear. I settled on some sweatpants with a belt and an oversized T-shirt and knew my first stop had to be a twenty-four-hour Wal-Mart.

I bought some size-four jeans and pretty tops that never came in my previous size. It was one in the morning and the salesgirl minding the fitting room looked tasty. I had her come in and help me fasten a top. Then I asked her to lick my nipples. She did, her eyes glazed. I sucked hers too, and sucked her dry in more ways than one. I stashed her body in the astral plane right there in Wal-Mart.

On the way home, I bought a triple chocolate ice cream cone and it tasted like dark grease. A part of me that remembered Häagen-Dazs wanted to fucking cry.

But to console myself, I went to a club and let this fine young white man take me home, the type of man that wouldn't have looked at me once when I was fat.

He had some strokes, pumping me good and hard. I still couldn't come. But the taste of human sexual excitement was yummy; it was as if I fed off that too. His gizm hitting the inside of my pussy held the thrill of potential life and blood. I buried my teeth in the side of his neck, just like I'd seen Sofia do. I don't think he noticed until it was way too late.

Over the next few days I desperately tried to find Jelly. She hadn't called or come around in weeks and that wasn't like her. No matter how hard we fell out, we always made up.

I needed Jelly. Not only because she was sure to have lots of blood in her oversized body but once I transformed her into a vampire too, maybe things would be more how they used to be.

Don't get me wrong, it's great being fine and all, but there is some stuff that I wouldn't mind—like fresh, crisp breezes, the sun on my skin, the crunch and sweetness of an apple, flower colors, the shared passion of a tender kiss, the scent of mown grass and feeling the cool blades under my toes and laughing at a joke with Jelly. In my new world, things like this no longer exist.

Remember when I said vampires live on the borders of the astral world? Many things I remember as a human are outside of my perception, the same way spirits, auras and certain energies are outside of yours. But weak human preoccupations should be for weak humans, shouldn't they? I'm strong and beautiful, and I can eat all I want.

Okay, I admit that I miss Jelly. I'm eagerly looking forward to killing her. What I'm worried about is that Sofia seems to have disappeared too. Her apartment is always dark, the curtains drawn. I'll destroy Sofia if she gets to Jelly before me.

Jelly is mine. And I'll be nice enough not to let her rot alone.

Culmination

I couldn't find Jelly anywhere. I was pissed when I saw that Jelly had moved from her house. She'd quit her job too. No notice, it was like she fell off the face of the earth.

I used every resource I had in my search, but the spirits were noncooperative, the demons recalcitrant. They fall over themselves to be at the beck and call of humans, but if one of their own needs something? Tough shit. We minorities never can stick together.

I was in a great mood when I unlocked my door that night with this fine black buck sniffing my ass. I knew he'd be one delicious bite. And who do you guess was standing in my living room, all big and bad in living color? You got it. Jelly. And the girl looked damn good. She'd taken off a lot of weight. Don't get me wrong, she was still mighty hefty. Jelly had to take off way more than that to approach normal proportions, but she did look healthy and fit in a Queen Latifah type of way.

"Tell him to go," she said, gesturing at the man.

He started to protest and I did too, because, shit, I was hungry.

"Then I'm outta here," Jelly said.

She moved toward the door. The bitch was serious. "Okay, he'll go. Get out of here, all right," I said to him without once taking my eyes off Jelly. She'd be far more satisfying than that brother, anyway. I sort of liked her new take-charge attitude. I opened the door and shut it behind him.

"Jelly, where you been?" I asked. I didn't wait for her answer, because she didn't seem suitably shocked at my transformation. "What do you think of the new me?" I did a pirouette.

She sniffed. "Not much. And call me Angelica from now on."

"Angelica, huh? It's a whole new you too. I see you got off some of that blubber. You're looking good. I hope you think I am too." I begged for her approval. I knew she couldn't have been talking about my appearance when she curled her lip.

"You no longer have a soul," she said softly. "Why, Keesh? You were better than this. But you always wanted to do it the easy way. I'm so sorry." A tear ran down her cheek.

What the fuck was the matter with her? Had she lost her mind? "What do you mean, my two-hundred-plus ass was better than this?" I demanded, running my hands over my shapely form. I turned the full blast of my preternatural sexual magnetism on her. "Want to see all of it?" I purred, and pulled down my top, exposing my breasts.

She sniffed again, louder, and pulled a tissue from her pocket, blew her nose and wiped her eyes.

Here I was, sexy and fine as hell and the bitch was crying like I'd died. Well, I had, but still. Shit, let me put her out of her misery. I bared my teeth and advanced on her.

"Don't move another inch or you'll regret it!" Jelly, 'scuse me, *Angelica,* cried out. I was so surprised at her threat, I stopped in my tracks.

"I'm sorry, Keeshia, but you damned yourself, and now I have to destroy you," she said solemnly.

I had to laugh. "How do you propose to do that? Sit on me and crush me to death with your fat ass?"

She pulled something from a holster behind her back and held it in front of her—like some sort of weapon.

"What the fuck is that?" I inquired.

She didn't bother to answer; instead, with one hand she opened a leather bag at her feet. She didn't take her eyes off me while she pulled out this black thing and threw it at my feet. I bent down to study it. It was Sofia's head. As far as doing us in, decapitation usually does it.

"Daaaaaaang," I said. This was disconcerting. Sofia was a powerful vampire, far older than I.

"Die, fiend!" Jelly yelled and brandished this bigass sword like she was some sort of motherfucking samurai or something.

So I did the smart thing. I ran, right through the goddamn picture window. She was on me too. Bitch was fast. I cut through the astral and couldn't lose her. Fuck, fuck, fuck. I was getting quite attached to my head and all that fly hair. It took a while, but I finally lost her in a crowd.

I knew I couldn't go back home. I went to the airport, removed a ticket from a kill and got on the plane.

I move from city to city now. I'm afraid to stay in any one place for very long, because I know Jelly is searching for me. In the astral, I hear whispers that our kind is being picked out and destroyed.

Jelly, the goddamn fat black vampire slayer. Buffy's scrawny, blond ass would probably shit.

Vamp Noir

ANGELA C. ALLEN

The air in the narrow, dark alley behind the overcrowded and run-down high-rise apartment buildings is a mix of stale piss, rotting Chinese food and the sweet tang of freshly spilled blood. A rusted fire escape dangles overhead, attached more by accident than design to the pockmarked and graffiti-covered brick wall beside it. Row after row of neatly ascending windows spill patchy blocks of light as dimly lit bodies move in the background, oblivious to the carnage below.

I don't recognize the first body lying spread-eagled and face-down on the jagged concrete. But the other one is familiar. His scent is easy to identify: a swirl of expensive cologne and healthy male pheromones now combined with the stench of involuntarily released human waste. He lies flat on his back, his eyes turned toward the mouth of the alley as if he had watched for me with his dying breath.

"May your God judge you lightly," I whisper now as I kneel beside him, brushing one gloved hand over his face and closing eyes already filmed over with the white cloud of death.

Enrique's lifeless face remains startlingly beautiful. In fact, not a single scratch mars his perfectly proportioned features. The sweep of thick, dark lashes, shapely full lips, neat goatee, smoothly arching eyebrows and flaring nostrils set against olive-toned skin form a symmetrical feast for the senses. He could have been a martyred young saint in repose. The only thing ruining the picture is the five-inch-long knife blade attached to the iridescent mother-of-pearl hilt sticking out of his throat.

"*Mami Chula,* you looking hot!" he had drawled teasingly at our last meeting, a quick rendezvous in a forgotten corner of the city. "Mmm, you got on those sexy black leather gloves. Baby, you know that dominatrix look turns me on," he'd said, smiling at me out of velvety dark eyes.

Remembering now, I trail one leather-covered finger down his cheek in farewell. "I think even your killer couldn't bring himself to destroy such beauty."

I turn to his nameless companion lying nearby. The body is stiff, the limbs hardened with rigor mortis, but with a careful push I am able to turn him over. His face and neck are a deep purple from the pooling of the blood in his prone position. But the mottling of lividity does not completely hide the signs of a brutal beating. His face is a nightmare of broken bones, lacerations and bruises. His own mother wouldn't recognize him. His right arm is bent at a physically impossible angle and I see a large wet stain on the front of his coat, low on his belly, which suggests a fatal hemorrhage.

"He took you by surprise, didn't he?" I murmur. "You were the lookout. He came from behind, the knife held down low, and before you could turn around, the blade was buried in your gut—you never had a chance."

In three months this is my first casualty. I'd been warned that couriers never lasted long; either they gave in to temptation and bolted with the package or simply fell victim to a heartless city that ate its young if they weren't smart enough to survive. Enrique had been surprisingly reliable for a petty criminal and sometimes drug runner. Every seven days he'd faithfully picked up a sealed package from his boss and dropped it off still sealed to me.

I called it a job; some people called it extortion. The FBI called it a "Mob tax" paid to organized crime. Being a Mob soldier wasn't my first choice but I was an outcast among my own kind. I was forced to create a place for myself with those humans who move among the shadows where I dwell, humans who embrace the darkness because it hides their secrets.

I'll have to tell the doctor we lost a payment, I think, just before my eyes spot a familiar shape a few feet away. I scoop up the brown-paper-wrapped package and discover the thick tape still intact, the envelope unopened.

What kind of thief kills two men and then tosses the cash?

The weekly payoff Enrique handed over contained thousands in untraceable bills. It represented a small fortune to the typical crack addict or street-corner prostitute that roamed this hardluck neighborhood.

I scan the area carefully before drawing off one black leather glove. My newly freed fingers flex with power, eager to touch, to feel, to know. I mentally gather the reins of control as I reach for the still-bloody handle sticking out from Enrique's throat.

I grasp the blade, my chocolate-colored skin contrasting sharply with the pale, iridescent handle as the power flows out of me and I am transported through a twisting curve of time and space back to the past.

Images spring at me like restless ghosts given a last chance to live again. I see a long, shining dagger slash down in a deadly arc; I hear the wet gush as unyielding metal stabs deep into unprotected muscle and tissue; I watch as Enrique pleads for his life.

Through Enrique's eyes I see a bulky figure approach, a stray beam from a lone streetlight glints on pale skin, a bald head, bristly jaw and reflects back from near-colorless, light eyes. In the background is the dead body of the lookout. Enrique is frozen with horror, his eyes darting from his slain friend to the approaching killer.

"Look, man, if this is about that girl, I didn't know she was doing anybody else," he says with a desperate laugh, backing deeper into the dead-end alley. "She was just a little something to pass the time, you know what I mean? I been with my lady for five years. We got kids and all."

"This ain't about some bitch," the killer says, drawing a gleaming blade from inside his ragged denim jacket with a deftness that speaks of long experience.

Through the lens of secondhand sight, the rank odor of his skin crashes into me in a multihued rush of colors, the black of unwashed flesh, sour sweat and bad breath forming a nauseous brew.

Adrenaline spikes through my veins on a hot rush, fueled by the reckless courage that fills Enrique. He suddenly strikes, leaping forward with a small but sharp blade of his own to find his attacker's thick neck. Instead of reaching its mark, Enrique's blade rips out the killer's gold hoop earring, leaving in its place a torn and bloody flap of flesh. The heavier man easily overpowers Enrique. He is pinned to the ground in seconds.

"Get the fuck off me!" yells Enrique, a thread of fear running through his voice as he begins to buck and twist uselessly under the heavy weight of his attacker. "Take it, take the goddamn money! Just leave me alone!" he pleads.

"Shut up! I didn't come for no money!" the man snarls, ripping the package from its hiding place inside Enrique's jacket and tossing it into the darkness. The quick movement causes a rivulet of blood from the killer's earlobe to fall on Enrique's upturned face like a crimson tear from Hell.

"Santa Maria, Madre de Dios . . ." we whisper reverently, the words of the rosary coming to our lips as our strength ebbs and

death draws near. We moan weakly as the killer's knife plunges into our fragile skin, slicing through sinewy muscle and severing vital arteries. Life-giving blood rushes in to fill the now-gaping hole, but our carotid artery has been cut and the damage is beyond repair. Our senses fade and our vision blurs as blood loss robs us of strength.

"*Mira! Mira!*" calls a voice with a thick Spanish accent from the sidewalk where two young men in puffy, black down jackets and thick-soled boots stand peering into the darkness.

Our killer moves away, blood dripping down his neck.

"Yo, man, you bleeding bad," Spanish Accent says as he cautiously edges deeper into the malodorous darkness. "You need a doctor or some shit like that. *Necesita ayuda!*"

"Stupid fuck! Get away from me," the killer growls, pulling free and shoving past him to stagger out of the alley, pressing his jacket collar to his ripped earlobe.

"Oh my God! Oh my God!" interrupts his until-now-silent companion, catching sight of the two men lying half hidden behind an overflowing trash Dumpster. "Hector, there's two guys who look dead!"

"Oh shit, oh shit!" moans Hector.

"Yo, man, we better get outta here before some cops roll by and say we did it," suggests his cynical friend. "My boy Pedro is locked up right now doing time for some crazy shit just like this."

We dimly hear the two almost Good Samaritans leave the alley, their strong, young voices fading as they hurry away from their grisly find, leaving us alone to face the darkness that waits at the edge of our sight.

"NO!" I say, pulling back from that black abyss. The power recedes as I return to myself and cross back into the consciousness of now. I lock the images away for later examination and rise to my feet.

While journeying into the past I have been blind and deaf to the present, but already I can hear the faintest vibration from distant footfalls. It is time to go. I push my still-tingling fingers back into the glove and move toward the high, barbwire fence at the rear of the alley.

With a running leap I somersault over the fence to land on the other side. I hear a yell of alarm as someone finds the bodies of Enrique and his friend. As I turn to leave, a small voice calls out. "Are you a superhero?" the round-eyed child lisps from her perch in a window a few feet away.

These humans are so fanciful, so ready to believe in the power of cartoons and fairy tales but unwilling to accept the reality of beings other than themselves when confronted with living evidence.

"No, superheroes aren't real—vampires are," I reply.

"Sheila, Dr. Micelli's been asking for you. What took you so long?" asks Tommy as he opens the door of the small but ornate two-story brick home crammed next to its neighbor in the densely populated hills overlooking the bay. I absently register the gun clearly visible in the shoulder holster strapped over his shirt.

"Enrique is dead," I say, starting down the marbled hallway.

"Did you kill him?" he asks matter-of-factly.

"No," I answer without turning.

"Sheila, there you are," breathes the Doctor in cultured tones as I enter his study, a lavish and soundproof room with an antique armoire full of out-of-date medical journals and a bar stocked with first-rate whiskey and fifty-year-old French wine. "I was beginning to worry. I trust all went well tonight?"

Dr. Anthony Micelli is the ideal of an aging but still-handsome professional, his gray-flecked dark hair carefully cut in a conservative but flattering style: tasteful gray slacks, a navy blue sweater and a crisp white shirt set off his Florida winter tan to perfection. To all appearances he is the epitome of a physician relaxing at home in front of the fire after a busy but rewarding day healing the sick.

That image is a lie. The Doctor's real business is not medicine but money laundering and drug trafficking.

An ambitious Micelli had cheated his way through classes at a small Catholic college and bought his degree from an even smaller medical school in the Caribbean. The well-informed knew he was the son of a notorious Mafia don. And the very well informed knew he had risen through the ranks of La Cosa Nostra to become boss of one of the most powerful crime families in the city. Not an ounce of marijuana or a gram of cocaine or heroin came into the city that wasn't cleared by the Micelli family.

"Enrique is dead. He and the lookout were both killed before I arrived. His killer didn't take the package. It's all here," I say, withdrawing the money and placing it on the desk in front of him, ignoring the third person in the room.

"Hmm, that's three couriers in one month," muses the Doctor, a faint frown creasing his forehead. "And you say the killer didn't take the money? I had assumed it was simple greed behind the first murder, but maybe it's more than that, maybe some new street gang needs to be disciplined. Tommy might have to look into this."

"You fucking kidding me? You wanna send out a capo to chase down some filthy street thugs who probably whacked each other over a pair of sneakers? Gimme a fucking break!" says the smoke-roughened voice of the man reclining on the sofa with a cigar clutched between the thick fingers of one hand. "We got bigger things to worry about here. We nominated Tony Jr. to be made and the Commission is meeting next week. We don't wanna piss anybody off in the other families. If they think we can't handle the business they might get scared; somebody might think we're weak and they can challenge us. No, Boss. We gotta keep this quiet for now."

"Sal, you're my consigliere now and you've been with the Micelli family more than twenty years. I trust your judgment," says the Doctor. "My first priority is my son and the continuation of this family. If anything should happen to me I want him to be able to take over."

"I'm honored to serve under you, Don Micelli," rasps Sal. "I'm gonna do everything I can to help Tony Jr. after he takes the Oath of Omertà and becomes a made man. Then we'll take care of that other shit."

"*A parola d'onuri vali sangu,*" intones the don in Italian. A word of honor is worth blood.

"Sheila, please forgive my lapse in manners. This is Salvatore Marzanzini, the new adviser to the family," says the Doctor, waving toward me. I give him the barest nod of recognition. "Sal, this is Ms. Sheila Seven, a new associate who helps us with collections."

"When did you start hiring *moolingnannes?*" he asks, raking me from head to toe with obsidian eyes set under graying eyebrows in a lined and sagging face.

"I keep up with the times, I'm an equal opportunity employer," says Micelli, laughing. I can see that Sal realizes he hasn't really answered his question but he isn't willing to risk pushing him over it.

The truth is I had carefully implanted the idea of hiring me into the Doctor's mind months ago. Unlike the paranoid delusions depicted in the movies, where victims are hypnotized with a single burning glance, the art of mind control is both time-consuming and exact. I had secretly visited the Doctor for weeks before our first carefully orchestrated public meeting. I had struck when he was most vulnerable, during the darkest hours of night, when the conscious brain shuts down and the subconscious takes over. It is only then that a vampire can breathe upon a human and sow the seeds of subliminal suggestion.

I can see Marzanzini drawing his own conclusions about my true job here. He thinks I'm on the payroll because I'm sleeping with the Doctor. I know what he sees when he looks at me, and it is a carefully cultivated image designed to deflect suspicion.

I deliberately shift my weight now, drawing his gaze to my legs outlined in supple, formfitting, black leather pants. I brush back a handful of long, night-dark braids and fold leanly muscled arms, the color of richest brown chocolate, left bare by the sleeveless vest I'm wearing. I check his reaction with a sideways glance from slanting, honey-gold eyes.

Sexual desire blazes from him despite his best attempts at concealment, snaking out toward me along with his scent, which swirls into my head on a flood of angry indigo blues and virulent reds streaking through the icy white of the truly amoral.

"Sheila, I have another assignment for you. Tomorrow night I need you to ride out to the Brooklyn Navy Yard around ten and pick up some election results. Sal will have everything ready for you," says the Doctor, rising and coming around the desk. "Tommy will meet you there in case there's any trouble," he adds.

"What kinda trouble I got fixing one little election?" Sal laughs. "It's in the bag, Don Micelli. I'm gonna be president of the Union of Ship Haulers and Plastic Fitters. That multi-million-dollar pension fund they got is already in my pocket."

"I'm sure you're right," says Micelli. "Just consider this a little insurance in case anyone decides to check the ballots. I don't want any evidence of our involvement on the premises. A paper trail for the feds to follow is the last thing we need."

"I know how to handle the feds, I'll have 'em fucking swimming with the fishes!" Sal growls.

sh up here and be at the Navy Yard tomorrow at ten," ...say, tiring of my little game with the overweight Sal and eager to leave. I have not yet fed this night.

"Good, good. I want to hear all about it when you get back," says the Doctor with a perfect smile that never reaches his eyes.

After leaving the study, I easily wind my way through the subterranean passageways that lie under the house, finding Tommy in the weapons room oiling his guns. He looks up with a ready grin as I enter the small space. Three of the four walls are covered with gun racks and the fourth holds specially built glass cases for storing ammunition.

Tommy "Two Guns" Celona is that rare individual, a cop who was also a made man. On paper he manned a desk at Manhattan headquarters. But in real life he worked full time on the other side of the law as a capo for the Doctor. He had fifteen years on the force and was looking to make twenty and retire with a full pension. He showed up for promotion days and cop funerals. He got a check in the mail every month and his departmental evaluations were outstanding. No one bothered to mention that the deputy inspector who rubber-stamped his attendance record was his second cousin. He wore two guns—a Glock Model 19 tucked under the shoulder and a sleek little SIG Sauer P-226 tucked in an ankle holster.

"Sheila, what do you think of our new consigliere? Sal's such an old-timer I think he was in the original version of *The Godfather*," he jokes. "When my brothers and I were young he used to take us on fishing trips and he wouldn't allow any of us to speak English—*soltanto italiano*. He said we had to remember our roots."

"What happened to the old consigliere?" I ask. I'd never had a chance to meet him.

"It's a sad story but I'll tell you now so you'll know the truth," he says, responding just as he should to the mental implant. My directive for him had been simple: trust me.

"The official version of his death is he had a heart attack, but that was just something nice for his wife and kids, to save the family honor and keep the name clean," he adds. "The God's honest truth is he was caught stealing from the don. About a month ago Sal found him with a stash of about half a million dollars. Marco was like a son to Sal, but when he drew on him he did what he had to do. He took him down. It was very traumatic for Sal. He still feels guilty about it."

"He was walking around with half a million dollars?" I ask in disbelief, knowing the Mob's fondness for small, untraceable bills. You couldn't lug around that much cash in one small suitcase.

"Not exactly, they found it at the apartment he kept for his *comare*," he says.

"So you're telling me this wise guy is so wise he hides a fortune in stolen Mob money at his mistress's place," I muse. "That's a pretty stupid thing to do."

"Yeah, if Sal hadn't told me he'd seen it with his own eyes, I never would have believed it either—Marco was the don's brother."

The long road that leads to the place where I sleep is surrounded by a thicket of desolate streets holding burned-out factories that see few visitors during the day and none at all during the night. The only rent-paying tenant is a city sewage plant that spits out toxic fumes that hang in the air like a warning to the sane to stay away.

This night the bleak silence is broken by angry shouts.

"Are you trying to cheat me, bitch! Are you? Because I know you made more money than this," the man screams as the weeping woman cringes behind the decaying hulk of an abandoned car. Her makeup has streaked her face, giving her the look of an olive-skinned raccoon. He towers over her, his dark hands clenched into angry fists that are covered in heavy gold rings.

"You were working that corner for six hours, Marylene. I want the rest of my fucking money!"

"That's all I got, I swear, Johnny-Boy," she sobs.

Neither one looks up the first time I ride past. When I swing the bike around, heading back in their direction, the man looks up with an angry scowl. I can see him trying to peer behind the tinted visor of my helmet to decide if I represent a threat or not. I roll to within a few feet of them and cut the engine.

"Nosy bitch, this ain't none of your business. You get back on that bike right now and I might forget I saw you," he commands in a rough voice as I swing my leg over to dismount.

"But I won't forget I saw you," I say, continuing to walk toward him.

"We're just talking. Everything's fine, miss. I don't need no help," pleads Marylene, looking up at Johnny-Boy as if checking for his approval.

"Help? I didn't come to help," I say, beginning to laugh despite myself.

"Stupid bitch, when I finish with you your crazy ass will be needing some help," he snarls, advancing toward me across the gravelly stew of shattered glass and small stones littering the deserted lot. "I'm going to teach you a lesson you'll never forget."

I wait until he springs forward, his body weight off center and falling before I turn, twisting in a graceful arc of motion as the power wells up inside me, coursing through my veins and ending in a surge of adrenaline so powerful that the impact of my foot hitting his thickly padded torso sends an audible crack through the still night air.

"Oh my God, oh my God, Johnny-Boy!" screams Marylene, peeking out from behind her fingers.

"*Arrghh . . .*" groans Johnny-Boy, grimacing and clutching his broken rib as he staggers back a step. He regains his footing and a twisted grin blooms on his face.

"Just for that, I'm going to carve my initials in that pretty face after I beat your ass," he threatens me in a vicious whisper, reaching into his pocket and withdrawing a butterfly knife that he deftly flips open.

He charges toward me, coming in with the double-headed blade held low, aiming for where he can do the most damage. As he closes in, I sidestep and grab his outstretched arm, snatching the dagger away in a movement so fast it appears as a blur and using the momentum of his own body, slam him to the ground, twisting his wrist as he falls so that once again a sharp crack cuts the air.

"Still think I'm here to help you?" I ask, crouching over him and grabbing his uninjured hand to pin it high above his head.

"*Arghhh . . .* you bitch, you broke my wrist!" he moans, gazing down his arm at the now limply dangling wrist in horrified disbelief.

"And here I thought you liked this game. Wasn't it your idea to play rough?" I say. Out of the corner of my eye I see his companion hit the road, stumbling over the uneven pavement in her three-inch high heels but still managing a good jog. "It looks like it's just you and me now."

This close, his smell is nearly overpowering, the blacks and browns swirling together like the fierce winds of an ocean storm, with the vermilion of human blood roiling in the center like the untouchable eye of a hurricane. I give in to temptation and lower my face, breathing in deeply the scent of blood, of flesh, of food.

"Get off me, you crazy bitch!" he defiantly shouts, spraying my face with spittle.

I catch his eyes, holding him with the force of my will. "You have something I want."

"Yeah, yeah, take it. The money is yours," he pants breathlessly. His eyes flicker rapidly as a look of sly cunning steals over his face. "What I said before, I was just playing, you know, just playing. That bitch Marylene made me so mad I wasn't thinking straight."

In my time among the humans, I have found that those who project an image of viciousness and cruelty are often the most malleable. The braggarts and bullies amount to nothing more than hollow shells who readily bow down before any force stronger than themselves. It is the outwardly meek and quiet ones who inwardly possess an iron will that refuses to bend.

The man is sweating now, desperation stealing over him, his onyx-colored eyes wide with fear. I can tell by the loud pounding of his heart that he feels the storm hanging over him, but his limited intellect is unable to comprehend the true danger.

His street-honed instincts whisper to him that one small woman is no threat; hasn't he always subjugated her sex with violence and intimidation? It's a hard world and the weak have to give way to the strong. But something beyond the five known senses is screaming that this time things are different.

"This is for Marylene," I tell him, grasping his jaw in an iron grip.

His scream echoes off the walls of the empty buildings around us as my upper lip curls back and gleaming, white incisors slide out. The sound is abruptly cut off as I find the pressure point on his neck, pinching it just enough to temporarily paralyze his vocal cords.

The first taste of blood is like a jolt of pure energy, red hot and steaming, streaking through my veins and into my starved cells on a wave of nearly unbearable pleasure. It curls through my belly and up to my brain, purring in ecstasy, arching and twisting in hedonistic delight.

It is a struggle to stop but I tame my thirst. I close the puncture wounds with a swipe of my tongue and wrench his head around to face me, issuing a single command: forget.

It is impossible to completely erase another's memory; the connection between synoptic nerves, chemical triggers and the memory banks of the brain itself are too deeply entrenched, but I can blur my victim's recall, giving the events the quality of a dream, where the details are hazy and hard to grasp, until remembering is like reaching for smoke.

Long hours later, the sun finally slips below the horizon and the coming night chases away the day.

I lie dreamlessly inside the wood-lined walls of the wine cellar. The air is fragrant with the smell of fermenting grapes. Dusty bottles of the finest merlot and aged whiskey rise all around me in solitary splendor, the forgotten treasure of some human long gone. The only sound in the sparsely furnished and austere room is the irregular thumping of my heartbeat, slowed to the infinitesimal pace required to support life functions, living yet not alive.

"Sheila," calls a deep, intriguingly accented masculine voice. A second, stronger heartbeat invades the room. It is the one person who has the right to freely come and go here in my underground home and not fear death.

My body temperature rises and my heartbeat quickens as I come to life. I rise from my sleeping mat and light the long, red tapers placed around the room before I sink to one knee, bowing my head respectfully.

The visitor extends one hand before my bowed head.

"I honor you and I honor your line," I whisper reverently as my tongue lightly traces the deeply etched lifeline in his palm.

"It is dangerous for our kind to dwell so long among humans," he says. "You must come back. You must come home."

The request is familiar, the pain a little less sharp each time he voices my own secret longing. The memory of the secret caverns deep underground where our kind nest and mate fills me with constant longing. Each time he comes he asks me to return. But each time I answer the same.

"By the order of the Council I have no home," I answer, my head still bowed and my gaze directed toward the floor. "Any vampire who stands accused of harboring a human must be punished. I am guilty of nothing and would do it again. The human I found had less than five years. I did not bring him forward to the Council because they would have ordered his death."

"That is the right of the Council. It is not your place as a non-power-holder to pass judgment on these matters!" says the man harshly. "It has only been three months' time. If you come back with me now I can still use my power as a Council member to sway them against a full Inquisition.

"You made this choice. No one expected you to choose a sentence of seven years' banishment in the world of the humans rather than submit to a trial by Inquisition," he adds, a note of accusation in his voice now. "It's not too late to go back. You can still prove your loyalty."

"No, this is my life now," I answer, without looking up. I don't need to see him to visualize his face, a breathtaking arrangement of skin the color of richest teakwood over bold, chiseled features and curved lips set under stormy gray eyes, his shining black hair worn long in the way of his warrior ancestors who roamed this land when it was still called the New World.

Silence stretches between us for long seconds and then I hear my name called in a throbbing whisper: "Sheila."

His hand falls across my shoulder in a heated caress that leaves a trail of fire in its wake. I rise to my feet, bringing my nude body against his fully clothed one and twining my arms around his neck as he towers over me.

The kiss is full of heat, scorching me both inside and out. His hands slide down my back and encircle my hips. I feel his heavy erection rising between us. I twist my hips against him, eager to feel him inside me. He rains hot kisses down the side of my neck as we sink to the floor, falling into each other with the ease of longtime lovers.

"I miss you," I confess on a broken breath as his lips find my nipple. I grasp handfuls of his thick, silky hair, swirling it over

my breasts and stomach in a sensual feast. The flick
light bathes us in soft shadows.

As we lose ourselves in the dark taste of passion, our
beats slowly synchronize until they beat as one.

All conversation stops the moment I cross the threshold of the
small, cramped trailer space that serves as the headquarters of
the Union of Ship Haulers and Plastic Fitters. Outdated and
peeling prounion posters are tacked to the paneling alongside
dusty calendars featuring half-naked women with improbable-
sized busts. The male faces in the room wear various expressions
of shock, surprise and hostility.

"Holy shit," breathes one man, his blue eyes widening visibly
as they travel over me.

"Sheila, come on in. You're just in time," calls Tommy, entering the office through a second door. "Sal's finishing up with the
ballots and should be out any minute.

"I believe you guys have heard of the newest addition to my
private security team," he drawls with the smug look of a young
boy showing off a new toy.

"This is Vinny, a friend a mine," he says, using Mob language
to signal that Vinny is a made man.

"What is this, some kinda joke?" says the scowling Vinny, all
dark eyes and thick wavy hair. "Did the suits at headquarters
give you Soul Sister for a partner?"

A round of derisive male laughter fills the trailer.

"This soul sister holds a black belt in tae kwon do and is a
crack shot," bites out an angry Tommy, springing to my de-
fense. "She can split the hairs on your ass with a nine. I'd trust
her with my life!"

An uneasy silence grips the room in the wake of his outburst.

Tommy's normally placid brown eyes are hard as stone, and I
can see by the men's faces that they've been reminded that
Tommy is no low-level Mob soldier to be taunted with im-

punity. He is a top capo with a kick-ass reputation and the power to make or break any man in the room.

"Hey, take it easy, *paesan*. You know Vinny ain't been right in the head since high school, when he got knocked out during the championship game," teases a handsome young man of medium height.

"Fucking goombah," responds Vinny with a half-smile and a toss of his head.

"Welcome to the family," adds the teaser, coming forward with a warm smile and a glint of pure male appreciation in his hazel eyes as they drop to my breasts encased in a corset-style, laced black leather jacket.

He catches my eye on the way back up. "Nice . . . gloves," he says with a grin.

I hear heavy footsteps approaching and turn my head toward the door at the far side of the trailer. Moments later Sal lumbers through carrying a box marked OFFICIAL UNION BALLOTS in his beefy hands and a half-lit cigar clamped between his teeth.

"Alright, it's done. The ballots have been counted and the winner declared," he mumbles around his cigar.

"Hey, Sal, you make that adjustment?" A guy in the crowd laughs.

"*Stutti zitto!*" Sal yells, waving the cigar angrily. "You think the walls don't have ears? You're going to bring the feds down on us, opening your big mouth!"

"Let me help you with that," says Tommy with a speaking look around the room. He deftly hands the box off to me and I slide it into a heavy canvas backpack.

"*Aspetta momento!*" Sal calls out as I open the door to leave. "Tommy, I just remembered. I got some other business to discuss with you. Youse better stay a while longer."

"Sure, Sal," says Tommy affably, waving me back in.

"No, no, in private. I mean, family business, *capisce?*" explains Sal with a falsely apologetic look toward me.

"It's no problem. I can handle this job alone," I tell Tommy.

"Alright," he finally sighs in resignation. "But I won't be long. I'll be right behind you. And remember, make the delivery directly to the Doctor."

I notice the glare of headlights behind me as I'm heading out on my bike back to the main road leading out of the pier. The vehicle slowly trails me but doesn't come close enough to ring any alarm bells. After a few minutes I idly dismiss it as some of Sal's boys who've also left early.

Most of my concentration is on finding my way back through the thicket of rusted, metal cargo containers and old shipping crates that litter the area. My bike's tires struggle for purchase on the pockmarked road surface, caked with years of oil and grease. I take a firmer grip as my back wheel abruptly slides hard to the right.

The sound of the revving motor is my only warning before the vehicle behind me suddenly speeds up, bearing down with predatory intent. It is so close that I can clearly make out the individual points of the spiked, metal grille mounted on the front of the large, dark SUV. Dark-tinted windows cloak the face of the driver.

The sharp edges of the spikes inch ever closer, ten feet, six feet—now three feet. I hang a quick left around a hulking metal container, my wheels fishtailing wildly as they slip on oily residue. They find traction just as the SUV swings around the same curve. I've gained precious seconds but I can't outrun him here as I could on the open road. The paths are too short and dangerously near the river. I have to stay away from the water at all costs.

I duck around a line of waist-high crates, the SUV still prowling behind me. Suddenly it roars into my peripheral vision, keeping pace with me on the other side of the crates. We race along separated only by a few feet of wood. Up ahead I can see the telltale gleam of moonlight on water. I turn the bike in a tight three-sixty curve, speeding back the way I came. The SUV swings wide to block my path, hitting an oil patch but quickly correcting. We are now on a head-on collision course, players in a dangerous game of chicken.

The seconds tick by with dizzying speed as I calculate and weigh my narrowing options. On one side is a gauntlet of heavy crates, on the other are the life-stealing waters of the sea and ahead are three tons of metal charging toward me with pulverizing force.

Seconds from impact I swerve, sending the bike skidding across the pavement and my body catapulting through the air. I crash onto the hood of the SUV, arms and legs flailing as I grope for a hold.

On the other side of the tinted windshield the driver wrenches the wheel, sending the car careening across the roadway. I bear down with all my strength, one hand clinging to the edge of the hood while the other grips the handle of the driver's side-view mirror. My incisors slide down as rage blooms inside me. The thin veneer of civilization is ripped away by my murderous frenzy. My fist smashes through the tinted glass, startling the driver into releasing the wheel. With a low growl, I wrap my gloved fingers around his throat and drag him out, hurling his body through the air with inhuman strength. I leap off the hood and the SUV speeds on its path, splashing off the pier and into the murky water.

The man on the ground coughs weakly as he turns his head. "Fucking mooley, I'm gonna kill you! You got no business here and we don't want you!" sneers Vinny. "Sal's gonna get rid of you! I'm gonna whack you myself."

I stand over his prone figure, looking down at him and struggling to master the killing rage screaming at me to tear him limb from limb. From my vantage point I can clearly see his broken leg, the knee twisted at what looks to be an excruciatingly painful angle. Vinny won't be driving again any time soon.

He stares up at me in mingled horror and fascination, blinking in disbelief and swiping a hand across his face.

I smile wider, letting him see my incisors.

"S-s-spooky fucking bitch, you're gonna put the *malocchio* on me!" he stutters, crawling away, using his hands to pull himself along against the weight of his injured leg.

"I'm not going to give you the evil eye. I'm a vampire, not a witch," I say, moving so fast he doesn't have time to scream before I sink my teeth into his neck.

A faint gurgle deep in his throat is all I hear as I take my fill, the rich blood sinking into me, my rage draining away on a wave of satiation.

By the time Tommy reaches the Doctor's house, I have been careful to erase all traces of my encounter with Vinny. The only clues left are the tears and rips in my black gloves, but those have been thrown away and replaced with an unmarked pair. When Tommy arrives I am in the garage polishing the chrome on my bike, my motions calm and unhurried.

"Hey, Sheila, did you see or hear anything strange on your way out?" says Tommy as he walks in. "Vinny was jumped as he was leaving the Navy Yard. They broke his leg and stole his car. The guys found him down by the docks, talking out of his head about witches and vampires."

"Everything was quiet when I left." I shrug. "How'd things go with Sal?"

"You know Sal, he wanted to know why outsiders were being allowed into La Cosa Nostra," says Tommy, clearly uncomfortable with the topic. "He's just an old-timer who wants things cut-and-dried like they were in the good ol' days of Prohibition when the Italians ran one neighborhood and the Irish ran an-

other. I told him Meyer Lansky was one of the most famous
Mafiosi ever and he was Jewish. How's that for racial fucking di-
versity?" He laughs.

The intercom on the wall crackles to life: "Tommy and Sheila,
please come to my study," requests the Doctor.

"On the way, Doc," answers Tommy.

"I've just gotten word that we've lost a fourth courier," says
the Doctor in greeting as we enter the room. "The other families
are starting to ask questions, suggesting we can't handle our end
of the trade and we're becoming a liability. There's rumors the
Commission may bring this matter up and use it as a reason to
vote against letting Tony Jr. be made.

"I want this killer stopped. The family can't afford to lose the
confidence of the Commission," he adds from his seat before the
fire, a brandy snifter held casually in one hand.

"This job is now priority one. I want them stopped. I don't
care what it takes. And, Tommy, when you find the person re-
sponsible, take care of the problem—for good," he finishes
tightly, his professional mask slipping to reveal the ruthless
Mob boss underneath.

The foul air in the alley has not improved. Even the cold air
doesn't completely dispel the stench. The level of garbage
spilling from the forgotten trash Dumpster is the same and the
lone streetlight continues to shine fitfully, threatening with
each flicker to fade altogether. The only change in the forlorn
landscape is the torn line of black-and-yellow police tape that
now litters the ground, mute evidence of murder.

Tommy's police-issue black sedan is brazenly parked in front
of a fire hydrant when I arrive.

"This where you found the vic?" he asks, shining his flashlight on a dark smear of dried blood in the rear of the alley.
Standing nearby, smoking nonchalantly, is Dmitri, his blond

hair and parchment-pale skin starkly illuminated under the gaze of the full moon.

He greets me with a cool glance from ice-blue eyes, his face wearing its habitual closed expression. The tall, Soviet-born Dmitri Federov was a former KGB agent and member of the Russian Mafia known for his silence and his skill with weapons. The doctor had hired him for both reasons.

"This is where I found Enrique," I answer. "But the lookout was killed closer to the street. He was ambushed from behind with a knife and the body dragged here."

"It makes sense. Kill 'em quick and then dump the bodies somewhere they'll blend in with the rest of the trash," comments Tommy. "It's not what I'd do but it's not a bad plan for an idiot perp."

"Alright, so we got a perp who's good with a blade and likes to attack from the back," he theorizes. "Everyone fan out and look for anything that sticks out, anything odd or out of place that can give us a clue to this guy."

Without a word, Dmitri obediently wanders off, flashlight in one hand, cigarette in the other, his eyes diligently scanning the ground behind the Dumpster.

I stake out an area near the far wall, every so often swinging the flashlight in a careful show of industriousness. My superior night vision allows me to easily cut through the shadows and zero in on small objects invisible to the two men, but I keep up the pretense of using the light for the sake of appearances.

The faint gleam of moonlight on metal catches my eye. I crouch down for a better look and see the earring half-buried under dirt and debris. I'm ready to dismiss it as simply a lost trinket, but then my mind flashes back to the images captured by the killer's blade, the man looming over Enrique, a flash of blood dripping from the killer's torn earlobe before all is swamped by pain and fear.

"Sheila, you got something?" calls Tommy.

"I think Enrique managed to rip this from the killer's ear before he died," I say, holding up the small gold hoop. "If he was wounded and bleeding, we might be able to pick up his trail."

"We're damn lucky you found anything in this darkness," he says, reaching out to examine the earring. "This place is a hellhole in the daytime and it's ten times worse at night.

"After two days, we'll need a shitload of luck to pick up his trail," he adds, rolling his shoulders under the weight of his gun holster and jacket.

"You never know," I murmur, rising and walking back to the street, haphazardly directing the flashlight along the sidewalk, kicking aside broken bottles and discarded beer cans while casting around for telltale signs of blood undetectable to the human eye.

"The killer was on foot and heading west," I say, spotting a ragged but steady trail, the fallen blood like neon markers, each droplet a ruby-red snowflake, delicately beautiful with an intricate latticework design that called to me in a wordless language.

"He can't have gone far on foot," says Tommy, as we turn the corner and veer off toward an overgrown lot. "He must have been headed to someplace within walking distance."

"It stops here," I say, coming to a halt before a rusty, metal manhole cover. The area is surrounded by overgrown bushes and weeds but the manhole's rusted metal surface is relatively clean.

"Fucking rat went underground," spits Tommy, but without any real heat in his voice. He gives a resigned sigh and leans down, grunting as he lifts the heavy manhole cover aside, revealing a ladder descending into a narrow tunnel, the walls covered in mold and fungus.

"Ladies first," says Tommy with a wicked grin.

After a few feet the narrow tunnel opens onto several overlapping train tracks. I climb down, Dmitri close on my heels. The air here is close and warm from the heat generated by the passing subway trains. It is also saturated with the smell of decades of decay, wet mold and the excrement of thousands of rats.

"Sweet Baby Jesus! This is disgusting," exclaims Tommy, descending behind Dmitri, his flashlight on a seething mass of rodents nesting at the bottom of a nearby wall. "How the hell are we going to track him down here?"

"He can't be far, it's too dangerous to walk on these tracks for long," I say. "The third rail is carrying enough voltage to light up a small town."

"Shit," moans Tommy, gingerly stepping across wooden railroad ties.

Squealing rats mark our progress as we plow through the inky darkness. There are no drops of blood to light our way. I must instead rely on my keen sense of smell to track the killer's path. After two days the scent is faint and nearly buried under the chemical tracks of others. Like a weaver with a basket of different-colored threads, I examine each one until I isolate his smell, sending my senses on a quest for any lingering traces.

"Damn, it's hotter in here than hell on the Fourth of July," mutters Tommy, wiping his forehead. "This place is a fucking cesspool. Only a crazy person would live down here."

"*Shhh . . .*" I hiss suddenly, holding my hand up for silence.

Half a dozen figures carrying glass-covered lanterns slowly shuffle into view. There are no visible signs of weapons.

"No shooting in the tunnel, you could kill yourself with a single ricochet," cautions Tommy as Dmitri stealthily eases a hand to the butt of the AK-47 strapped to his side.

"Stop right there," yells Tommy in a hard voice of command. "Don't give us any trouble and there won't be any problems. We only want to ask a few questions."

One of the raggedly dressed men, with straggly brown hair and deathly pale skin, gives a high-pitched giggle, the sound echoing in the cavernous tunnel and sending shivers down my spine.

"This is the King's territory and only his subjects are allowed into the Kingdom," intones another man, marginally better dressed in jeans and a tie-dyed T-shirt. His hair is a psychedelic rainbow of orange, red and blue stripes.

"Fine, he's the King of Siam and I'm King Kong," scoffs Tommy. "We'd like to talk to the King and ask him some important questions."

The ragtag group huddles together for a few minutes, exchanging furious whispers before their apparent spokesman, Rainbow Hair, reaches a decision.

"His Majesty will see you," he tells us. "But you must swear to never reveal the secret of the Kingdom to our enemies."

"Sure, sure, you got it. We solemnly cross our hearts, hope to die, promise to never reveal a thing," gushes Tommy sarcastically.

"You have to wear blindfolds," adds Rainbow Hair, pulling several lengths of thick cloth from under his T-shirt. Dmitri throws Tommy a dirty look from narrowed eyes but doesn't resist as the ragged group surrounds him.

Soon the men are marching us through the hot darkness, our path twisting and turning in a series of concentric circles before reversing course and moving in the opposite direction. Finally, we hear the sound of many voices speaking at once and echoing back as if in a huge cavern. We are prodded up several steps and pulled to a stop.

"Remove the blindfolds," orders a deep masculine voice.

The cloths are yanked off with more speed than safety and Tommy winces as several strands of brown hair are removed with his blindfold. He blinks owlishly as his eyes adjust to the light flooding the ornately decorated hall.

An interlocking-cross pattern of pale blue, dull yellow and burnt carmine terra-cotta tiles covers the high, vaulted ceiling. The walls are solid marble and the floor is finest granite. A dusty gold and crystal chandelier hangs overhead like a relic of a bygone era of elegance and grace.

"Where the hell are we?" asks an awestruck Tommy, tipping his head to take in the faded glory around him.

"Welcome to my Kingdom," says the tall, lean man sitting at his ease in the tattered red velvet chair. His vivid hazel eyes set in a face of mocha brown lend him a faintly exotic air.

"I am the King and these are my loyal subjects. They will all be important members of my court when the transition of power is complete," he pronounces with a regal wave of one arm in the direction of the milling throng.

The crowd is predominantly male, but here and there a lone female can be seen. Most wear cast-off clothing and a variety of scars and tattoos stands out in sharp relief against skin unnaturally pale from the prolonged absence of sunlight.

"This place is beautiful. I can't believe we're still in the subway. Where is this?" asks Tommy, openly gawking as Dmitri silently scans the room.

No weapons are in sight, but all around us I can sense the red-hot pulse of anger and the subdued threat of violence.

"This was once the private milieu of the rich, built solely for the purpose of sparing the privileged and the powerful the necessity for sharing space with the unwashed masses," proclaims the King in mocking tones.

"Holy shit! This is the old train station under City Hall," exclaims Tommy. "I thought this place was destroyed years ago."

"It's been closed for nearly one hundred years but I plan to restore it to its former glory," says the King, rising to his feet on the makeshift dais.

"The new Kingdom will be filled with plenty for all. There will be an end to corruption and mismanagement," he adds with religious fervor, his hazel eyes fixed on some grand sight only he can see.

"I will rule by majestic right and dispense justice to my loyal subjects. All will be able to lay their petitions before me and be heard."

"You're fucking crazy," says Tommy flatly.

"No, I'm mad, there is a difference," he returns. "Mad from years of people passing me by on the street, pretending not to see me as I rot in my own filth. Mad from the indifference of our leaders who promise everything and deliver nothing. I'm mad at the world and determined to take revenge."

"And so your solution is to hide down here like rats," I say, drawing his gaze. He strides over to me in two flowingly graceful steps.

The King smiles. "We are not hiding, merely awaiting our time until the true ruler assumes the throne. The transition of power is a tricky thing," he adds with a wag of his finger. "But enough about the future. What brings you top dwellers belowground?" he asks.

"Why don't you ask him?" I say, nodding at the large, bulky man with a bald head and a torn earlobe half-hidden behind the King's chair.

"Tiny Tim?" he says, turning to glance at the man. "What does he have to do with you?"

"If he's clean, nothing," says Tommy. "But if he's been interfering in Mob business, he's ours. For starters, I wanna know how he got that split ear."

" 'Am I my brother's keeper?' " quotes the King, shrugging his shoulders in a deliberate show of insolence.

"Maybe you didn't hear me clearly," replies Tommy in a menacing whisper. "I said 'Mob business.' That means I can snap my fingers and have enough men down here to make this place a distant memory if you don't stop talking in riddles and start making sense real fucking soon."

" 'Uneasy lies the head that wears a crown when alliances are forged that take their toll in blood,' " says the King. " 'And always the sword of Damocles hangs overhead.' "

"What the hell are you talking about?"

"Do not ask me to name your enemy. You have only to look among yourselves to find him," drawls the King in a bored tone.

In a flash Tommy's gun is out, the gleaming black barrel pointing dead center on the King's forehead. "I oughta put you out of your misery," he snarls. Gasps and shouts of alarm fill the air.

"You could indeed but we are many and our name is legion," says the King, matching his unflinching stare, hazel eyes boring into brown.

As the silent standoff continues, the tension in the room rises until it reaches a perilous plateau, teetering on the breaking point.

"Fucking nut," says Tommy finally, shaking his head in disgust. "It'd be a waste of good ammo to shoot you."

As the two men back down from a direct confrontation, the tension in the hall eases and audible breaths of relief are heard. Dmitri's battle-ready stance relaxes fractionally and I feel my own pulse level ratchet down a notch.

"Look, we've lost four men. We just want to ask if you or any of your guys know anything," tries Tommy, clearly striving to mend relations and appear nonthreatening.

"If the hero would cut the Gordian knot, he must first find its heart," answers the King enigmatically.

"The hero would gladly fight, but like Julius Caesar on the ides of March, he has been betrayed by one he loved," I say, wrapping my words about Marco's death in a metaphor about the famous Roman general murdered by his trusted friend Brutus.

"Ah, beautiful and smart!" he exclaims, moving toward me and smiling into my eyes. "But the general must follow his orders, even though they lead to death. Tell me, my beautiful one," he whispers, reaching out one finger to lightly trace a path down my shoulder to dangerously near the swell of my leather-covered breast. "Would you yield to Caesar?"

A growl erupts from Dmitri.

"Ah, I see this one is forbidden fruit," laughs the King, moving away. "No matter, I have my lilies of the valley to keep me company."

"Enough of this Julius Caesar crap. Who's the bastard who's trying to bring down the Micelli family?" demands Tommy.

"Anger is outrageous and hatred a pity, but who can stand against envy?" says the King, his slight figure moving with lanky grace as he paces.

"Goddamn it!" explodes Tommy.

"And was this general reluctant to follow these orders?" I quickly cut in, taking a stab in the dark and hoping to draw more clues from the mad King.

"Yes, on occasion I believe that he has been most strongly reluctant to do so," he answers. "But like the faithful Abraham, we must heed the call. When the mighty Abraham was called to sacrifice his son Isaac, did he hesitate?"

"Let me get this straight," breaks in Tommy. "You made a deal to go out and whack these guys because if you said no they'd kill you?"

"A clever analogy but not strictly true," says the King, turning his head to smile at Tommy. "And now, I'm afraid that like the oracle at Delphi, your time for questions is up. I thank you for your visit, but you'll understand if I don't invite you back."

"Yeah, our time is up and we're leaving," says Tommy. "But if I so much as hear a rumor that we've lost another man, your time will be up—forever."

Lazy drifts of white smoke spiral up from the slim, hand-rolled, Cuban cigar the Doctor holds in one hand while the light sparkles on the beveled crystal edges of the glass of whiskey he holds in the other.

Tommy and I stand stone-faced on either side of the study door, silent symbols of lethal power. He is fashionably stylish in a dark suit that covers both his guns without bulging. My black leather catsuit doesn't allow for any weapons underneath.

From my position across the room I watch a fleeting trace of longing cross Dmitri's face as a cloud of fragrant smoke reaches him. He stands empty-handed and at attention in a recessed corner. He is dressed casually in a black sweater and black cargo pants, but his clothes do nothing to disguise the AK-47 assault rifle he carries at his side, the distinctive reddish-brown of the weapon's plastic magazine visible to everyone in the room.

His presence tonight, along with mine and Tommy's, is more for show than action. A meeting of the Commission is a formal and solemn occasion where all the heads of all the local Mafia families come together to decide who will be allowed in and who will be turned away.

I don't know the future, but already I can feel the volatile and angry energy in the air and almost see the black haze of jealousy and hatred mingling with the smoke fumes.

"This evening I put forward my son, Tony Jr., for initiation into La Cosa Nostra," the Doctor announces now, striking a carefully studied pose in front of the fireplace as all eyes turn to him. "He's been trained and has proven himself to the family. He's ready to take the Oath of Omertà and become a made man."

As if on cue, a handsome young man with striking blue eyes steps forward. He gives a nod of his head as all eyes in the room turn toward him.

"I personally stand for Tony Jr.," rasps Sal from behind a cloud of smoke, breaking the silence. "The kid is one hundred percent; he'll make the family proud."

"Thank you, Sal," says Tony Jr., a well-rehearsed smile blooming on his face. "I want to let everyone know that I respect the traditions of my grandfather and my father. And I intend to—"

"What's this shit I hear about the Micelli family can't handle business no more?" interrupts a large, red-faced man whose nearly three-hundred-pound bulk takes up half the sofa. He looks at the Doctor with all of the arrogance of a man who can and did run the city through an invisible network of bribes and murders.

Like animals on the hunt, the other members of the Commission, lounging on sofas and chairs and leaning against the wall, snap to attention, watching the Doctor's face like hounds questing for the scent of first blood.

"Jimmy has a valid concern," begins the Doctor, a look of intense annoyance crossing his face and hardening his eyes. "As some of you know, we have recently lost several employees under less than optimal circumstances. I have received a report from my security team that the killer was a rogue element from a fringe group living underneath the city. They assure me the threat has been dealt with and eliminated."

"Exactly." Sal nods. "Don Micelli lost revenue and trained employees but the situation is under control. We might have to whack a few more nuts to keep 'em in line, but it's finished. I say we move forward with voting on Tony Jr.'s nomination. Everybody in favor—" begins Sal.

"*Aspetta momento!*" calls Jimmy as a rumble of discontent rolls through the room. "I ain't made up my mind that this thing is settled. Where there's smoke, there's fire, see? And I want to know who was behind these murders. If there's a contract out on the Micelli family, they're a liability now. If they can't take care of business no more, people on the street will hear that," he adds. "Pretty soon, we don't have no respect and the Russians and the Mexican cartels are taking over our territory."

"Jimmy's right," says one man, looking at the Doctor through narrowed eyes.

"Yeah, we gotta get to the bottom of this," adds another, nodding his graying head sagely.

Tony Jr. looks to his father, a question in his eyes.

"Gentlemen, there's no need to be alarmed," soothes the Doctor, his cordial tone not matching the fury I can see burning in his dark eyes. "I will personally ensure that this matter is taken care of to your satisfaction. My security team will have orders to use whatever means needed to solve this problem—including lethal force."

"Good," agrees Jimmy. "Because until you do, there'll be no vote."

"I think I know who's behind the killings," I say, riveting all eyes on me as I step away from the doorway and farther into the room. "I believe it's someone here in this room—someone on the Commission."

"Who is this woman?" asks one man incredulously. "If she was a man, I'd have her killed for insulting my honor."

"You've got balls, sister," laughs the fat Jimmy, his belly shaking with genuine mirth.

"I told you she'd be trouble," mutters Sal, a scowl on his face.

"Sheila, you do understand that you have just accused a member of the Commission of breaking their oath of loyalty to La Cosa Nostra?" says the Doctor somberly. "If what you say is true, there is a traitor among us."

"It's true and I can prove it beyond a shadow of doubt," I say, meeting his gaze.

"You have twenty-four hours to bring me proof." Addressing the group, he continues, "The Commission will meet here again tomorrow night. If what she says is true, we'll deal with this according to the code of La Cosa Nostra." He pauses before adding, "But if what she says is not true, I'll kill her myself."

I have only twenty-four hours to find a killer. The King's cryptic comments about an enemy float through my mind. According to Sal, the traitor in the family was Marco. But Sal killed Marco more than a month ago . . . right around the time the Micelli family started losing couriers. It can't be a coincidence that the killings started after Marco's death. I must go back to the beginning, tracing the trail of blood back to Marco's grave.

The small boating dock is deserted at this hour, the small creatures of the night the only witnesses to our arrival. Any other eyes are wise enough to look away and quickly forget anything they might see here.

With the ease of long experience, Tommy and Dmitri ready the boat for travel. They have both been here before. I have not. This place is anathema to my kind, the presence of our enemy too near. Tonight, I brave the beast in search of the answer to a riddle. What memories lie in the mind of a dead man.

The roar of the motor drowns out Tommy's voice as we pull away from the deserted dock, the small fishing boat darting around a line of fluorescent orange safety buoys and picking up speed as we hit the open water. At low tide the water is calm and the current smooth.

"I'm going to open up the motor to full throttle," he yells now, suiting action to words.

Neither Dmitri nor I answer him, Dmitri out of habit and me out of fear. I am afraid that the act of speaking will further drain my dwindling strength.

We have only begun our journey to the private island where Marco is buried and already it is all I can do to remain upright. Next to sunlight, open water is the most dangerous foe of any vampire. Dying by sunlight is a clean death, quick and instantaneous, over in an instant. But crossing running water is cruel torture, sapping our great strength and weakening us until our bodies simply stop functioning. Even now my senses are so weakened I can no longer hear the trip-trip of Tommy's heart or the deeper thud of Dmitri's pulse behind me.

My power leeches away the farther we travel from land. When the last hint of horizon disappears from view, my eyes close and I feel myself slump forward, my head too heavy to lift, braids falling down to veil my slack face as I direct all my energy to drawing air into my oxygen-starved lungs. Like a puppet on a string, I feel my boneless body gathered up and cradled close to a hard, male body. Foreign words in a strange tongue are whispered in my ear, the deep voice stealing inside me and filling me with warmth and heat, surrounding me, protecting me, lending me strength as I fight the devouring pull of the sea.

"Hold on, Sheila! It's only a little way more," yells Tommy.

Long minutes later, I dimly hear waves breaking on shore. The drone of the motor dies away and the boat rocks wildly for a moment before it steadies. I feel myself picked up and carried. I am gently placed on a patch of soft grass, the odor of living things rooted in the soil floating into my nostrils. Strength and vitality slowly seep back into my limbs, quickening my heartbeat and flooding my muscles with adrenaline. I open my eyes to see a worried-looking Tommy leaning over me. Dmitri stands aloof at a distance, smoking a cigarette and looking out over the water.

"Hey, are you okay?" Tommy frowns with concern. "I swear I never saw anybody get so seasick so fast."

"I'll be fine," I say, rising to my feet and ignoring his outstretched hand. "You didn't have to carry me."

"I didn't," says Tommy drily.

I am surprised into stillness at his words. I know he is telling the truth because he cannot lie to me with the mental command I have implanted in him. But I gave no commands to Dmitri. He operates under his own free will.

The ever-silent Dmitri shoots me an enigmatic glance before tossing down his cigarette, grinding it out with one boot heel and striding off toward the small rise ahead.

"Tell me again how this is going to help us find Enrique's killer," asks Tommy. "My money is still on that nut underground. I'm not exactly happy to be digging up the grave of a dead man. Marco may have broken his vows to the family but he still deserves some respect." Tommy crosses himself.

"I told you, the King may be crazy, but he is only the body of the snake, not the head," I answer. "His riddles were filled with odd hints about conspiracies and betrayal. If we solve the riddle, we find the real traitor to the family and the person behind the killings."

"And you think a field autopsy of Marco's body has the answer?" he asks.

"Yes," I say, letting him come to his own conclusions about what that process will actually entail.

"Right, we better get moving, we have three hours until high tide," says Tommy, hoisting a shovel over one shoulder and flipping on his flashlight.

After nearly an hour of digging, the gaudy gold casket is uncovered. Stepping on the casket handle, Tommy climbs out of the grave, his warm breath visible in the cold air as streams of white fog. A shirtless Dmitri stands wedged between the dirt wall and the closed casket, his shovel poised to pry off the lid.

Tommy quickly crosses himself as the casket opens with a groan and a whoosh of air scented with death and formaldehyde rushes out. Inside, Marco's decaying body lies on a bed of white quilted satin, a large, ornate gold cross clutched in his hands. After only a few weeks, the corpse resembles a mass of white, gelatinous pulp. The airless environment inside the casket has kept external predators out, but the internal bacteria and the inevitable processes of human decomposition have covered his flesh with a viscous liquid.

"God! I think I wanna be cremated," groans Tommy in disgust.

"You're sure there was no autopsy?" I ask.

"No, like I told you, Don Micelli filled out the death certificate himself."

I climb down next to Dmitri, who, despite the noxious gases given off by the corpse, has seized the opportunity to light up. The brief flare of the lighter flame as he cups it to his mouth gives his face a pure and austere beauty at odds with the surroundings. By contrast, Marco's face is an obscenity; the features blurred beyond recognition and the head itself a misshapen ball of discolored and swollen tissue. Strangely, his clothes are almost pristine, the white shirt only a little wilted and the black suit jacket and discreetly patterned tie virtually unmarked.

"I'll take it from here," I tell him. Without replying, he heaves himself out of the grave, the long muscles of his back fluidly bunching and relaxing under his pale skin. I hear Tommy complaining about the foul smell as they move away, heading upwind of the open casket.

Once they are out of viewing range, I quickly begin unbuttoning the black suit jacket, laying it open and undoing the white shirt underneath. The entry point for the fatal bullet is a small hole with blackened edges. There is relatively little damage on the outside of the wound, a mark of how well the hollow-point-tipped bullet did its job. It entered the body cleanly and once inside proceeded to tear through the vital organs with the force of a small hydrogen bomb.

I strip off my leather gloves and plunge my bare hands into Marco's chest, ignoring the cold, spongy feel of his decaying organs and pressing past his ribs and into his chest cavity until I feel his heart. I find the bullet near his spinal cord, lodged neatly between two vertebrae.

At the touch of my fingers on the metal casing, I am wrenched into the past and images slam into me with a jolt. A carousel of memories crashes into my mind at high velocity—Sal's face, the cigar dangling from his lips, a terrified Marco speaking rapidly and then a young woman's face twisting in anguish, her words a tangled mix of Spanish and English.

"That's not his money," says a young woman in her late teens with a thick Puerto Rican accent.

"Shut up! I'm not talking to you," accuses a red-faced Sal.

"Sal, I swear, I don't know where the money came from," says

Marco, tall and handsome like his brother Don Micelli, but without the killer edge. He looks at the suitcase full of bills in clear bewilderment. "I never seen this bag before in my life. I don't even know how it got here. I never bring money here, you know that."

"What I know is you got half a million dollars that don't belong to you," screams Sal. "Youse been stealing from Don Micelli and stashing it here with your little whore!"

"*No soy puta!*" cries the teen, her face crumbling. "*No es verdad!*"

"Hey, you got no call to talk to Altagracia like that," scolds Marco, gently wrapping one arm around the weeping girl. "She ain't done nothing to you."

"C'mon, *paesan,*" he cajoles. "We've known each other for too many years to fight over money. In this business, crazy shit happens all the time. Whaddaya say you pack up the suitcase, take it to Don Micelli and we can straighten things out tomorrow."

"I'm telling you your days of cheating this family are over. You're not walking out of here alive," screams Sal, the veins standing out on his forehead.

"Sal, I'm telling you I didn't steal that money," insists Marco. "It's late, I'm tired. You take the money and in the morning we can talk to my brother. We'll straighten this shit out like men, *capisce?*"

"No!" shouts Sal, pulling out a shiny 9-millimeter Glock.

"*Madre de Dios!*" Altagracia wails as the bullet hits Marco squarely in the chest, sending him staggering back, blood already bubbling from his mouth as the bullet tears through his arteries and his lungs fill with blood.

I hear Sal scream, "*Puttana!* Get over here, you're coming with me. I'm going to make sure you never open your mouth again . . ."

My body feels so cold suddenly, like the temperature in the room has suddenly plunged twenty degrees below freezing.

Random thoughts and pictures fill my head, the curve of Altagracia's breasts when we make love, memories of my four
daughters when they were babies, my wife Constance's face on
our wedding day, playing tag with my brother, my immigrant
father's pride when I graduated high school and his Italian accent, still strong after twenty years in this country, when he
hugged me and said for the first time I could remember, "I love
you."

"Why?" we ask Sal with our dying breath, our heart breaking
with sadness and the pain of betrayal.

"*Cafone!* I'm sick of taking orders from you and your brother.
You think I can't run this family? I taught you both everything
you know about the business. With you out of the way I'll be
consigliere. And when I get rid of your brother, I'll be the don,"
Sal vows.

"Hey, Sheila, how's it going down there? You need a hand?"
calls Tommy, impatience in his voice.

I swim back to the present and shake off the last of Marco's
blood-soaked memories.

I refasten all the clothes, taking care to cover the new, much
larger hole in his chest. The soggy flesh around the hole sags in-
ward now, but there's nothing I can do about that. Finished, I
clean my hands, draw on my gloves and clamber out of the
grave. Dmitri shoots me an inscrutable look as he begins to
shovel dirt onto the closed casket.

"Well?" prompts Tommy.

"Who was with Marco when he died?" I ask.

He shoots me an impatient look. "Sal was with him. He's the
one who found him with the stolen money."

"Yes, but where was Marco at the time?" I say, drawing out
the question.

"At his girlfriend's apartment," answers Tommy.

"So where was the girlfriend while Sal was pulling the trigger
on her sugar daddy?" I ask.

"That's a good question. I don't know." Tommy frowns. "Sal never mentioned her. And nobody's seen her since Marco died."

"Maybe there's a reason nobody's seen her," I suggest. "She was the only other person there that day, the only witness to what happened between Marco and Sal."

"But what does that have to do with the killings?" Tommy asks, his face reflecting his confusion as he follows my line of questioning. "You said that the person behind the killings was someone in the Commission."

"I think Sal's behind the murders," I say.

"No! That doesn't make sense, I don't believe it," he says, shaking his head, his brown eyes widening in disbelief. "Sal has always been like a father to all of us. When my own dad was killed by some street punk trying to make a name for himself, Sal stepped in to help my mother raise me and my brothers. He took us fishing, for God's sake!"

"Tommy, listen to me," I say, moving closer, tentatively feeling my way through the thicket of his human emotions. I can hear his quickened heartbeat and sense his tormented anguish. "The Sal you knew then is not the same Sal who killed Marco," I say. "That's why we have to find Altagracia. She has to tell the Commission the truth about that night and what she heard."

"Okay, I can call in some favors down at police headquarters and get an APB put out on her," suggests Tommy, running a hand through his hair. "I'll say it's for shoplifting or some petty shit like that. We can also swing by her and Marco's old place and work the neighbors, ask if they've seen her recently."

"Alright, that sounds like a solid plan. While you and Dmitri handle that I'll chase down other leads," I say.

"You have other leads?" Tommy frowns, a question in his voice.

"Yes," I answer without elaborating.

He shrugs and turns toward the boat. "Whatever we do we

better make it quick. High tide is coming in and the clock is ticking."

The return trip across the water is worse than before. The tide has roughened and swells rock the boat continually. I sit in a frozen stupor as we reach the halfway point between island and shore. My heartbeat is dangerously slow.

For the first time since I have come to live among the humans I taste fear, rising acrid and bitter inside my weakening body. What a delicious irony, to escape the Inquisition, the Council's thinly disguised trial by torture that proves the loyalty of those lucky enough to survive, only to die surrounded by water, alone and unknown. With that last despairing thought, my mind sinks into a state somewhere beyond the finite limits of life but not yet entering the vast infinity of death.

When I feel hard arms enfold me I cannot even summon the strength to open my eyes. The boat pitches wildly, a rogue tide hitting us broadside. The salty spray splashes onto my face like icy drops of fire.

"Shhh . . ." croons a deep voice from the man seated behind me as I unconsciously moan and try to turn my face away. A warm hand rises to cradle my cheek, gently wiping away the burning taste of the sea before tucking my face into the shelter of a broad chest.

"*Strigoi*," whispers the voice, using the ancient Romanian name for my kind, the name given to the first blood drinkers in that faraway land where we were spawned so long ago from the seed of a dark prince.

A warm wrist is pressed to my mouth, the tantalizing promise of fresh blood lying just under the skin calling to me. Against my wind-chapped lips the soft skin feels as smooth as the most expensive silk. I open my mouth the merest fraction but do not have the strength to feed. The sea has stolen it.

"Drink," gently implores the voice. "The blood is the life."

Like a boomerang the words echo in my head. The blood is the life. The blood is the life. From somewhere I summon the strength to open my mouth and weakly sink my teeth into soft tissue, my sharp incisors opening a vein. The blood trickles down my throat to my thirsty cells as I slowly drink. The wrist is taken away after only a few moments, but it is enough to call me back from that dark purgatory of nothingness. My heartbeat quickens; I open my eyes. We have reached land.

Dmitri's arm drops away. Cold air rushes in to replace his warmth as he stands up. In seconds he is leaping onto the small dock and busying himself with ropes and knots to secure the boat.

He stops momentarily when I ease to a standing position beside him. Tommy passes us both, making a beeline for his car.

I grasp Dmitri's arm before he can pull away. I push up his coat sleeve to bare his still-bleeding wrist, two small puncture wounds marking the spot where I fed.

He gives an imperceptible jerk at the first touch of my tongue on his torn flesh. I slowly swipe my tongue across the marks, bathing the wounds until they close cleanly with no discernible trace of injury.

"Thank you," I whisper, meeting his ice-blue eyes.

For a few seconds only, a light flush paints his face and I glimpse a scorching heat lurking in the depths of his gaze before he veils his eyes. When he reopens them, they are once again the impenetrable blue I have come to know. Without a word, he brushes past me.

He is waiting when I arrive at dawn, his strong arms reaching out to hold me. I wrap myself around his body until there is no space between us. We interlock like two parts of a whole, connected from groin to lips.

"Beloved, are you hurt?" he says, breaking away from the kiss. "I felt you weaken; I felt your life force in danger."

"Then why didn't you come?" I cry, hating myself for letting him see my pain. "I nearly died tonight and you weren't there to save me. As a power holder, you could have sent me a share of your power to strengthen me."

"Sheila, you know the Council forbids contact with anyone who has been banished," he says.

"I'm your life mate!" I scream, my open palm cracking against his face with a sharp sound.

His eyes slide away in shame.

"It has been difficult for me since you were accused of breaking the law," he says. "I know it is difficult for you to bow to the Council in all matters. But you must learn obedience. The Inquisition is dangerous, but if you—"

"—survive it I will be judged innocent? My loyalty confirmed?" I finish, not bothering to hide my scorn. "Do you know what it's like to be driven from the world you've always known? To have your kindred turn their backs on you and to be shunned by your own life mate," I say, forcing him to look into my blazing eyes. "I will never submit to their barbaric tests. I did not break the law and will serve my seven years' banishment rather than bow down to arrogant dictates of the Council.

"I have found a new life among the humans," I add.

"I love you," he whispers.

"Then you love an outcast. Unless you are prepared to join me in exile, it would be better for both of us if you didn't come again," I say, hardening my heart.

The underground tunnels are as hot and humid as before, the thick air closing in on me as I retrace my steps, searching for the secret lair of the King.

I am sure that with Marco's memories I have now solved the murderous riddle of his death at Sal's hands. There is one more piece to the puzzle that I must put in place before I can present my evidence to the Commission. Instinct tells me the missing piece is here, buried under layers of dirt and soil in an effort to hide the truth. The King's words echo in my head, a bizarre map that when unraveled leads straight to Sal. The girl Altagracia is the key and I must find her before my time runs out. She is the key that ties it all together. I have sent Tommy and Dmitri ahead to the station to wait for my arrival. We are all conscious of the swift passing of time. I pick up my pace through the winding tunnels. It is the booming sound of his voice that leads me to him.

"The time is now, my soldiers!" says the King. "We must take up arms and bring justice to all the enslaved citizens of this corrupt city. We are the righteous leaders of the Kingdom Come!"

A quick look around the corner into the large hall reveals the charismatic King surrounded by several dozen followers gathered about the dais. They look at him with rapt faces as he expounds on his vision for the future.

I pull back and continue my search down a darkened hallway leading off from the main hall. Dust lies thick in the side passages, clumped in corners where spiderwebs gleam overhead and the sound of scurrying rats can be heard.

At the third such passageway I catch a whiff of an odd smell that teases my senses. There is a faint flower essence, faded and elusive but oddly familiar. As I stand there I recall Marco's last memory of Altagracia. She wore a light floral fragrance.

I ease inside the room, the only light a single lantern placed on a small stool. In the far corner of the dimly lit room is a crudely constructed wooden cage. The sole prisoner is a badly disheveled girl wearing a ripped and torn blouse atop grimy jeans. Her skin is nearly gray with fatigue and shock.

Before I can move closer, I hear heavy footfalls approaching. I slide back into the deeper shadows of the room, my black leather top and pants blending into the darkness. After long minutes, the heavy figure of Enrique's killer, the man known as Tiny Tim, lumbers into sight.

His eyes widen as I spring, covering the distance between us in one strong leap.

"Stupid bitch, I'm going to kill you!" he rages, all but frothing at the mouth with incoherent fury, a look of vicious determination settling over his unshaven face.

"Bring it on." I smile.

The bullet he fires from the cheap pistol he pulls one-handedly out of his waistband rockets past with a high-pitched buzz to bury itself in the wall behind me.

"Are you aiming for the wall or did you just get lucky?" I say tauntingly. Before he can lift his weapon a second time, I wrap my gloved fingers around his wrist and close them with a vise-like grip, grinding the fragile bones under the skin into broken pieces.

I clamp my other hand around his thick neck and lift his bulk until only his toes touch the floor.

"Black bitch! . . . K-k-k . . . kill you!" he chokes out defiantly even as his face pales to the color of dirty chalk.

"Your insults are as pitiful as you are," I tell him, deliberately letting him see my incisors slide out.

"Noooo," he wails as I suck the blood out of his thrashing body. As I let him fall in an insensate heap to the floor, I hear more footsteps heading in my direction, drawn no doubt by his screams.

Altagracia lies insensible in the cage. She never looks up as I break through the thick boards and metal nails of her prison.

"Altagracia! I work for Don Micelli and I know what Sal did to you," I say, hoping to stir her to action with the mention of Sal's name.

"You're here to help me?" she asks with cautious optimism, her dazed eyes holding little hope. I can see that she is desperately weak from her ordeal and in no shape to attempt an escape.

"Yes! I know why Sal wanted to keep you quiet," I say, spinning around to aim a kick at the man creeping up behind me, machete in hand. My booted foot connects with his pelvis and I hear the bones snap like twigs. "I know Sal murdered Marco."

I quickly grab her arm and pull her from the cage, hefting her slight weight in my arms with ease. I enter the hallway leading back to the main tunnel and break into a light run, hoping to get out before the others arrive. I am not so lucky.

The sound of frantic shouting fills the air. "Where is he? Did you see him?" yells one man. "He got Tiny Tim and stole the girl."

A pack of men appear in front of me, quickly spreading out to encircle us and cut off our escape route. I cannot see any firearms but I'm taking no chances this time.

I place Altagracia on her feet. She wavers but finds her balance.

"Hold on!" I growl, pivoting to throw a hard elbow at the man foolish enough to charge me and a roundhouse kick at the person unfortunate enough to move into his place.

"Get behind me!" I shout, steadily backing toward the dark mouth of a side tunnel. The number of bodies chasing us is still formidable, but fewer and fewer rush to attack as they see the fate of their comrades.

I give one final bone-smashing kick to the leg of a particularly persistent pursuer and spin around to grab Altagracia's arm.

"To the left, to the left, cut them off!" yells a large man, a broken baseball bat in his beefy hand.

"I really didn't want to do this but you leave me no choice," I mutter, pulling the Glock from my pocket. The crystal chandelier tinkles and sways as gunfire echoes around the cavernous room, bullets falling like lethal raindrops on surprised faces.

The hollow-point bullet rips into the back of the man raising his arm to fire a small pistol, tearing through bone and tissue like the head of a mercilessly marauding army.

I take advantage of the resulting confusion to swing Altagracia into my arms again and make for the main tunnel. Once I'm out of sight of the others, I give my power free rein, using the energy to race through the darkened, rat-filled tunnels, the girl in my arms blessedly oblivious.

As we reach the light of the train station, I gradually slow until I am walking again. At the platform edge, I rouse Altagracia and urge her up the stairs. Around us on the concrete platform are a few late-night riders who sit or stand with bored faces.

"Just a little way more," I tell the exhausted girl, who is nearly comatose with fatigue.

When the train doors open, I deliberately choose an empty car. When a young boy attempts to enter I give him a look so vicious he quickly turns away. I ease a limp Altagracia down onto a seat bench. She has a weak but steady pulse.

"Altagracia, I need you to wake up," I say firmly.

"What? What?" she mutters. "I'm so tired. I have to sleep."

"No! Altagracia, you can't go to sleep now!" I snap, even as she sags spinelessly in the seat.

With a grimace and a quick glance at her closed eyes and pale face, I bring up my arm, peeling back the leather to expose my wrist. A quick twist of my teeth and a thin line of blood wells to the surface.

I pull her head up, forcing her slack lips to my wrist. "Drink and be strong," I whisper, hoping the mental command will be strong enough in her semiconscious state. As she slowly begins to lick the blood, a flush fills her wan face and her eyes open.

I take my wrist away and pull my glove over the wound.

"I had the strangest dream that I was drinking blood," she says with a wide-eyed look at me. Only a spot of telltale color lingers on her lips like the stain of some exotic lipstick.

"We don't have much time," I tell her. "My friends are meeting us at the next train station in a few minutes. We have to get you back to Don Micelli's house so you can tell the Commission what you saw the night Sal shot Marco. I need you to tell them the truth. Are you up to doing that?" I ask.

"I loved Marco. He was a good man." She sobs quietly, burying her face in her hands.

Tommy and Dmitri are waiting at the station as we pull in—Tommy with a worried frown and Dmitri calmly smoking a cigarette despite the large NO SMOKING signs posted in the area.

"She needs medical attention, but she'll do," I say, moving back so that Tommy can see Altagracia's slight figure behind me.

"Jesus, you did it. You really did it!" he says with a smile. "I thought you were crazy but you were right."

"Now we have to finish it!" I say.

A weeping Altagracia collapses in a heap in the middle of the Doctor's study. Only her face is visible; from the neck down she is enveloped by the folds of Dmitri's coat. It dwarfs her much smaller frame, the cuffs turned back several times to bare her fragile wrists.

"This is Marco's mistress, Altagracia Concepción," I announce, letting the murmurs die away before I speak again.

"Two months ago she was with Marco when Sal came to the apartment and accused him of stealing half a million dollars from the don," I say. "She was the only person who witnessed what happened that night. She's here to tell you the truth about Marco's death."

The room erupts with shouts. A maddened Sal is on his feet, screaming profanities in Italian and English. When he makes a move toward the still-crying Altagracia, Tommy draws his gun.

"Tommy? What is this?" says Sal, his face graying in shock. "You would draw on your old Uncle Sal?"

"Sit down and let Sheila finish," he growls in reply, bitterness in his voice.

The shaking Altagracia remains huddled on the floor.

"My dear, perhaps you'd like a drink of brandy to steady your nerves," offers the Doctor in his smooth, patient voice.

"Altagracia, I'm here with you. You don't have to be afraid anymore," I whisper to her, gently grasping her arm to help her upright. After a few seconds of uncertain swaying, she steadies and raises her face.

"*Mentira!*" she accuses, glaring at Sal.

"She's sick with grief. She's not right in the head no more since losing Marco," says Sal, shaking his head sadly.

"Sal, I think we owe it to Marco's memory to at least listen to her," says the Doctor.

"Start from the beginning," I tell her, moving back to let her stand on her own.

"He came to the apartment that night," she begins haltingly. "I let him inside because I know he and Marco are good friends. I was in the kitchen when I heard him shouting. He was saying that Marco had done something very bad. That he had took money from his brother.

"When I came into the room he had a big suitcase with lots of money. He opened it and said, 'See, here's the money you stole from the don,' but Marco kept saying how he didn't know where that money came from," she says, her voice beginning to waver. "He called me names, ugly names, and Marco said for him to stop and that they could talk to his brother in the morning and straighten everything out. But he just kept shouting and calling me names and saying Marco had stole the money! *Pero está la mentira!* Marco never stole from his brother!"

"Why didn't you come forward and tell me this when my brother was killed?" asks the Doctor, an odd look on his face.

"He took me away!" screams Altagracia, her face growing red. "After he shot Marco he grabbed me and covered my mouth and face with towels. I begged and pleaded but he made me go with him to some strange place under the ground. And they put me in a cage!"

"It's okay," I croon as she collapses to the floor, folding into herself like a flower bending under the strain of too much weight.

"Sal paid a man called the King to get rid of her so that no one would ever know the real story about why Marco died," I explain. "But the leader took pity on her and instead of killing her he simply took the money and imprisoned her in a cage underground.

"Sal also paid the King to have his men kill Micelli couriers so that the Commission would lose faith in the family and reject Tony Jr.'s nomination. His ultimate goal is to control the family.

"Marco was just a warm body standing in your way," I say, walking toward Sal, who now wears a hunted look on his sagging face.

"No, no! This *puttana* is making stuff up," he says, turning his eyes toward the don. "She thinks her lies will get some kinda blood money out of the don."

"Your real target has always been the Doctor," I add, talking over his protests. "You decided that you would run the Micelli family and that if need be you would kill to do it.

"You wanted Altagracia dead because you believe the old saying: 'Three can keep a secret—if two are dead,' so you paid the King to kill her and dispose of her body, but for some reason he didn't follow orders. He kept her alive."

"What is this? Who you gonna believe, Don Micelli? Me or this fucking *puttana?*" demands a desperate Sal. "I worked for this family for years. I've always been loyal to you. This *moolingnanne* just joined the payroll yesterday."

"I always knew in my heart that Marco would never steal from me," says the Doctor. "I let your lies blind me to the truth."

"Fucking *cafone!*" yells Sal, jumping to his feet. "You don't have the balls to lead this family. You're too soft!"

"No, Sal, you're the one who's a piece of shit if you think you can ever be the head of this family," he says. "Always you have wanted to be primo, to be number one without earning that honor.

"From this day forward, your name will never again be spoken in this house or by anyone in this family. From this day on, you are dead to me."

Two men with guns drawn lead the still-screaming Sal from the study, a litany of curses falling from his lips.

"Tommy, go and get Tony from his room," says the Doctor. "He deserves to know what happened here and why the Commission won't be voting tonight."

"Got it," says Tommy, exiting the room. As he leaves, whispers and looks fly around the room. Jimmy finally nods and rises to his feet just as Tommy returns with an expectant-looking Tony Jr. His handsome young face is open and guileless, more clean-cut cherub than future Mob kingpin.

Jimmy clears his throat. "Don Micelli, it's your right as head of your family to take care of this," he begins. "But I want to ask that you allow the Commission to step in and handle this situation. A good man was lost because of lies. A man without honor has hurt us all.

"In the memory of Marco, may the Holy Madonna watch over his soul," he makes the sign of the cross and all in the room follow suit. "I speak for the entire Commission when I say we unanimously vote to accept the nomination of Tony Jr. to be a made man."

A big grin breaks out over Tony's face. He looks like an all-American high school student who's just been made football team captain. I feel a rush of elation at this news but push it down and keep my expression blank. Tony has been my secret project for months. He is both young enough and ambitious enough to achieve my goal. Already we are linked. With Tony under my mental command, I plan to make the Micelli family a global force in the drug trade with tentacles in every country. I will make Tony *capo di tutti capi,* the Boss of Bosses.

"God bless you," murmurs the Doctor piously. As the men continue their conversation, I put a hand under Altagracia's arm and lead her from the room.

We walk up the stairs into a guest bedroom decorated in soothing blues and greens, the heavy damask drapes drawn against the night.

"Please, don't leave," she begs when I turn to go. "When I'm alone I feel like I'm back in that horrible cage with no one to help me."

"Would you like to forget? To have the memory of everything that has happened since Marco's death become like a dream to you?" I ask, looking at her haunted and tear-drenched eyes.

"Yes!" she breathes.

"Then close your eyes and let yourself fall asleep. I promise that when you awaken, everything will be only a vague memory, something you can't remember even when you try," I say, guiding her to the bed and smoothing the covers over her as she lies down.

Dmitri is alone in the weapons room when I enter. His pale eyes track me as I close and lock the door behind me.

"You called me *strigoi,*" I say, coming to stand where he sits at the table with his legs splayed out before him. "That is one name for my kind. Vampire is another. I don't know how you know, but I have decided that if you were going to make the knowledge public you would have done so a long time ago."

His eyes are intent on my face but he doesn't speak.

"I am an outcast among my own kind, banished for something I did that violated the rules of our kind. The world of humans is my home now." I pause. "It has been difficult learning to live among you, but I have found that you are not so different from us. I think I can survive here but I do need one thing that I do not yet have."

I move into the space between his legs, allowing my gloved hands to fall onto his broad shoulders. I look into his ice-blue eyes.

"I need someone I can trust, someone who knows the truth but does not fear the power of the vampire," I whisper, bending closer until my lips are only a breath from his. "Are you that man, Dmitri?"

"Yes," he answers in a deep voice made hoarse by passion, his eyes blazing with desire. His arms encircle and pull me into his embrace as our lips meet in a heated kiss.

Human Heat: The Confessions of an Addicted Vampire

THE URBAN GRIOT

My Origins

I read an article in the newspaper some time ago that made me reflect on my tortured predicament. The writer commented on the sexual tension of fictional vampires. And he was right, there is plenty of intimate tension amongst us. However, my life is not that of fiction. I exist, and not only in the dark shadows of my New Orleans birthplace but during the luminous daytime hours of human folly.

This article made me think back to my origins as a vampire. I had not done so in many years now. What was the point? There is no escaping my fate. Only death can save me. But as far as I am concerned, I am already dead, and the next realm of death I do not care to know. So I continue to dwell amongst humans, tortured by my addiction for their heat and the taste of the sweetest bloods of passion.

Passion was how it all began for me. I was surrounded by it. I was such an insanely handsome and adventurous man in my numbered days as a human that it drove women, young and old, mad to have me. I see it all now. The selfish cravings of lust were my fate from birth.

I was born of exotic blood to begin with, a mixture of African, French, Spanish and American Indian. They called us Creoles, an American invention of a new human race. We were a nation within nations and a culture within cultures. But even amongst the vast beauty of the Creoles, I stood out.

Martelli Daniel Sosa. Who could imagine the creation of such a striking specimen of bronzed skin, crystal-gray eyes, ivory-white teeth and a face of perfect symmetry, crowned with a mane of dark curls? How could they not stare at me? And how could I not become accustomed to the attentions they gave me?

I spent most of my early human years as an orphan, which only increased their desire for me. It seemed that I belonged to everyone but myself. The only memory I have of my mother is that of a sick Creole woman on her deathbed. I remembered that she looked pale and old, older than a mother should look. But I do not remember myself feeling sorrow in her death. I felt more relieved by it, as if her death was good for her. It was the nature of things.

I never knew my father. But I was told that he was not a well-liked man. My father had failed to realize his place in the world. He was rumored to have been killed by a mob of offended and vengeful white men. Maybe they had hung him. But his body had never been found. So I imagined that they had burned my father alive and piled him into a heap of dark ashes to be thrown away into the wind.

Of course, without the supervision or protective care of parents or relatives, I was left to the mercy of strangers, all of whom had moral dilemmas and human desires to overcome. Many of those human dilemmas and desires were not controlled, which led to my first sexual encounter. Or affair, I should say. Because it was bitterly secret and ongoing.

On one of the hottest summer days of my human memories, Meredith Bennett, a wealthy, blond-haired maiden with eyes as blue as the ocean, called me to a quiet place behind her family's grand white mansion. The images of her floral umbrella, white dress, white laced gloves and fine, tailored shoes return to me often when I rest. I view the encounter as the beginning of the end.

"Martelli, could you please come with me?"

Meredith was years older than I, but even in my innocence, I was never afraid of her. I was only suspicious of her intentions with me. I understood that I was not of her race or class. So I stood there bewildered in my cotton overalls and tattered shoes, while my skinny brown arms dangled nakedly at my sides.

"Why would I want to?" I questioned her.

Meredith approached me and pulled me by the hand with all of her urgency.

"Come with me, and I promise that you will not soon forget it."

I stopped her tug on my hand with superior strength, even in my boyish frame.

"I will not soon forget what?"

Meredith's blue eyes glared at me, determined. Young and wealthy white daughters were well used to having their demands granted, particularly with the darker, African and Native races of New Orleans, of which I was a member.

"You will do with me as I tell you," she insisted, and pulled me forward again.

I became curious, as any adventurous boy would be. So I allowed her to have her way with me. Once we stood under a large oak tree in the shade behind her estate, Meredith reached inside of my loosely fit overalls and pulled on my small genitals.

"Do you have any idea what this is for, Martelli?" she asked of me.

At first, I was surprised by the sharp pain of her trespass and hastily pushed her away.

Meredith laughed, a wicked, girlish laugh that continues to haunt me.

"He-he-he-he-he-he. Boy, I promise, I will not hurt you."

She took off her white gloves and reached for my private parts again, managing to stroke my insignificant penis with her soft, pink fingertips. Before I could move from her reach, the stroke of her gentle fingers excited me. Soon I could not control the rush of blood that surged through me and caused my dutiful erection.

Meredith smiled and looked into my astonished eyes for reassurance.

"That is what it does," she told me.

Before I could calm the desperation of my scrambling thoughts, Meredith sank to her knees and tasted my erection at its tip, sending shocks of bliss exploding through my unprepared body.

"You like that, do you?"

Meredith seemed excited by my pleasure as she continued to devour me. I found myself unable to move. I could feel the anticipation of something powerful, the most ungodly feeling a young human male could ever possess. When I had reached that point, it felt as if a thousand tickling feathers were exploding through the length of my shaft. I was driven so wild by this insane period of pulsations that it shook me in my stance and moved the earth where I stood.

Meredith eyed me and was pleased by my urgent release. For explanations that were beyond my conception, I reached down and stroked her cheek and chin, as if to thank her for exciting me in such a way. It merely seemed the correct thing to do.

For my appreciative tact, she smiled and said, "You will be a great lover, Martelli. I am sure of it."

And she was right. By the time I had reached my full growth as a man, I had loved hundreds of women of every race, class and creed within the province of Louisiana. I had mastered the human art of love and seduction, and I had loved them all. Possessively. Until I met my match.

Abigail, an astonishing mixed breed herself, coffee-brown, with hard dark eyes and wavy hair as black and mysterious as the night, was not from Louisiana. No one knew her birthplace or family name, only that she was free and unruly. They called her "The Gypsy Woman." And for whatever reason, they feared her.

I had never met the woman, actually. I had only heard stories about her. But then she appeared over my horizon, like the morning sun, wearing a burgundy dress and no shoes.

I will never forget her first words to me as I stood in the busy fish market of the Mississippi River.

"I have been watching you, and waiting for you to become a man for a long time now."

She looked no older than I was, but her words made her seem as if she was much older.

I asked her, "And why have you waited?"

I would have charmed and loved her in a heartbeat. She was breathtaking. I could see how any man or woman could fear her. Her alluring beauty was intimidating. However, she had met her match now, and I would not turn away.

She smiled and touched my chiseled arms with her hands when she answered me.

"Some of our worldly desires are better served in time. You will live long enough to realize as much yourself."

"You speak as if you know my future," I responded.

She said, "I do know it. And I have protected you long enough to have your extended future for myself now."

I was immediately amused by the woman. She seemed my equal in vanity. Nevertheless, I felt a need to establish clarity in her words.

"You've protected me when? And from who?"

As a grown man, I stood over six feet tall, with solid, muscular mass. And I was not easily tussled with.

She asked me, "How do you assume that you've been able to court so many women without repercussions from envious men? You have courted many treasured and wealthy daughters, Martelli, as well as beautiful wives."

I was stunned. I had rarely thought of the repercussions of my lovemaking. She was right. I had been trouble free in my various relations with women. But now I was curious.

"And how have you protected me?"

Abigail was a beautiful woman by any standard in the world, but I did not at all view her as a woman to be feared physically.

She only answered, "I have my ways."

We seemed to converse in private at that moment. Her dark eyes had hypnotized me. I paid attention to her alone. No one else existed.

That was quite unusual for me. Even when I appeared to give a beautiful maiden my full attention, my mind's eye had always wandered. Not so with Abigail. My mind could think of only her, with images of our naked and intertwined bodies in a serpent's dance.

She read my thoughts and asked, "Is that how you think of us?"

What could I tell her but the truth?

"I think of every woman in a serpent's dance."

"But I am not every woman," she told me.

Before I could respond, Abigail had disappeared and left me standing there in a daze. I came to my senses and searched for her like a desperate hound.

"Did you see the beautiful woman in red? Where did she go?" I asked an old fish salesman.

"What woman?" he responded, confused.

"She was just here, standing in front of me."

The merchants and buyers at the fish market began to look at me as if I were a madman. Had I imagined her? Was it all an illusion?

I spent the rest of the day attempting to convince myself that she was real. But when the daylight hours had faded, I had lost my battle of faith. I no longer believed she existed. So I no longer searched for her.

I sat out alone under the full, illuminating glow of a silver moon and wondered what my fate would be in life. And she read my thoughts again.

"You will continue to love and be loved for thousands of lonely nights amongst the humans."

Abigail appeared in front of me as mysteriously as she had before. This time she wore clothes of virginal white, as did I.

I told her, "I no longer believe in you," and turned away.

Abigail laughed at me.

She said, "I did not realize how spoiled you have become in your ways. You seem to lose patience far too easily."

I said, "I have patience only for that which is real."

"You mean that which is easily attainable and requires limited patience," she responded.

Her words filled my ears with a smothering warmth, as if she was right behind me. I turned to face her and found her standing beside me. Her movements seemed as swift as the wind. I took note of it.

"I chase no woman in vain."

"Yes, I know. And since you have grown so accustomed now to having your way, I shall be forced to have you wait much longer than I had initially expected."

I told her, "You can expect to wait for an eternity as far as I am concerned. I do not play games of which I am not the master of its rules. If you have watched me for so many years, as you claim, then you should know this about me already."

She nodded and conceded.

"Yes, but I seem to have underestimated how . . . bullish you are."

"I am not bullish at all. I am only an expression of true manhood."

Abigail did not bother to comment. Not immediately. She seemed to allow my words to settle on her mind a spell. Then she looked at me in what appeared to be a face of sorrow.

She said, "I was a true woman once. And my arrogance took it away from me. I have not been the same since. That is . . . until you."

She had puzzled me. If she was no longer a true woman, then what was she? And she spoke as if she was twice as old as she appeared. So I began to wonder what childhood she had had to allow her such creative explanations of her fate.

"And now you will have me wait with more arrogance," I told her in spite. At that moment, I cared less about her personal history. I could only think of my own connection to her, and what I wanted.

Abigail looked at me for the first time in a stare that I could deem as threatening. Her dark eyes turned into sharp, narrow slits.

She said, "I pity you as I pitied the innocence of myself once. But I am no longer innocent. And I now know the ways of the wicked. So let us not prolong the inevitable."

In a blink of an eye, she kissed me. It was the most engaging kiss that I had ever felt from a woman. And it left me paralyzed in wonder.

A cold chill rushed through my bones as I found myself

falling weightlessly. I felt inebriated without drink. Her kiss was that powerful. And I remember my eyes drunkenly locked on hers before she viciously attacked my neck with sharp teeth that poked holes into my ripe veins.

"Uunnhh!" I growled in vain. I squeezed her firm body with all of the strength that I could muster, trying to push her away from me.

But I was powerless to release her grip upon me. My eyes rolled skyward toward the moon and the stars above us. I remember the pain of her hungry bite, as well as the rigidness of my body as she drained me of precious, warm blood, leaving me cold and weak.

I had lost all of my defensive energy. My body hung limply against the strength of Abigail's. I had no idea a woman could be as physically powerful as she was.

"Now you will know the true meaning of loneliness and desire," she told me.

My fresh blood stained her lips, teeth and tongue as she spoke. She then bit her own lip with her sharp-edged teeth and kissed me again, intertwining her own blood with mine.

The warm mixture of fresh blood squirted into my open mouth like a spring and nearly choked me. I was forced to swallow.

"Uurrgghh!" I responded desperately. I could feel my life vanishing before me in a repulsive drowning of blood.

"Relax," Abigail whispered. "It is too late to struggle now. It has begun."

She bit into her lip deeper and produced more of her blood to feed me with. And I drank it, helplessly, until my insides constricted and burned with pain.

"Uuunnnhhh!" I wailed.

Abigail released her hold upon my weak body, sending it crashing to the dirt, where I squirmed like a serpent in turmoil.

"*Uuurrrlll!*"

"Ha ha ha ha ha." Abigail mocked me with her laughter.

Her laugh was deeper and richer than Meredith's, but just as unforgettable. And when I had regained my senses, after what seemed like an eternity of agonizing pain, my entire body yearned to taste more of Abigail's warm blood.

The Hunger

Abigail's bite and blood-filled kiss began a drastic change inside of my body. I felt sick with nausea, cold at the bones and empty within my gut. I reached for my neck to find that I had stopped bleeding. The holes from her bite were still present, but they no longer pained me. And they were much smaller than I had imagined them to be.

"What have you done to me? What kind of demon are you?" I asked Abigail weakly from the ground, where I continued to lie in recuperation.

She answered, "I am a vampire," with her teeth still exposed to me. "And I have shared with you my gift of eternal life."

Within my mouth, I could feel the strengthening of my own teeth and jaws. They seemed increasingly tight.

"You witch! I did not ask to join you in a living hell! What gave you the right to defile me?"

"I chose you because of your great passion and hunger," Abigail informed me. "And I have always viewed you as my proper mate."

However, she had no idea what she had done. I had been hungry my entire life out of necessity, hungry for everything, including my freedom, the freedom from possessive desires. So I had learned to use the desires of others against them. In particular, I had learned to use the desires of women. And I had made myself appear more passionate than I was in reality, which was more vengeful. I had loved women to counteract their own lustful possessions of me. But in secret, I dreamed of peace and equilibrium, to be loved without possession.

In a flash, I rose up against Abigail, only to have the fingernails of her right hand clasped tightly around my throat. She held me extended above the ground as her sharp nails broke my skin.

She said, "You are still weak and young, Martelli. But in time you will be very powerful."

I said, "I wish to be powerful now to rid myself of you." I managed enough strength to twist myself free of her hold. She then shoved me with such monstrous force that I tumbled backward through the air, landing hard against the earth.

"Aarrgghh!"

Before I could rise again, Abigail was quickly upon me.

"Do not be foolish, Martelli. There is far too much for you to learn. You need my counsel," she warned me.

However, I was angry and determined to fight her.

"I never asked for your counsel!" I spat, as I rose against her a second time. I was swift enough to grab her neck between my own nails. But with a violent slice of both her hands into my chest, she opened up twin gashes that were inches long and deep.

"Aaahhhh!" I squealed in pain, immediately letting go of her.

Abigail ate hungrily of the blood that squirted from my opened chest.

What a bloody mess she had made of me. I readily expected

to die when she had finished. It was the end of all life for Martelli the man, as well as the demon.

But I regained my consciousness and found myself resting inside a barn with filthy pigs, fowl and cattle. And I was much weaker than before. But when I looked down and felt for my chest, it was nearly healed. So was my neck. They were both miracles.

"You must eat now and regain your full strength, Martelli."

It was Abigail. She was still there with me.

I looked up to face her to spite her again, but I was far too weak to continue in my challenge. She seized a young pig and opened the tough hide of its neck with one ferocious bite as she stood above me. Fresh blood poured out of the squealing pig and into my dry mouth. And as I drank, the other animals inside of the barn became frantic with fear.

I had no choice. I was now a vampire, whether I wanted to be or not. So I emptied the pig of its blood and desperately moved on to the next one, and killed with my new, powerful teeth for the first time.

"Yes, Martelli. You must eat until you are full. And you may find me after you have cleansed yourself of such foul blood of animals."

At the moment, I cared not about her insult. I only knew that I needed blood to fill the aching hunger within my gut. I savagely attacked and killed several squealing barn animals and drank their blood until I had satisfied myself and felt strong, stronger than I had ever felt as a human.

The changes that I noticed within me were astounding. The vampire blood had heightened my senses. I could now see, hear, smell, taste and feel at least three times more sharply than before. I looked around me inside the barn and could see the major veins of every animal with pinpoint accuracy as they continued to scramble for their lives, away from my demonic thirst for their blood. I could clearly hear the tempo and the stress of their animal heartbeats. I could smell the stench of their fear, and the wretched foulness of their unwashed bodies. I could taste the panic of their warm blood pulsating through my enlarging veins that rapidly transformed their blood into a form of vampiric energy. And I could feel every newfound inch of my recuperated body, even the pesky mosquito that hovered near my ultrasensitive skin, only to be captured in an instant within my nails and quickly eaten to test the sharpness of my razor-edged teeth.

But as I stood there in the middle of the chaos inside of the barn and swallowed the tasty snack of mosquito blood, my new senses began to overwhelm me. It was all too much and too fast. Maybe I had overdone my first blood-hungry meal. The panic, stench, fear, taste and noise of the animals began to irritate me beyond my tolerance.

"Eeeaarrrkkkk!" The noise grew louder and ate at my throbbing nerves until I was forced to cup my ears and scream out in madness.

"What have you done to meeeee? You witch! You wiiitch!"

As I moved forward to escape the torture of those squealing animals, I had no idea how powerful I had become. I literally flew from the barn and broke the hinges of the doors that contained me with no more than a forceful extension of my arms.

Blooommm!

"Where are you?" I hollered into the darkness. Abigail had taken me to a deserted acreage of farmland, away from the population of New Orleans. I was ready to begin my search for her, this time to exact my revenge for changing me into such a vile being. I cared not who spotted me, for I had not asked to become a vampire.

"Where are you going?" Abigail questioned me from behind.

I moved quickly to seize her as soon as I heard her voice. I planned to snap her body in two with all of the new blood power that surged through my veins.

"You will pay with your life for what you've done to me," I growled as I secured my grip upon her neck.

But when I searched her face, I saw and smelled the fresh blood of a human that still wet the side of her lip. The raw aroma of her feast enchanted me. My nose flared wide, and I began to crave the sweet blood that I sniffed inside of her.

She smiled and laughed as my hold became weak upon her.

"Do you see the difference that human blood makes?" she asked me. "Animal blood can make you strong, indeed. However, it is not the preferred."

She did not have to explain to me what she meant. I could sense it. I fell weak with hunger within her arms again. I could feel the fresh human blood racing excitedly through her veins. And I wanted it. But as soon as I spotted the vein from which to draw the blood from her neck, Abigail fought me fiercely.

"I am not a powerless maiden to be robbed of the blood of my feast," she proclaimed as she shoved me away from her.

I was so hungry and engaged in my quest that I never fell backward. I maintained my balance and attacked her as fiercely as she had pushed me away.

She then attacked my throat with her lethal nails again. I grabbed her long fingers before she could strike and pushed them away from me while squeezing the bones within them.

"*Uunnnnhhh!*" she squealed.

I was obviously stronger than her now, and still ravenous for her blood. Yet, she was still as swift in her movements as I was in mine. And as I lunged toward her neck again with my teeth to take her, I found her own teeth locked in a battle with mine. It struck me for a moment as animalistic, and it startled me long enough for Abigail to toss me backward over her shoulder.

I was not able to stop myself from a bad landing on her second counterattack. She was indeed a clever fighter.

"You will not have me tonight until you are cleansed of that foul animal blood," she reminded me.

I paused and took the first sniff of myself. I reeked of animal foulness. But so what? It only made me more determined to have the fresh human blood that I smelled within her. And it would serve her right to have my animal stench upon her, draining her of her sweetness. I planned to punish her for including me in her living hell in as many ways as I could make possible.

I smiled at her and leaped back to my feet, still surging with vampiric energy.

"So, you will deny me of fresh human blood, even as I reek of panicked animals?"

She backed away from me as I slowly moved toward her.

She said, "You have been asleep and feasting on beasts for several nights now."

"And I will now feast upon you," I told her as I attacked her again.

Abigail stuck her hand directly into my mouth and grabbed my tongue with her nails, drawing blood from it. She then pulled my tongue forward from my mouth. I growled in pain as she attempted to lacerate my tongue with the nails of her free hand. I grabbed her arm and twisted it away from me, squeezing her wrist defensively like the head of a serpent.

"Aaahhhh!" she squealed in pain, as I crushed her wrist.

Suddenly, in the middle of our standstill battle, I felt weak. I was panting like a spent hound. She had forced me to use much of my new energy in a reckless tussle with her. And my grip upon her became weak again.

Abigail could sense my distress and began to laugh at me once more.

She said, "There is still much you need to learn, Martelli. Much indeed. For animal blood fades far too easily, and it is only to be used as temporary fuel, until more human blood is consumed."

She had given me the information that I needed to defeat her, I was sure of it. And as I could sense the elements stirring within her, I was certain that she could sense the same within me. So I slowed my breathing and my vampiric blood flow to fake exhaustion.

I breathed deeply and told her, "Please, let me have some human blood. I beg you. Why do you continue to torture me?"

She said, "You must learn to hunt for your own."

"I understand that. But as of now . . . as I am again weak . . ."

I dropped to my knees as Abigail pondered my fate. I then began to sense the excitement that she held for me. Her heart rate increased with the curiosity of sharing fresh blood from her veins with me.

She said, "It is not a vampire's way to beg."

I responded, "What choice do I have when you continue to fight me?"

She was determined in her struggle to deny me. She bared me her fanged teeth in another smile when she responded, "Then you admit that you are not my equal."

How could I be her equal? I had just become a vampire, while she had been one for many years already.

So I agreed with her assessment.

"Yes, I am far from your equal. You are my master, and I am your pupil."

She nodded to me with all the pride of a queen.

"And I shall teach you what you need to know, starting with the choices of blood," she explained to me.

But before she could begin her lecture, I used my remaining strength to latch on to her exposed neck with my teeth. She had let her guard down. I had sensed it.

"You deceived me!" she yelled, as I bit into her neck with my teeth.

It was too late to fight. I had already punctured her vein, and the sweet human blood squirted freely into my hungry mouth.

I expected Abigail to fight me in vain as I drained her of her precious blood, but she did not. She became submissive, moaning and cuddling me as I feasted.

"Ooooh, Martelli. You . . . youuu . . ."

She reached for my groin, not to attack me there, but to feel the throbbing of blood energy as it filled every part of me, including my masculine pieces.

"Do you feel the heat?" she asked of me.

My eyes began to roll upward toward the moon in lust.

"Yessss!" I hissed into her neck. I dared not let go of her until I had satisfied myself.

And as she held on to my masculine parts, I noticed that they as well had grown more powerful than before, and more sensitive.

Our serpent's dance had finally begun. It was an ungodly seduction upon the hard rawness of the earth. Abigail pulled my filthy clothing from me, and I pulled her clothes from her, so that every naked inch of our brown vampire bodies could intertwine.

"Mar-tell-leee. Mar-tell-leee," Abigail continued to moan as I mounted and slithered upon her.

Imagine a thousand strokes of pleasure throbbing through every inch of you, transforming your body into a giant worm of a thousand orifices. Every touch was climactic in itself as the shared, warm blood of prey shot through our bodies and heated us in the frigidness of the night. Even the insects of the earth envied us, and crawled upon us to have their share of the bliss.

I began to stroke Abigail diligently, and dutifully, and consistently. And she stroked me in full submission, and squirmed, and moaned. We stroked into the virgin earth together with the wind stroking us, and cooling the rapid heat that emerged from our open feast of each other.

I panted breathlessly, in disbelief of such raw and purposeful devouring. It was as if life itself had needed us to fertilize it and each other through our hungry sexuality. And I had no idea how long it had lasted, I only knew that Abigail had outlasted me, and she had carried me to a secret lair to rest me in my very own coffin until it would be time for us to awake . . . and feast again.

The Ways of a Vampire

When I awoke in my coffin, starved by new hunger, Abigail was there to help raise the lid.

"You must learn to conserve your energy if you plan to survive as a vampire, my darling Martelli," she greeted me.

She wore another virginal dress of flawless white, and had clothed me as her twin in a white shirt and dark pants.

"And how is a vampire to conserve his energy with such blood-soaked passion from you?" I teased her. I no longer thought of her death. I accepted my fate as a vampire now, and I needed her to assure my survival as well as to match me in my passions.

Abigail smiled as I arose from my dark coffin.

I looked around me and noticed nothing familiar in this dark place. I could smell the stench of death.

She said, "You must allow yourself to become familiar with the smell of death, for death is key to your survival."

I told her, "I am already familiar with the smell of death. I have been around it all of my life. Must I rise to the smell of it as well?"

Abigail nodded to me. She could understand my irritation. Nevertheless, she countered, "Then think of it as a reminder to yourself to heed the lessons that I give you, or you will soon join those who have died around you."

She had a point, and there was no more need for argument. So I accepted her logic to benefit my own survival.

"Put this on," she told me in reference to a burgundy gentleman's jacket with golden trim.

I looked it over before trying it on.

"Nice taste. But whose is it . . . or was it, before me?"

Abigail turned away from me and became elusive.

"Let's just say that you remind me of someone."

I looked in her direction at her smooth brown skin and striking beauty, and I understood more than what she was willing to tell me at the moment. After all, I had been experienced with the many moods of women.

"So, as he has impressed you, you have impressed me, and I shall impress someone else."

Abigail became violent in her look again.

I grinned smugly and approached the gentleman's jacket she wanted me to wear. Abigail had set out to make me her companion, but it would have been far more fruitful for her had she chosen to court a more loyal man. I could only wonder how much she had thought out her predicament with me before she acted to include me in her dwelling. Although I had been a vampire for less than a week, there was no reason to believe that my attractiveness and cunning as a human would not be increased now that I was a vampire with enhanced senses and strength.

I went with Abigail back to the populated city of New Orleans after the sun had gone down, and carried with me a heightened perspective. Not only did I assume certain conclusions about the humans we pondered to feast upon, but I could now sense their truths and falsehoods as well. I could see straight through their many façades. I could hear their heartbeats when they lied, became fearful or tried to hide their excitements. I could touch them ever so faintly and read all of their deepest emotions. And I sensed how sweet or sour their blood would taste when consumed.

As one could imagine, I was like a child in a candy store with humans, a candy store of easily attainable blood. And New Orleans was known as a late-night town.

"Martelli! Martelli!" an old friend called in recognition once we reached the center of town.

I had known Ericka Chappell for the majority of my life, and she was quite excited to see me again. She was a white maiden with a sprinkle of Native American blood, giving her the deep, dark eyes, olive tone and dark hair of an ethnic woman. However, her father, Mr. Harvey Chappell, was a staunch Englishman and a wealthy man, which had solidified Ericka's place as a white American woman.

I stopped with Abigail on my arm and introduced the two women.

"Ericka, this is Abigail."

Ericka was surprised and read the situation immediately, but did not speak on it.

"I'm pleased to meet you," Abigail told her with an extended hand.

Ericka took her hand and exchanged pleasantries.

"The pleasure is all mine."

But she could not deny her curiosity.

"So, you two are soon to be married?" she asked of us.

Abigail looked into my eyes and grinned. She considered that we were already married, as intertwining vampires.

"Yes, you could say that," she answered.

Ericka appeared stunned by Abigail's answer.

"Oh, well, I guess you two have that much in common."

She meant it as a slight to both of us, but more so to Abigail, "The Gypsy Woman." Ericka had always flaunted her family's wealth and found it hard to fathom that I would not want at least some part of it. It was all a game for Ericka, but she had just slighted the wrong woman.

"And who do you have a commonness with, my dear?" Abigail asked her snidely.

Ericka was stunned again. Abigail and I were still colored people, and of a lesser New Orleans class, who were supposed to regard her with the proper respect.

She said, "I beg your pardon."

"I beg yours," Abigail responded.

I smiled and stepped between the two women to defuse a rising situation.

"Well, I am not afraid of you *or* your magic," Ericka hissed at Abigail.

I intervened and asked my old friend, "And what magic would that be?"

I was curious to see how much she knew.

Ericka looked at me as if I should have known.

"She makes people afraid of vanishing and dying mysteriously. But I am not afraid of her at all," Ericka huffed at me. But she was afraid. She was a little drunk too. I could smell it on her. She was also without panties under her dress. I could smell that as well, as I am sure that Abigail could.

As a crowd of onlookers began to stop and listen in on the conflict, Abigail quickly walked away, leaving Ericka and me alone.

Ericka looked at me sternly and whispered, "How could you be with such a woman, Martelli? I had such great hopes for you."

Ericka had great hopes for everyone, and she had shared her bed with many.

"I am in a better place now," I told her calmly. "But what about you? Are you still searching for peace?"

Ericka stammered to find words. "Well I . . . I just . . ."

She then stopped and stared at me.

"I always considered you as very handsome, Martelli. Believe me when I say that."

Ericka was utterly confused. She had no idea what to do with her father's wealth and influence, and it drove her to reckless habits and decisions.

I told her, "I don't doubt that you believe it, my dear. However, I do believe that you need to find what it is that will truly make you happy."

She looked at me with vulnerable desperation.

"You are not interested in me for yourself, Martelli?"

It was a dangerous question. And even if Abigail did not hear it, I am sure that she would know. She knew it before Ericka had spoken to me. The woman was ripe to die in lust.

"Are you certain that you would be satisfied with me?" I quizzed her.

"Oh, yes, Martelli, I am so very certain," she assured me.

However, in her state of inebriated desperation, Ericka was liable to say anything to anyone.

In my own deviousness, I tempted her to confess her demons. I whispered, "Have you been denied a good spanking recently?"

Surely Ericka knew what I meant. She looked at me with blissful eyes and confirmed it when she began to laugh.

"How did you know?" she asked me. "Is it that obvious?"

The young woman was practically falling over me in public. And she was still very alluring, just confused about her place in the world. Humans are all orphans and gypsies in their own ways. It's a wonder that any of them understand the confusions of each other. I rarely understood my own conflictions as a man, but they had been simplified as a vampire: seek, prey and consume.

I asked Ericka out of my own curiosity, "If I offered to take you to bed with me tonight to experience the strongest passion you have ever known, would you say yes?"

It was a rhetorical question. I knew her answer as soon as Ericka had recognized me in town that evening. It was her fate to be taken. She was begging for it. Her blood was so ripe and so strong that night that I began to crave her madly as we continued to speak. I sized up the major vein in her neck and could nearly taste her tainted blood before I even touched her.

She asked me, "Would you? But what about your woman? Would you betray her for me?"

Ericka wanted only to hear something pleasing that night. She would have believed me if I had told her I would sell her a piece of the moon.

I told her, "My only desire is to give you what you need that would make you happy."

She looked into my gray eyes as if I were a dream come true.

"You wouldn't lie to me, would you? That would be so very bad of you, Martelli."

"No," I told her. "I speak the truth. I would like to share something with you that you have never experienced."

She placed her gloved hand across my chest.

She said, "I want to experience it."

In my ignorance, I immediately began to lead her away by her gloved hand. I cared not who had spotted us. I only desired to feed my hunger. So I led Ericka away from the crowd of town and into more private pastures.

"Where exactly are you taking me, Martelli?" Ericka questioned.

She was giddy with excitement. She had no idea what would become of her. My teeth were already beginning to tighten with anticipation of my feast.

"We are going where you can scream without anyone to hear you."

Ericka thought of it as a joke and began to laugh out loud.

"Martelli, I had no idea you were such a devil."

I grew impatient and turned to her too soon and too eagerly.

"Well, now you will know," I told her.

Ericka spotted my sharpened teeth, ready for the kill, and she froze. Not a sound arose from her mouth. She was in a state of total shock. I stared at her for a moment in bewilderment before I decided to feast on her.

Just as I lunged at her neck with my teeth, Abigail appeared and shoved me forcefully away from the woman.

"Leave her be," she told me, "Her blood is spoiled by drink and depression."

"Nonsense," I responded. "Her blood is ripe."

I was irritated that Abigail had stopped me. I could already imagine the taste of Ericka's tainted blood making its way into my vampire system, quenching my growing thirst for her. I cared not that she was drunk or depressed. She had excited the demon within me, and I needed to consume her.

I pushed Abigail out of my way and started back toward Ericka. The woman continued to stare at me as if in a daze. She could not believe what was before her. I could not even smell the stench of fear. She had none. She wanted me to consume her in whatever demonic way that I saw fit. She really was depressed, and suicidal.

"Martelli, what has happened to you?" she asked of me. "What have you become?"

Although in a stupor, she even approached me. That amazed me and halted my hunger. Could she not see my teeth and my vile, animalistic appearance? Was she not at all repelled by me?

Before Ericka's or any of my own questions could be answered, Abigail reacted to my moment of confusion and seized the maiden by the neck to strangle her.

"No!" I protested. But I had responded too late and too passively to save the woman. Abigail had strangled her as quickly as possible.

"Had her blood been ripe, she would not have died so easily."

I knew not what to think of it at the moment. I only watched as Ericka's cold, limp body crumbled lifelessly to the earth.

I then looked to Abigail. "And what will I eat now?"

Abigail answered simply, "Other prey."

She then heaved Ericka's body into the air and carried it over her shoulder to our hidden place of rest. When we arrived, Abigail led me into a hideous pit of corpses and tossed Ericka's body atop the pile. The stench of rotting humans was so strong there that I moved to cover my nose, only for Abigail to slap my hand away.

"Get used to it," she told me. "The smell of death should never repulse you. You should learn to invite it. For it will mean that you have feasted well, and that you are still alive."

Alive. I could not imagine the word having the same meaning as before, when I was still human. Were we really alive as vampires?

"We are more alive than humans will ever know," Abigail answered, reading my thoughts again. "We may rest while humans are at play, but when we are awake, they are no more than blood-filled children to us. You see how easily she came to you?" she asked. "There will be many more like her, Martelli, and many who are better suited to consume."

"How do you continue to know what I am thinking?" I questioned her. I had no such power over her.

She smiled at me with exposed teeth.

"Because I was once like you. And we are kindred spirits," she answered. "The many thoughts that you now think, I have already thought them.

"And do not worry, Martelli," she added. "We will surely eat. For there are hundreds of thousands of humans who would suffice to feed us."

"And how many of those thousands do you plan to eat for yourself?" I asked her in jest.

She answered, "As many as my belly will allow me to consume before I meet my cold and agonizing death."

Virgin Blood

Abigail trained me to hunt for the surging, vivacious blood of human gamblers, those who saw gold in mere stone. So we feasted upon idiots, mistresses, slave owners and love-thirsty whores, like Ericka Chappell, whose blood radiated with boundless energies of submission, possession, loyalty and naïveté.

We then would share our hungers between us, mounting, stroking, humping and devouring each other in our own ravenous desires. It appealed to me then that Abigail would have us choose blood that would make our cravings for each other more purposeful. Or at least more purposeful for her. She had chosen me as her mate, but I had not actually chosen her as mine. Maybe she had even been jealous of Ericka Chappell's passion for me, and so she had killed her to keep the virus of jealousy-spawned blood out of our vampiric cohabitation.

However, I had grown bored with Abigail's premeditated and wicked touch, as well as with her cold-hearted demeanor. For she seemed only pleasing to me while we danced to the passionate drums of the serpent. She had rarely set my mind at peace. And I had found that even vampires desired stimulating conversation every once in a full moon.

"Do you still think as I think?" I asked her one night in our laziness.

Abigail turned to me and attempted to suppress the truth. For even she realized I could not be held captive for an eternity. I had been her mate for some three decades. That length of time for me to remain faithful to her purpose surprised even me. But time had much less vulnerability to vampires than it did to humans. Humans grew old and weak, dying as mere shadows of their earlier years of prime existence. But vampires aged only in wisdom and experience. Our prime years were in our age, and I had become anxious to explore more of the world with what I had learned of it as a vampire.

Abigail responded, "You disappoint me with your boredom, Martelli. You are still young yet."

"And you are not as old as I once thought you were," I countered. "You are far too selfish in your ways to be as old and as wise as you'd like me to believe. Selfish to not even introduce me to other vampires."

She became angry with me. "For what purpose, Martelli? I have my own set of rules and my own codes of existence. I do not need them meddling in my affairs with humans."

"Am I a part of your affairs with humans?" I asked her. "Do you still view me as such after all the years that we have been together?"

We had even been forced to move our dwelling several times to adapt ourselves to human technology and advancements. I now posed as a night-shift photographer, where I could hide behind the lens of a camera while studying my prey. And Abigail was a head maiden of entertainment, enticing young ladies of the night to serve the personal whims of men who could afford to pay for them.

We lived in a fine stone-built house, still away from the major population of New Orleans, where we could maintain our privacy. We used other facilities within the city to entertain and prey upon humans, never allowing our place of rest to be jeopardized by investigations. We had even built a coffin large enough for us to rest beside each other. Another one of Abigail's splendid ideas.

"Of course you are not human. Not anymore. However, you still hold certain thoughts of favor toward them. And I have noticed these favors."

She was right. I had swayed in my emotions with certain human women. And Abigail had caused them to die in ways that humans could accept, such as automobile accidents and falls from opened windows. She dared not feast upon these women, for I would smell their blood in her and drive her jealous with envy of their wonder.

She said, "You must continue to cleanse yourself of such cravings for them."

But it was already too late. My eyes burned when set upon one woman; my nostrils flared for the scent, ears toned to the voice, fingers longing to touch and tongue anxious to taste the exotic treasures of a young Creole named Ira.

I had met the young, caramel-coated woman in a photo shoot with her father and a white man who was her entertainment manager. They were desperate to make her a singing and performing sensation, but she was not yet polished enough. At least not as a singer. Nevertheless, her look and presence were to die for, with curly reddish-brown hair that fell in healthy tumbles over her shoulders. Her large, maple-brown eyes teased me as she stared into my camera with the poise of a woman and the zest of a child. Even the small mole on her right cheek was perfect. And I could not stop myself from thinking about her, even as my thoughts betrayed Ira to Abigail.

Casually, Abigail told me, "I still manage to protect us, you know."

"How, by killing humans who dare to challenge or investigate us? I can do as much for myself now."

She grunted. "Our privacy is not as simple to maintain as you believe."

"Is that a threat?" I asked of her. Perhaps she was reading more of me than I thought, and she had already begun to calculate leaving me to my human passions and alone to defend myself.

Abigail spoke no more of it.

So I anxiously awaited the next photo session with Ira, her father and her manager. But they never called me again, forcing me to find her on my own. Which was not at all a hard task for a vampire. I could locate her radiant presence just by thinking about her under the full use of my heightened senses.

I followed her trail of energy and scent to a recording studio on Charles Street near the French Quarter. The New Orleans area had begun to industrialize with the naming of many streets and sections. I sat outside the studio against the sidewalk with my camera until I could sneak a word with the young maiden. Ira was no more than sixteen at the time, and her father was very protective of her.

When I felt her presence nearing the entrance door, I prepared myself to act surprised to see her. But as she approached, I could sense distress from the abnormal sound of her heartbeat. And when I viewed the loss of spirit in her face, her distress was confirmed.

"I'm singing the best I can," she confided to the wind as she stepped outside of the studio doors alone.

I had no time to waste. I was certain that someone would be coming soon to comfort her before I would be able to connect with her if I did not act immediately. So I threw myself at her feet.

"Ira. How have you been? You look gorgeous as always."

She wore a simple sky-blue dress so she could sing and perform without hindrance, and no shoes, the sign of a free-spirited woman. Abigail despised shoes herself.

Ira looked at me and was embarrassed by her emotional outburst.

"Martelli. What are you doing here? I thought you no longer wanted to take my pictures."

I could not believe what I was hearing from her mouth, nor from her heart. She was actually happy to see me. I could sense it.

"No such thing," I told her. "I would never tire of taking pictures of you. Who told you that?"

"Well, your agent called and told us that you were busy with other projects."

I stopped and thought before I spoke. *My agent?*

However, I had no time to deal with such insignificant matters. I could deal with that later. At the present, I only cared to connect souls with my new interest.

I said, "That's nonsense. I would be a foolish man to deny such a beautiful young lady my professional services. I would take your pictures for free if your manager could not pay me for them."

Her heart fluttered and she smiled at me.

"Well, I'm glad to see you. But they are working me to death in there," she informed me.

I thought fast and asked her, "Would they mind if I took pictures of you while you sing? I could call it *The Work of Genius.*"

She laughed a girlish laugh and said, "Oh, you flatter me. Come along and I'll tell them myself. You can help me to relax."

"But I don't want to intrude," I told her.

"Oh, nonsense. I must have you. I always thought you were a great-looking photographer," she confessed with glee. "I couldn't imagine replacing you with some pig-faced pervert. You were always such a professional with me. Even while I flirted with you madly."

"Oh, well, I did notice as much," I flirted back. The demon in me begged to allow it. And as she guided me inside the dimly lit studio to join them, her soft touch on my arm told me that she would love me dearly.

"Father, Herman, look what the cat brought in to boost my spirits."

I smiled and nodded to her father and manager. There were at least eight other young men in the room with them. They were all recording engineers and musicians whom Ira was to perform her songs with.

With my presence in the room, I could suddenly hear the violent heartbeats of several of the young musicians, black, white and Creole, who immediately took emotional offense to Ira's liking of me. I pitied the fools, but I was not there to lose to them. I planned to seize the prize unabashedly.

"Martelli," Herman, her manager, greeted me with an outreached hand. He was short and plump with dark brown hair and wire-framed glasses, wearing a gray business suit. "We thought you were no longer on the job for us. And we hated to have to replace you. You do such great work, as if you can read her emotions before you snap the picture. No one else has been able to capture her versatility like you do. It's a gift, I tell ya'."

"It sure is," her father agreed. He was a fellow Creole man with dark brown, wavy hair combed to the right, with a part to the left. He wore a business suit as well, of fine brown wool.

"Well, I'm here to make amends by snapping pictures while she works," I told them.

Herman said, "Be my guest, Martelli, as long as you continue to make her look good."

We all laughed before I moved to secure a corner of the recording booth from which to shoot Ira and her band of jealous musicians. My presence did not help Ira's voice much. She needed vocal training, not a recording session. There was still much for her to learn about singing.

"I / went down the road / and found / my heav-ven . . . I / went down the road / and found / sweet joy . . ."

It was a beautiful song. And even though Ira had difficulty nailing all of her notes, her singing of the song appealed to me in a matter of purity and rawness. Sometimes the honest and natural note, even if wrong, can be more perfect than the right note delivered to perfection.

I began to feel as if Ira's song was being performed specifically for me. It was our song. It was a song of our love. No one else inside the room mattered to either one of us. And as Ira continued to sing our song and stare at me through the lens of my camera, I began to envision us, not in a serpent's dance but in a swan's dance upon the peaceful waters of a lonely pond. We were white swans upon the surface of the water, flapping our wings playfully as we spun ourselves into blissful circles.

"Rrrrnnnnkk!"

A wrong note was violently stroked by a blond-haired guitar player, destroying the tranquillity of my vision. And it was played not in honest mistake, but in calculated envy of Ira's obvious attentions toward me.

I gritted my teeth and promised myself that the blond-haired boy would die a thousand deaths if he meddled in my affairs with Ira.

"Shit, Joseph," one of the recording engineers blasted him. "That was our best take yet."

Ira smiled, no longer stressed about her performance.

She said, "You see what I mean, Martelli? They are working me to my death. And I have yet to even be loved by a man."

She had knowingly thrown fire onto a gasoline-filled house and had burned the ears of every desirous young man inside the room. A woman who knows her power over men has a dangerous weapon. Ira was showing me just how well she could wield it.

I only smiled at her, knowing that her heart raced the

strongest for me. Nevertheless, she had presented me with a challenge, a challenge that I would take with all of the possessive zeal of a full moon. I even decided to toy with my competitors.

I told her, "I am quite sure that Joseph would die to love you."

The blond-haired boy looked at me with anger in his eyes and in his heart.

He said, "You're just a photographer. What do you know about anything?"

"I know much more than you could ever imagine."

It was just what Ira wanted, a noble fight amongst men for her love. Only I was much more than a man.

Herman walked out from the engineering booth and said, "Hey, what the hell is this? Are you guys gonna make music or what?"

Joseph complained, "This guy's distracting me with his camera. Why do we even need him here? This is not the time for pictures. I don't even like my picture taken."

Herman looked at me with a decision to make. He was obviously fond of what my expressive pictures could do for Ira's career, a career that he realized would be more about her look than her voice.

He turned back to Joseph.

"You can sit out for a while and let Martelli take the pictures with the rest of the guys. Then you can get back in there when he's done."

Joseph was incensed. "What do you mean? I don't have time to hang around here while he takes pictures. This was supposed to be a music session, not a photo shoot."

The boy was begging me to end his irritable life. I could clearly see that he would cause me problems if I did not bother to handle him.

Herman finally told him, "Well, do whatever you please, Joe. But if you don't finish the song, you won't get paid."

Joseph looked at me and stormed off with his guitar.

"Damn nigger blood," he spat as he headed toward the door.

His last words seized Ira's attention, along with that of a few of the band members.

She said, "I have nigger blood too, Joe. So do many of us here. Do you feel the same way about me, and about the rest of us?" she asked him.

The boy looked conflicted. Did he love her, or did he only love his own desire for her? I had to ask the same question of myself. We were both vampires in our lust for her.

He answered, "It's the photographer that I don't like. The rest of you are fine. But I just can't stand the way he looks at you."

"And how does he look at her?" Herman asked the boy. "He's a photographer, for God's sake. He's supposed to look at her."

Joseph looked at me again and was still conflicted. I began to worry that maybe he did see something unusual about me, which was all the more reason to kill him. But I dared not threaten the boy with bodily harm, not in front of Ira and the rest of them. So I maintained my peace.

"I just don't like him. He seems creepy."

I was forced to at least defend my character.

"Why, because I am not a band member and I choose to make my living by capturing the perfect picture from my camera and not by strumming the wrong notes from a guitar? Sir, if you do not like to take pictures because of your own deep insecurities, then you may admit as much. But please do not attempt to push your insecurities off on me. I am quite sane, and your outburst, on the other hand, has surely presented you as the mad one here. Or the jealous one, I should say."

When the band members began to smile, along with Herman, Ira, the engineers and her father, I knew that I had won their collected favor over Joseph and could relax.

Joseph did not walk away as I expected him to.

"I'm not afraid of taking pictures," he announced to us. "And I have no insecurities about them."

He then retook his place in the band, with the obvious intention of assessing my continued cravings for Ira. His presence now served only to make me uncomfortable, which I am sure was his plan.

I was able to maintain my poise and ignore the lad. Nevertheless, my flirtations with Ira would have been more purposeful without his nuisance.

I was incensed at Abigail's attempt to sabotage my relations with Ira. That night I waited for her at our house until she arrived after midnight.

Before I could speak a word to her about my complaints, she uttered, "The complications that you lead yourself into with humans will cost you a pretty price. I am only trying to save you from your self-inflicted agony."

Her quick words had preempted my anger. She was admitting her evil deeds before I could rightfully accuse her. That was rather tactful of her. I immediately realized that I was not dealing with childish humans in my anger, but with a seasoned vampire who remained my master.

I responded civilly, "Did not you involve yourself with the complications of humans when you protected me, only to poison me with your wicked blood and force me to become your mate?"

Abigail ignored my disrespectful question and searched my eyes for the truth.

"Is that your intention, to make this girl your mate?" she asked of me.

I answered, "And what if it is?"

I was ready for the challenge, to leave Abigail. We both realized that our full moons left together were numbered.

"I would first warn you that her love of you may not be as it seems."

"My love of you was not at all solidified before you defiled me," I reminded her.

Abigail looked at me with desperation and pity. She then grabbed my face in her hands and said, "Martelli, I care enough about your future to guide you away from the path that you seek, even when I know that it is your fate. Human emotions cannot be trusted."

"So why did you trust mine?" I pushed her hands away from me.

"Because you were alone," she answered. "No matter how many women you loved, you were still alone. So I trusted that you could accept solitude as a vampire, solitude with me as your only companion for life."

"Well, I will have that solitude now with her," I stated boldly.

Abigail breathed deeply, my words a great wound to her heart. She then backed away from me and looked defeated. I had never seen her look that way.

"I will weep for you, Martelli. I have loved you for a long time, and she does not."

"Nonsense. You speak this only out of jealousy," I told her.

Abigail shook her head in all sincerity and said, "No, I speak this out of truth. She is virgin blood, Martelli. And virgin blood cannot be mastered. It is too volatile, too sweet, and far too deadly."

"What do you mean?" I asked her. "We have never tasted virgin blood before?"

"Never," Abigail answered. "There are certain rules that are not to be broken."

I knew that Ira was a virgin. I was attracted to her purity. I would be the first, and I would be the last. So I planned to ignore Abigail's warning.

I said, "You have possessed me more than you have loved me. And now it is time for me to find my own *true* love."

Abigail viewed me in silence before she spoke her last words to me.

She said, "You will now find that true love is the strongest possession there is, or has ever been." And she turned to leave me.

As Abigail had stated, it was my fate to chase Ira. After all, Abigail could not hope to kill every maiden that I lusted for to join me in hell. My cravings for my own mate were inevitable. We both knew it. So I went out to seduce her that very night, and immediately I regretted my continued ignorance.

I could smell the heat of Ira's blood before I had even reached the city. It was boiling and passionately reactive. The blood of a human could only react in such a way in its lust. So I transferred my attentions to the object of Ira's desire, recognizing the familiar scent of Joseph, the guitar player. He had beaten me to the seduction, and I had been far too preoccupied with questioning Abigail to sense Ira's betrayal of me.

I unleashed my fangs in the darkness of the night and flew up to the window of a cheap, downtown motel. And there, inside of the bedroom, Joseph tried his best to rob Ira of her precious virginity, and the powerful innocence that radiated in her virgin blood.

"Joseph. Oh, no. Oooh," Ira moaned as she fought him.

His pink lips and hungry tongue devoured her ready breasts. Her perfect brown nipples slid in and out of his mouth.

"Oh, Joseph. I am not ready," she whispered in confession.

Joseph complained, "Then why do you continue to tease me?"

It was confirmed. Ira had made the boy her love slave.

He then spat, "Are you ready for him? Martelli? The photographer?"

I awaited the answer myself and listened to the truth of Ira's heartbeat.

"I don't know," she told him. She was still undecided.

I felt a touch of despair in her lack of connection to me. It was my own fault. I had not spent enough time with her. And I had allowed her to slip out of my sight while my enemy for her affections continued to live and prey upon her.

I vowed to myself that I would never make that mistake again.

Joseph said, "But you do know that you love this," and he began to suck her breasts with more recklessness.

"*Oooh, yesss,*" Ira moaned to him.

I allowed myself to smile. The boy was quite ravenous himself. I had a new respect for Joseph now, even though I would soon kill him.

He told her, "I love you so much, my dear Ira. I just can't stand to see you with anyone but me. And I would give you anything to love me."

The heat the two of them produced was the strongest I have ever witnessed. Human blood had no limitations; it was alive and self-replenishing. And virgin blood was the most radiant type. Abigail was right. The smell of it alone drove me to near insanity. So what would its taste drive me to do?

"*Pleeease, Ira. Pleeease,*" Joseph begged her.

His lips and tongue licked farther down her belly toward her moist cave of treasure.

"*Joseph. Joseph,*" Ira continued to moan.

However, she no longer possessed the strength to fight him. He had won her over, and was near her point of penetration.

"*Ooooh, yessss,*" Ira moaned again, while desperately grabbing the sheets with both hands.

Her defenses were depleted. And I could take no more.

I broke through the window and took Joseph into the air by his neck, sucking the heated blood from his vein as lustfully as he had sucked the blood-boiling skin of Ira. Joseph cried and whimpered in vain, like the helpless boy that I imagined him.

Ira watched me in my vile attack of Joseph and let out a scream of horror with all of the power in her singer's voice.

Time was of the essence. I discarded Joseph's drained body and immediately jammed my blood-stained tongue down Ira's throat to stop her from screaming. It was an act of desperation. I sucked the loose blood from her mouth and consumed it to stop her from drowning. I then filled her sweet insides with my masculinity to show her the full capabilities of a lust-filled stroke.

And as I began to stroke her in her panicked silence, I could feel the warm looseness of her virgin blood running rapidly from inside her legs. Without full control of my senses, and in the blissful heat of desire, I sank my teeth into her soft neck and tasted her addictive virgin blood for the first time, sucking it from her more violently than I had intended.

And, oh, it was so sweet, so sweet, so sweet, that I forgot my own demonic strength and sucked out all of her life before I could share my vampiric blood with her to make her my mate.

I looked down at her and panicked.

"Ira? Ira?"

Immediately, I opened up my veins to feed her my blood and reawaken her to the dark side, but it was too late. She was no longer alive to feed from me.

"Nooooooo!" I screamed, only to invite her band members into the room. They had used the shabby hotel as a brothel for the many women whom they would entice.

"Oh, shit! That's Martelli. What the hell is he doing?"

"Hell, look at his teeth. He's a vampire!"

I was so distraught over Ira's death that I had not bothered to hide myself from the human witnesses. I would now have to kill them all or flee for my life. But I chose to flee with Ira in my arms, believing that I could bring her back to life with more effort and patience.

So away I flew to my house with her to try in vain to bring her back from the dead. But I was no Frankenstein. And I wept on my knees at my new loneliness. For I had lost Ira without the reality of her love, and I had lost Abigail, who really did love me.

The Addiction

Abigail had been selective enough with her prey to dwell amongst humans without much of an uproar from them. But I had undone in one insane night what she had been able to maintain for decades. And our house, hideaways and all of our belongings in New Orleans were sought out and destroyed in a mad search for us.

It seemed that I was indeed still the young fool in need of prolonged training. However, Abigail was no longer there to provide me with it. And as she had foreseen, after tasting the sweetness of virgin blood, there was no going back for me. I could no longer stomach the taste of idiots, or whores or mistresses and their masters. So I left New Orleans in haste and settled down in the warm, tropical paradise of southern Florida, a haven for Catholic schoolgirls who were taught to give themselves only to their husbands.

It was a virgin oasis, particularly rich with Spanish girls whose parents were fresh off the boats from Puerto Rico, the Dominican Republic and Cuba. I altered my look by cutting off my dark curls—a tedious affair, because my hair would grow back quickly as a vampire—and I began to wear stylish glasses and the flashy clothes of a gigolo. I got a new gig as a producer of pop music.

Everyone wanted to be a pop star in the new America, and as I had learned from my experience with Ira, the sexiest of young maidens were forever being pushed in the direction of adored invincibility, an invincibility that often included abstinence. Young boys, with their possessive control, were dangerous walls of jealousy to any girl's quest for stardom. Even deadlier was the powerful seed in them that forced untimely pregnancies. So I allowed myself to become the trusted interloper, hinting of homosexuality to dull the senses of overprotective managers and family members who might serve to block my goals of seduction.

Oh, yes, in times of increased human technology and advancements, it was a means of mere survival that a vampire adapt to more serviceable lifestyles. So I learned all that I could about the creation and engineering of popular music in an effort to continue producing songs of seduction for the sweet, heated blood of virgins. But by the time I had settled into my new life and routine in Florida, fate once again caused me to flee for my life. For I had unknowingly chosen the wrong family to prey upon.

"Oh, I just love that song so much, Poppi," Samia Vargas crooned into my ear at my recording studio.

Poppi Groove was what they all called me in the music industry. It was a catchy name, particularly for the Spanish population that was so plentiful in the various counties of south Florida.

I looked up into Samia's beautifully tanned face, and I could already envision her strong, young nails digging into my back and shoulders as I stroked her and sucked her sweet blood. Even the smell of her breath was sweet, a mixture of rice and beans with pineapple soda.

"I made this one specifically for you," I told her.

Samia playfully smacked my right shoulder.

"Stop playing me out, man. You didn't make that for me."

"No, seriously, I did. I know what you like now," I told her.

"Well, it sounds like a perfect heartbeat or something," she commented.

I smiled with all the innocent charm of a gay man.

"Don't you find heartbeats to be sexy? I know I do. Heartbeats speak the truth," I stated. "And we all want that, don't we?"

"I know that's right," Samia responded. "There are way too many liars out there. And they're all out to try and get your funky goods."

The girl stood close to me in blue jeans that were so tight they restricted some of the circulation in her blood flow. As a homosexual man, I could tell her so without much alarm from Domino, her career-managing older brother.

"Speaking of funky goods, I think you could stand to wear some looser jeans to move around in a little more naturally," I advised the young pop singer. "And hasn't anyone ever told you that tight panties can lead to yeast infections? That's why I try to wear nothing but loose-fitting, quality briefs, if anything."

Samia laughed, right as her brother Domino reentered the room. He would take frequent breaks away from us to smoke cigarettes or talk business on his constantly ringing cell phone. He was a well-crafted young man, who had covered much of his muscular body in colorful tattoos of gang affiliation.

He stopped to listen in on the organic party beat that I had created for his little sister.

Boomp-boomp—boomp/Boomp-boomp—boomp/Boomp-boomp— boomp/Boomp—boomp.

With the added guitars, horns, cabasa and thunderous hand claps, the full song production was certain to impress an excited crowd.

Domino looked at me and nodded his approval.

"Yo, that shit is hot, man. You keep it coming and I'll keep the cheese on you."

"The cheese is well accepted," I responded to him from my producer's chair.

Samia gave me a touch of breathing room away from her well-curved and virtuous body. As I continued to age, it seemed that more young women were gaining delicious curves.

Domino looked toward his sister a spell. "And stop talking that gay shit to my sister, you hear me? You might start giving her freaky ideas and shit," he warned me.

"Whatever," Samia snapped back at him. However, he was serious. I could read it from the stillness of his heart and the evenness of his scent. He was a killer. Yet, he could never kill as many as I had. So I had no fear of him.

He looked at me again and said, "Yeah, that was fucked up what happened to that singer Rochelle in that airplane crash, man. That's why we're taking nothing but tour buses to travel. I'll have that motherfucker fixed up, man, and spray-painted with a bunch of hos on there. But no airplane rides for my little sis'. Fuck that. She's too valuable."

I smiled and nodded to flatter him. I had not much to say about Rochelle. She was another virgin prospect that I had produced hit songs for. And her shocking plane crash was not by chance. That is all that I am willing to say about it. I was relieved when Domino's cell phone rang, breaking his attention from my recent tragedy.

"Hold on," he told us. "Yeah," he answered. "Who? Naw, man, I told his ass not to do that."

He walked out of the studio, leaving us alone again.

Samia rolled her eyes in his absence.

"He's such a fuckin' hypocrite," she hissed to me. "I mean, he can have girls over at all times of the night, but I can't even have a boyfriend."

I smiled at her. These were the conversations I longed to have with young maidens.

I said, "It's the old double standard at work. And it's been the same for thousands of years. The promiscuous woman is a whore, and the promiscuous man is a stallion."

"Well, what he doesn't know won't hurt him," Samia informed me. She quickly looked back toward the door to make sure that he hadn't heard her.

I knew that she had not been able to explore much on her own. Nevertheless, I was curious to know how wide her imagination could wander.

"Oh, well, do tell," I told her. "The more juice I have on you, the easier it is for me to custom-make songs that will fit you to a tee."

Samia grinned, her heart racing with passionate secrecy.

"You mean you would write a song about my secret boyfriend?" she asked me.

I faked surprise. "Secret boyfriend? I thought that I was your boyfriend," I told her.

My flirtation shocked Samia more than I expected it to. She gasped for air. I guess I gave young maidens more credit than they had earned. The ease with which I was able to seduce them had always surprised me. Then again, youth was indeed wasted on the ignorance of the innocent.

She said, "Oh my God, that's so embarrassing."

"What's so embarrassing?" I asked her.

"I mean, if you weren't . . . you know."

"Gay?" I asked her.

She was too bashful to even speak it.

"Well, yeah. I mean, some of my girlfriends were even like, 'Girl, if he wasn't . . . ' you know."

"Gay," I stated again.

I found a certain pleasure in her queasiness about the assumptions of my sexual orientation. For although I preferred the blood of women that I found to be attractive, I had devoured the blood of just as many men, if only to keep a balanced flow of energy that held masculine edge. Even her brother, Domino, was attractive to me in that way. His macho blood was quite strong.

Samia remained giddy in her revelation to me. Even as a gay man, I had managed to slither into her sexual daydreams. I could even smell her funky goods, as she called it, beginning to moisten during our conversation. But it was not funky at all. It smelled rather tasteful and sumptuous. And it had gone untouched by others.

"So, you find me to be attractive as a man?" I asked Samia bluntly.

She could no longer bear to even look at me.

"Well, that's . . . I mean, that's pretty obvious," she answered.

I said, "Well, I'm flattered. And if I were straight, your brother would definitely not leave me alone with you to make our music. Because I would surely jump your bones and suck them dry like a greedy fat man at a barbecue grill. You are just that sexy."

Samia laughed as hard and as loud as she possibly could. She had no idea how literal my comment was to be taken.

"You are crazy, man. *Loco!* I could hang out with you anytime," she told me.

And when she touched me, she also told me that I would be allowed to kiss, lick and softly explore her if I chose to do so.

Domino reentered the studio once again and stared at us. He

was completely sold on my homosexuality. He deemed me utterly harmless to his sister. And my genuine attraction to his vibrant fervor only helped to sell my role to him. For I did like the lad, almost as much as I liked his sister. However, Domino was far from virtuous.

He shook his head at my lingering stare. "I don't get you guys. But, fuck it, man, that's your lifestyle, not mine. Just keep making the music and don't fuckin' look at me like that."

He eyed me threateningly until I looked away.

I turned and smiled at his sister to strengthen our bond. It was only a matter of time before I would have her. And possibly her brother as well.

All was in place for the continuation of my plans with the Vargas family when, on a particularly windy night, Samia surprised me with a distressing phone call.

"Poppi, Poppi, I don't know who else to turn to," she told me.

The first alarm that I could think of at the moment was pregnancy. But there was no way in hell that I would have allowed that to happen. I would have sensed it. I had been locked on Samia's body chemistry for weeks. However, as she continued her distress over the phone, I arrived at the next conclusion, the spilled blood of her brother, Domino, from gunshot wounds.

"What has happened?" I asked Samia. I did not want to give my extrasensory perceptions away, so I was forced to play ignorant.

"My brother's been shot," she confirmed. "I'm at the hospital with him now. He's all I got, Poppi. He's all I got."

I hated hospitals. There was far too much soiled blood there for me to stomach. And far too many chemicals from medicines mixed in the bloods. So I stayed clear of hospitals.

I asked her, "Do you need a place to stay? Or, you know, just someone to talk to about it?"

I was not going to the hospital. I was set to pass on any invitation to join her there.

She responded, "Yeah, but I'm afraid to leave him. He might . . ."

Her fear was understandable. She would never be able to live with herself if she missed the last opportunity to be with her brother and caretaker. Samia and Domino had no mother or father in the States. They had only each other and friends.

I asked her, "Where was he shot? And what kind of condition is he in?"

But I already knew those answers. Domino had lost plenty of blood; a major organ was punctured. His condition was critical.

Samia answered, "They shot him in the chest and he's lost a lung. The doctors are trying to save his remaining one."

I asked, "And where are your friends?"

"They're here, but they don't know how to handle anything like this, Poppi. They're screaming and crying and calling for revenge. I don't need all of that right now. That's why I called you," she told me.

Shit! Her desperation had me thinking insane thoughts. I had not shared my blood with many, but the thought of it had obviously surfaced in light of Domino's situation and my connection to his sister. How would Samia respond to her brother coming back to her as a vampire? And how would she respond to me for transforming him?

I was conflicted with human affairs once again. What would I do?

"I'll be there," I told her.

"Thank you, Poppi. Thank you."

I hung up the phone and stared at my dark walls. What kind of vampire would Domino Vargas be? He was a rather strong-willed man, and I expected as much from him as a vampire. But what of Samia? If I shared my blood with her brother, then I had no choice but to transform both of them.

"Then so be it," I told myself. It was their fate.

But when I arrived at the hospital, I found that I was not alone in my quest. A vampire of much higher rank had beaten me there. I could smell the strong vampiric blood within him. Parts of it were even familiar to me. He was a Vargas relative. I could clearly smell their connection.

"Their father," I whispered to myself.

I stopped there, no more than ten yards outside of the hospital entrance, in a panic. And before I could make a decision on how to handle myself, he was upon me.

He spoke to me from behind, "I am their grandfather's father."

I waited for him to reveal himself to me, and he did. He was as tall as I, and handsome, but he was much older than any vampire I had ever witnessed before. He had the wrinkles of aged skin and a full mane of long, flowing gray hair. It blew in the wind as he spoke to me.

He said, "I was not a young man like you when I was reborn. And, as a human, I had my children late in age. But I am here now to reclaim the seed of my human blood spawned many decades ago."

I wondered immediately if he knew my intentions with Samia. Once I had thought of it, I realized that he did know. For I had revealed it to him in my thoughts.

"I understand," he told me. "I have heard of you and your abomination of virgin blood. But we are kin now, more so than I am kin with my own human seed. And I could still benefit from your services."

He spoke to me with respect and tact, but I still did not trust him. Human or not, I understood that his seed had his loyalty, and I had been ready to prey upon them.

"Yes, but you have changed your mind now from your initial purpose with them," he answered me. He continued to read my thoughts. His intuition was stronger than Abigail's.

"So, what would you have me do?" I asked him. For I was nevertheless in his debt, because of his superior rank and poise regarding my addiction. We both realized that his blood was much stronger than mine, and that he could discard me with ease. So I stood there at his mercy, a possible enemy.

He said, "I will go to the son, and you will go to the daughter. And after you have consumed her humanity, you shall leave this place, never to set eyes upon us again. For if you do, it will surely mean your death."

I understood him immediately. He would allow me to live simply because he would not drink of the volatile virgin blood to which I had become addicted. But I was indeed still his enemy.

He said, "But you are not my enemy. As I have said before, I understand. And although I am of higher rank, as I was reborn from the powerful jaws of a stronger vampire than you were, we remain vampire kin. However, many years will pass before the son and daughter will forgive you for your obvious preying on them. And I believe that I would fail in protecting you from them. But I do promise you that I shall withhold from them your origins. And when they have found out on their own, I would have you pray for their forgiveness."

There was no more that needed to be said or understood. It would be done. I would take Samia Vargas into my hungry jaws and transform her human blood into my own. And afterward, I would flee for my life and never return.

I went to the daughter and found her waiting outside of the emergency room with several of her friends.

"Oh, Poppi," she called to me. She immediately wrapped her arms around me in blind faith. I began to feel guilt for her fate. However, there was not much time for me to waste with her.

I said, "Allow your friends to stay with your brother. They have your cell phone number and will surely call you if anything goes wrong. But it is important for me to talk to you away from here. Something has come up regarding your future that needs to be discussed in private between us."

Samia searched my face with wonder.

She said, "A major label is interested in our demo?"

She wore all of the hope in the world across her face in her time of despair. For she needed a reawakening of her spirit.

"Yes," I lied to her. What difference did it make now? She would soon become my enemy. So I gave her what her spirit craved.

She stopped and breathed deeply.

"Oh my God!" she expressed. Her hands covered her face to hide a fresh set of tears. They were now tears of joy instead of sorrow.

She said, "If Domino just makes it through, man. If he just makes it through."

"Yes, I believe that he will," I told her. And I began to guide her away.

"So, you have a contract waiting for me at the studio?" she asked me. "How come you didn't tell me over the phone? Don't we need to talk to my lawyer?"

Her mind was moving rapidly toward business, so I decided to use my most powerful tactic: passion.

I immediately turned to Samia and kissed her lips to paralyze her as Abigail had once done to transform me. I figured it would be the quickest way to get her out of the hospital and back to my place. And it worked. I was able to guide Samia away from there and back to my place like a dog leading a blind baby.

By the time Samia had overcome the shocking surprise of my lips and tongue on hers, I had stripped her naked and stretched her out upon my bed. Her beautiful, untouched virgin body was a landscape of vivacious curves. She was the serpent without an illusion.

"Where am I?" she asked of me frantically. "I must have fallen out. The last thing I remember was you . . ."

She then realized her fate in her nakedness.

"What are you doing, Poppi?" She sat up and covered herself. "I thought you didn't like girls."

"No. I do like you, so much that I have decided to share with you a contract of eternal life," I told her as I spread her legs with my strength. Samia had already dreamed of such and I knew that the quickest way to transform her was through her own blissful desires.

She pleaded, "Wait, Poppi. No. I can't do this. I can't . . ."

But it was already too late. Her fate had been decided. So I pushed my powerful, elongated tongue into her womanness.

"*Ooooh, Pop-pi,*" she moaned obediently to the probing of my tongue inside her. I then caressed her breasts with both my hands, causing her to arch her neck and body backward, as she allowed me to have my way with her. Her body began to sway in the rhythm of her rapid heartbeat as she thrust her hips downward into my ravenous mouth.

"*Ooooh, yeeeaaaah, Pop-pi.*"

She then reached down between her legs and ran her hands wildly through the curls of my hair.

"*Ooooh, do me, Pop-pi. Do me, Pop-pi,*" she moaned insanely.

I readily filled her with my enlarged manhood and drove her into more insanity.

"*Oh, yesssss! Síííí, Pop-pi, síííí!*"

"I am Martelli," I finally revealed to her. "And I am a vampire, like your grandfather's father."

I wanted her to know who and what I was. However, Samia was far too taken by her own lust to care. My identity became oblivious to her as I sunk my teeth into the soft skin of her neck.

She grabbed my head to hold me there as she moaned.

"*Nnnmmmmmmmm!*"

And I wept while still inside her, stroking the perfection of her womanness, engulfed in the heat of her desire, stripping her completely of all her purity and devouring her sweet, warm virgin blood, while her new master floated inside the room above us to inspect my work.

"That is enough!" he told me forcefully. "I shall feed her with my own blood now. Vanish from here before I change my mind."

I slowly released my seductive bite from Samia's neck and my overheated body from the radiance of her inner source. I watched her as she continued to squirm in lust upon the bed, as if a ghost had continued to stroke her. She was hot for rebirth, and I began to desire to keep Samia for myself. She would become my new Abigail in her heat.

"No, she will not," I was told, the father's claws suddenly at my neck. "Take the deal you were offered in honorable kinship or die here."

"But she will love me!" I screamed in disobedience.

"She will love blood, and your blood will not be as strong as she will desire," I was told by her new master. For his transformation of her would make Samia a more powerful vampire than I could ever handle.

I was tempted in my desperation to fight him, but I could not seem to release his mighty claws upon my neck, proving that I was no match for him.

"If you cannot break the grip of an old vampire within an old body, then imagine what the son will do to you in a young, strong body when he finds you here with his beloved sister."

His point was well taken. If I wanted to live another full moon of hunger for prey, then it was best that I leave rather than challenge the strength and vengeance of a fresh-blooded vampire with more powerful senses and strength than my own.

I weep now often when I think of how many opportunities for love I have wasted in my bloodthirsty lust. The way of a vampire is still more complicated than I could ever have imagined, as much so as the daily conflictions of humanity. And as I continue to read books and articles inside the dark library of my home, I can smell the exotic scent of another virgin who calls me to possess her sweet virgin blood, and to consume her human heat.

Whispers During Still Moments

LINDA ADDISON

"I need to tell you something," Adina said, straddling her latest victim on the dank ground in the alley. He had been handsome, with a strong chin and high cheekbones. He'd also been arrogant in his tailored blue suit and perfect haircut when they had met at the Greenwich Village wine bar earlier in the evening. The designer sunglasses tucked away in his suit pocket were going to look good on her.

Now, his ruined face gurgled. Blood dribbled from the sides of his mouth, streaking his blond hair. She didn't usually eat meat, but his kiss had been so sweet, his tongue so tender, she had to take it. More important, his eyes were still intact, though glazed over by blood loss.

"Don't go yet, listen . . ." Adina said softly, leaning close to him, licking the blood from his face. It was cooling in the night air, but it was still savory. She whispered in his right ear, in her native African Amharic language, giving him part of the secret: *"Fumiya ayzie, kambui sipo."*

Trembling with release, she growled, ripped his throat and

drank his warm blood. The ritual filled her body with tingling energy. As Adina swallowed his sweet blood her organs revived, her muscles and skin became younger, stronger, as if she were connected to the endless force of the Earth itself. This was the gift granted to first-generation vampires by the Whisper, their secret to apparent immortality.

She stretched, enjoying the increased vigor, wiping the blood from her mouth, licking it from her hands. A scent made her glance into the shadows of the buildings. The sweet, sour smell made her stomach twitch. Something ran away.

She jumped up and chased the figure down the alley, but it was gone by the time she reached where the darkness ended and the streetlights of the Village intruded. The sidewalk was full of people. Standing in the shadow of the building, she couldn't tell which way the creature had run. The smell, the hot tendril of its motion, simply stopped as if it had disappeared into thin air, not something a normal human being could do.

She inhaled the watcher's scent. Could this be a first-generation vampire? That odor was familiar; it had been stalking from a distance but tonight came closer. The sensation of ants crawling under the skin of her neck and scalp tickled her as the thing ran away. Once it hit the street her physical sensing of it abruptly ended. No, this wasn't a First. There was none of the maniac anxiety building inside of her, a typical reaction when one First met another.

The scent was primal, and even though it wasn't an animal, the being wasn't a normal human. They couldn't run that quickly. Could the thing have been a Remade, a human made into a vampire by a First?

Adina walked back to the body. She rubbed the back of her neck as tingling danced lightly up and down her spine, another feeling she had when near another First. Whatever the creature was, Adina had been so engrossed in the ritual and feeding that she hadn't perceived being observed before. It had dared to come so close Adina could still sense the thing's body heat where it had huddled in the shadows. A shiver went through her. How did the strange being elude her? She would have to be more careful. Even a First could be destroyed.

She used the dead man's clothes to wipe the blood splattered on her black leather halter, bare midriff and leather pants. The blood didn't come out of her belly button and silver belly ring easily, but what little was left wouldn't be obvious against her dark brown skin. After shoving the man's body into a large trash bin, she put on her black leather jacket and his sunglasses.

She patted her close-cropped hair in place and straightened her clothes. The alley was quiet, with only the sound of rats scratching in garbage, the wind moving scraps of paper and the distant murmur of traffic disturbing the peace.

Adina walked out of the alley rejuvenated and intoxicated. The fall air was cool, so good against her body, running warm with fresh blood. The Village street was crowded with people out for dinner or movies or just enjoying the crisp air of September. They reminded her of flies flitting around dead carrion, feeding off the remains of an Earth they had little regard for, rushing through their days. So many of them. So much food.

Two thousand years earlier she had been too aware of their lives, but the millennia had worn away her bond to them. Once she had cared for people, those in Sama, her home village in the Wello region of Central Africa. In time, everyone she cared about died. Each loss, each love ended by illness, old age or disinterest wore her heart thin. She questioned more than once the point of caring for anyone, of falling in love, until the pain and sadness were no longer worth it.

The last time she loved one of them was hundreds of years ago. Tacuma had dark, sad eyes, a quiet voice, beautiful dark brown skin and strong shoulders that Adina loved to caress and kiss when they walked together. She was convinced he knew there was something different with her, but Tacuma never questioned Adina. Not when she went on excursions at night, not even when she asked him to leave his village and move to an unpopulated area. Moving was the only way she could hide the fact that she didn't age.

Tacuma truly loved Adina and would do anything she asked, without questioning the reason. Every time she looked in his eyes she saw his death, so Adina ended the relationship with him. She closed her heart and accepted the Earth as her only partner.

The patterns of people's births, lifes and deaths flickered over the years, like fireflies. Humans had managed to add some years to their life spans over the last thousand years, but death still came soon in comparison to her life. Hunting and feeding became the center of her pleasure. The Earth and the Whisper didn't change. They were her only true friends.

Adina walked slowly through the crowded streets, the rushing of blood singing to her like the river of her home village hundreds of years ago. Occasionally when a man or woman glanced at her, blushed or took a deep breath as they passed by, their heartbeat quickened. They couldn't always know why they reacted to her, unconnected to their animal spirits. Although their minds didn't know they were prey, their bodies did.

Adina closed her eyes for a moment and continued walking. Even with no sight she could sense them like the warmth of bright lights. Easy to avoid, blood running in their bodies like electricity. She licked her lips, sucked in air for a deep breath— their scent spread on the Earth like an infection. Food, gasoline, cologne, garbage, leather, cotton and the rubber of their clothes and shoes were thick in the air. It was disgusting.

She fingered the gold figure on the chain around her neck, the symbol of Mercury, fire, like her, the great destroyer, cleanser of the Earth. The heels of her boots clicked against the concrete sidewalk, but underneath the Earth waited. She could feel it, her oldest companion, next to the Whisper in her dreams. She sighed. Whether they were a blessing or a curse didn't matter. She could no more control the Whisper than she could the Earth or her blood hunger.

Adina felt someone watching from a distance, probably the creature from the alley. She had the same tingling in her neck and spine. It wasn't a First, but there was something about how sensitized she felt to its presence that was similar to being in the vicinity of another First.

She stopped in front of a clothing store and looked at the people passing by reflected in the window. She saw nothing unusual about anyone. Whoever it was could be across the street or blocks away. How was she being blocked from targeting its position?

In the past she had been followed by a Remade, who had been studying her, hoping to find some way to live the extended, virtually immortal lives of a First, wanting desperately to link into the Whisper. Adina killed her when the Remade wouldn't leave her territory.

This thing watching her now was different. There was impressive power in it. Nothing had challenged her in hundreds of years. This could be interesting.

Taking her time pretending to window-shop, Adina walked down Eighth Street toward the West Side. The side streets were quieter. People were home in the apartments over the closed shops, and all the sidewalk action was along the main avenues and streets, where the restaurants and clubs were located.

There was a deep growl from an alley between two buildings on a side street. Normal humans couldn't hear the sound over the city noise, but it vibrated clearly in Adina's ears. Curious, Adina turned into the small empty street and followed the growl down the alley. She crept up on a tall African American man with thick, long dreadlocks holding a knife to the throat of a short, older Hispanic man with his hands bound behind his back. The bound man's sharp features were contorted in pain.

A quick rush of adrenaline made her tremble slightly, her reaction to being near a Remade. The older man was a vampire, his growl a call for help. His acrid scent permeated the alley with fear and disorder. This level of chaos usually came from a vampire who's less than a year old and had had little guidance from his Maker. No wonder he had been captured.

"Tell me where, now," the younger man said, letting the knife draw more blood. The dark blood of the Remade surged out of the neck wound like thick gravy, joining the puddle of blood on the ground. Judging from the thick consistency of his blood, Adina guessed he hadn't fed in a while. The young man was bleeding out the vampire.

Adina frowned. The blood of Remade was bitter. She had tasted one once, before killing her.

The older man wavered and looked in her direction, his dark, deep-set eyes locking onto hers, pleading for help. The knife holder glanced quickly in the same direction but returned his attention to the vampire. Adina was in the shadows of a building and knew he couldn't see her. This wasn't the person who had been watching her earlier; he was a normal human being with no apparent special abilities other than being cunning enough to capture an incompetent Remade.

She shook her head and growled so low the human couldn't hear her, but loud enough for the vampire to get the message. He slumped to his knees. It was clear he understood Adina wouldn't help him.

Adina slipped away. Whatever the young man's mission, let him kill the vampire. She didn't want the competition in her territory anyway. Hopefully he wasn't stupid enough to cross paths with her. But if he did, she'd consider adding him to the collection she kept in her basement. She smiled. Of all humans, vampire hunters were her favorite to play with.

●   ●   ●

Chun Zhang kept his distance, even though he suspected Adina sensed him watching. He wasn't prepared to face her yet. Firsts were acutely aware of their surroundings. He needed to have a good sense of her movement around the city. Her feeding ritual was the same as the few other Firsts he had observed. He wanted to check out her house. This would be harder now that she knew he was trailing her, but not impossible.

When she ducked into the alleyway he considered following, but didn't believe she was going to feed twice in one night. Even from two blocks away, he could feel she was sated. Instead, Chun maintained his distance, retained the hot tendril of psychic energy he picked up from Adina and made sure he didn't project his exact location. Chun was very good at finding lost people, and even better at tracking Firsts once he had a taste of their energy. Usually he needed to be in physical contact with something of the person, but the psychic energy of Firsts when feeding was so strong he could shadow them without ever touching anything they owned.

He felt guilty, as always, at having seen her kill. That never changed. But he couldn't have saved the young man. No point in thinking about that. He had to keep his mind on the mission: destroying her. This was a first-generation vampire, rare and powerful. He needed to capture the ritual words she gave her dying victims before finishing her. The more words he collected, the closer Chun got to being able to use that power against them and perhaps even become fully human again.

He fought the dread that crept into his gut when he thought of using the words. But the fourth Noble Truth of Buddhism gave him reason to hope: to end suffering he must change the way he thinks and perceives. He had to believe learning how to use these words would end much suffering. There was little else to hope.

He couldn't get close enough to hear what she whispered

tonight, even with his enhanced hearing, but Chun could tell it wasn't English. Probably her native African language. Following her from a distance for a few weeks, he watched her shop for clothes and jewelry, uptown and down. She called herself Adina, which meant "She Has Saved" in Amharic. A fitting irony.

It made him sick to see men and women alike attracted to her, when at any moment they could become her next meal. Not that she wasn't attractive, with her long, muscular limbs, wide hips and skin the color of coffee beans, her almond-shaped brown eyes and full mouth that were on the verge of smiling all the time. She walked with a roll of her hips that often drew attention. Like a ship cutting through ice floes, people noticed her when she passed. Although she could have been hundreds of years old, she looked barely twenty. After feeding, she shone with life, the life of her latest victim.

Whether he liked it or not, the cost of destroying a First was to watch a few fellow humans die. Nisi, his teacher and his love, had made that clear. She'd called a few days ago to say she would be in town this week. He needed to see her. Nisi made him feel human. Their love, even with the distance their work required, gave him reason to continue. Although he was stronger and faster than a normal human, Chun suspected he might need Nisi's help with this First.

In the long run, destroying one First saved many humans and broke another link in the making of other vampires, since they were the only ones who could remake humans into vampires. This was what he had to keep in mind. Humans had a better chance of surviving the vampire plague if the First could be eradicated.

A shudder went through him; a sharp pain throbbed in his forehead. One of his debilitating headaches erupted. Time to go home. Once the headache started, there was a good chance the rest of the seizure would come and he didn't want to be on the street when that happened. He hailed a taxi.

Home was a small, two-story building tucked in the downtown meatpacking district. The building was perfect, with its old-fashioned coal furnace and thick brick walls. Blocks away from the residential area, it was full of activity during the day and deserted at night. The perfect place for him to live, far enough away from vampire hunting grounds, especially those of a cocky First. They rarely felt the need to hide in the dark corners where humans didn't go. They enjoyed flaunting their virtual immortality, sometimes even becoming part of social circles that made them visible to anyone looking for them. Adina owned a small house off a private courtyard in an upscale part of the city. She practically glowed with overconfidence.

Chun stumbled into the kitchen through the side entrance of his house, locking the inner and outer doors. Ping, his dog, a large white-and-gray German shepherd–wolf mix, padded down the hall to meet him. Chun reset the perimeter alarms before going down the stairway in the kitchen, to the basement to collapse on a small bed. Ping whimpered, sensing the attack and nudged him gently with her nose.

"Good girl," he slurred through the pain, patting her head.

Chun pulled open the drawer of the small table next to the bed and took a capsule out of a jar. He popped the pill into his mouth, took a gulp of water from a water bottle, shoved his plastic mouthpiece in and curled up on the bed. Ping lay down on the floor, next to the bed, waiting for the attack to end.

He wasn't sure the ground herbs in the capsules helped, but Lucky Falcon, the Navajo doctor who'd given the pills to him, had promised they wouldn't make him feel worse and they could assist the recovery process, so Chun promised to take them.

He couldn't go to regular doctors and tell them that the blood of a vampire, mixed in with his own, periodically became dominant, and as this blood entered his brain Chun had seizures. On the other hand, it was also the same infection that gave him the abilities to be an efficient hunter of their kind. *What doesn't kill you makes you stronger.*

The storm exploded in his body. The seizures began as the vampire blood fought to take over his body. Kidneys, liver, heart, lungs, every major organ resisted the blood that now flowed through them. His mind floated into a dreamlike state, away from the gripping headache and spasms. His thoughts drifted from words to images and memories, swinging back and forth in time as the attack blossomed full force.

. . . Chun as a child, in China, riding high on his grand-father's shoulders, his grandmother scolding them to be careful, looking up at clouds shaped like dinosaurs . . .

. . . In their first home in California, aluminum siding and clean cement sidewalks, a mountain of leaves in their backyard in the fall . . .

. . . Chun in college, his heart skipping a beat when he first saw Tina . . . sitting on the bed on their wedding night, the room filled with candlelight and the scent of fresh roses, Tina so beautiful he had tears in his eyes . . . walking on the beach with his wife at night . . . his mother cooking meat dumplings . . . blood . . . everywhere . . . blood . . . a man knocking him out with one hand while sucking the life out of his wife . . . someone singing "Happy Birthday" in a dark room . . . coming to lying next to his wife's body, her blood soaking into his clothes, a pale man kneeling over Chun drawing on his chest with her blood . . . cutting into a rare steak, the blood seeping onto the plate in the shape of a leaf . . . the sharp pain of a bite through his skin, his scream . . . Tina throwing her wedding bouquet, the white roses arcing in the air . . . "She died too soon. You must listen, I have something to tell you," the man said to Chun and then whispered in Chun's ear in French, *"Avec envie, légère-ment"* . . . blood . . . the vampire's face covered in his wife's blood, shuddering with pleasure as he caressed Chun's neck, baring his teeth for the last bite . . . red, white and green balloons in a bright blue sky . . . a glint of metal, the vampire's head falling from its body . . . his wife's laughter . . . blood . . . a large brown-skinned woman standing over Chun with a sword . . . blood . . .

Ping licked his hand, recognizing the end of the attack. Chun slowly sat up and took a couple of sips from the water bottle. He knew better than to stand up immediately. It usually took him about twenty minutes to recover fully. He put his head down and breathed slowly, waiting for his body to readjust as the vampire blood became passive again.

Nisi was his savior. She had destroyed the First that had killed his wife and had almost killed him. Unfortunately, her blow had spilled the vampire's blood into Chun's open wounds, infecting him. It wasn't her fault; she'd thought him dead. He would have died, but the First's blood brought him back to life.

Nisi had easily carried him to her car that night, and to her home. She was strong enough to cut off the head of a vampire, and yet gentle with him. Realizing that regular doctors wouldn't know how to treat his wounds, Nisi called a neighborhood doctor, Lucky Falcon, to guide him back to life. Falcon was a Navajo healer, well versed in the traditional and untraditional methods of curing people.

Within a few days Chun had miraculously recovered from most of the wounds. Nisi told him what she knew about vampires. Chun would have thought her mad if he hadn't been through the hell of the past few days. He couldn't deny the violent memory of the attack, or the way he had changed. Everything was different.

Lying in her bed, Chun knew where Nisi was in the house, and when she left. Wrapped in her sheets, he could feel her move through the city, as if a string were attached between them. The ability to sense these things was one of the many things that had changed since the vampire attack.

Nightmares filled his dreams when he slept, images of face-less, maimed bodies, their screams and moans often forcing him to wake in a sweat. Once awake, voices filled his head, as if the walls had disappeared and he was hearing conversations from the houses in the neighborhood. If he woke in the middle of the night, he could walk through the house in the dark and see everything clearly. One day he tripped on the way down the stairs and grabbed the wood railing, pulverizing the wood. There were times he had felt as if he was losing his mind; the ex-periences he had couldn't be real.

Falcon stopped by almost every day, checking Chun's wounds and talking to Nisi. Chun could hear them clearly, even when they were on another floor. When Nisi began telling him what she knew about vampires and hunting, he told her about the new sensations.

"I knew you were changed by the blood," Nisi had said, as they sat on her couch. "No one heals as fast as you did, except—"

"One of them?" Chun said. "I've heard every word you and Falcon have said. I know you're afraid I'll change into one of them."

Nisi caressed his arm. "In the beginning, but now we know you're still human."

"But I'm different."

"Yes, stronger, your hearing, sight, all more like them, but no blood hunger." Sunlight streamed from the window over them. "You can still walk in the daylight."

"So far," he said.

She shook her head. "I don't think it'll happen and Falcon agrees with me. He needs better equipment to test your blood, but he's convinced the fact that the vampire was killed as the blood entered you prevented the complete transformation from happening. It may also be something special about your blood, he's not sure. But he's pretty certain you aren't going to change into a Remade vampire."

"If I do become one of them, you have to destroy me. I couldn't stand living like the monster who killed my wife."

Nisi nodded. They held each other. The scent of lavender water she wore surrounded him like a warm blanket.

The three of them spent the next few weeks discovering how the mix in his blood had altered Chun. He was stronger, faster and could heal more quickly than regular humans. All of his senses were heightened. If he was physically in contact with someone's belongings, he could track them.

"You're almost a superman," Nisi told him a couple of weeks later. They laughed together. It was not long after that Chun asked her to teach him about killing vampires.

When he told Falcon the words the vampire whispered, he had his first seizure.

He came out of it with Falcon and Nisi sitting by his bedside.

Falcon shook his head and said in Navajo, *"Ant iihnii."* Witch people.

"The Firsts each have a spell that keeps them strong and young," Falcon said. "Sounds have power. The power speaks to the blood, the blood to the body. This is how the Firsts live forever. You have that blood in you now. This curse saved you. Everything has light and dark to it. Perhaps you can use this to find the weakness to their strength, a way for us to destroy them."

"Falcon, you know I don't believe in the idea of magic words," Nisi said, helping Chun drink water. "I believe in the sword that spills their blood. This whispering ritual is just something they do."

"It doesn't matter what you and I believe. There was a time when you didn't believe in vampires. Chun's new abilities may be the way to another weapon."

He turned to Chun. "You know the truth in your blood, in the words you spoke, yes?"

Chun nodded slowly.

"But I'd like to learn the sword in the meantime," Chun said, smiling at Nisi.

Nisi taught him how to handle a sword, and what she knew about first-generation vampires and the Remade. This woman from a farm in North Carolina didn't look anything like the cliché of a vampire hunter from the movies. Just a little taller than he, she was stocky, wide with muscle, with strong, large hands gentle as butterfly wings over his body and capable of swinging a steel sword with the accuracy of a samurai. Her short brown dreadlocks made her look fierce as they practiced the fighting forms.

In those weeks of training she also healed his heart. Somehow, in facing the desperate future they would live as hunters, they found a place in each other's souls. Her eyes reflected a deep loss. She hadn't talked about it, and he didn't need her to, unless it would ease her pain.

When they made love, Chun wanted to fall into her body like water and become the air in her lungs. Every kiss, nibble, caress between them sent tingling through his spine. They took their time, stroking the kindled passion until they were intoxicated with desire.

Touching her soft skin with his lips was enough to arouse him and take his breath away. His fingers traveled over her body, slowly exploring each curve, barely making contact. Chun loved to listen to her breath quicken and heart race as he caressed her. Each moan from Nisi's deep voice poured heat into his body. Living this strange existence made sense when they were together. Nisi was the only light in the dark world he traveled through.

He missed her, but understood why they had to work apart. The human race needed both of them working separately to get rid of this scourge.

"Nisi will be in town any day now," Chun said, scratching Ping under her chin. "She'll be happy to see you again." He still had a slight headache, and his shoulders, ribs and knees ached.

Ping followed him upstairs to the first floor and sat patiently in the kitchen while Chun prepared her food.

Chun made himself two thick roast beef sandwiches after putting Ping's dish on the floor. Seizures always left him hungry.

He pulled the subcompact computer out of the cabinet over the stove to review combinations of the words collected from other First vampires. The program shifted the words randomly into different groupings. Collected words were entered phonetically in the language used by the First and then translated into Navajo, a language Chun felt was more secure since few people knew it. It didn't seem to matter what language he spoke the words in. The sounds reacted with the First blood in his body. It took these two things together to create a response.

He spoke them out loud, typing in his reactions to the word combinations.

"T'aadoo la'i yilkaahi." His fingers and feet grew numb, and heat flowed over the tips of his nose, ears and neck.

"Naa nish aah" left him flush, a little breathless and excited, the way he felt when he was around Nisi.

He did this, carefully, every day, in hopes of putting together the words in a pattern he could use to destroy all vampires, or at least Firsts. The only combination he avoided was the pattern of sounds of the First who originally attacked him. The two times he uttered them out loud had produced seizures.

There was no way, at this point, to test the effect these words would have on Firsts, but a reaction in him had to mean something. No one knew why the ritual rejuvenated only those with First blood. Chun followed research on the Internet about the positive effect of certain sounds and vibrations on healing normal humans. He couldn't help feeling that the answer to curing himself and destroying all of them lay in these words. Maybe if he collected enough of them he could rid the world of vampires. Maybe he could become fully human again and have a normal life with Nisi.

He tired quickly. Finishing his sandwiches, Chun checked the alarm system again and went to bed.

Adina sat in the corner of the run-down jazz club. The quartet on the low stage played riffs that reminded her of Coltrane. Music was one of humans' redeeming qualities. Jazz or rock or classical, she enjoyed the flow of music filling the air, the change of sound waves rippling and churning stillness.

"Do you mind?" a young man said, pointing to the empty chair opposite her.

For a moment she was going to tell him to move elsewhere, but she recognized his scent as the one questioning the vampire in the alley earlier. His long dreads were loose around his shoulders; his cinnamon-colored skin glowed with youth in the black turtleneck sweater. This couldn't be a coincidence. What game was he playing?

She nodded and turned her attention back to the stage.

He turned around to watch the musicians and didn't say anything until the set was finished. When the group went on break, he ordered a Black Russian and offered to buy Adina a drink, though her glass of white wine was still full.

"I can see you're here for the music, not the drinks," he said.

"And what are you here for?" Adina said, her newly acquired sunglasses hiding her eyes, but smiling slightly.

"The music, a little human comfort." He clicked her glass gently with his glass. "Here's to music."

"And you assume I'm human?" Adina asked, still smiling.

"I don't like to use the word 'assume,' you know the saying, 'Making an ass of you and me.' But you do give the semblance of being human. Are you perhaps a ghost haunting the club?" he asked, smiling now.

"Perhaps something like that." Did he think flirting with her would be enticing? She tasted the air around him. He had something else going on. If she hadn't just fed, this one would have been on the menu tonight.

"Are you an artist? Let me guess," she said, tapping her long red polished nails against her glass. "A writer."

"Bingo, you got me. And you, well, that's not going to be so easy." He leaned forward, squinting to see her face in the light of the small candle on the table. "A model or an international art dealer. Something unusual, not someone who works in an office building or anything mundane. You need the run of the whole planet." He took a sip of his drink. "Do you always wear sunglasses in the dark?"

She removed the glasses and set them on the table. "I'm sensitive to light. It's brighter than you think in here." His skin had the scent of someone about twenty-five years old, yet he maneuvered the conversation like someone older.

He lifted the sunglasses, then replaced them without touching her skin.

She raised an eyebrow behind the dark lenses. He was playing this very carefully, in no hurry to make his move, whatever that was.

The next set started with a version of Miles Davis's "My Ship." Adina closed her eyes and listened to the trumpet, drums and keyboards while breathing in the young man's scent. There was no cologne, just the natural musky odor of his body mixing with a slight fragrance of coconut oil from his long dreads. The heat of his body radiated through her. She imagined making love to him, his heat entering her cooling body. Hot lips on hers, his tongue, warm and wet, and in orgasm the sweet taste of his blood in her mouth and against her skin as her teeth ripped into his flesh. The trumpet caressed her thoughts, playing in between her images of them together.

She opened her eyes. He was engrossed in the music, his back to her. He nodded to the beat, his long dreads moving gently.

The steady pulse of his heart mixed with the music, adding to her desire to taste him. The band filled the second set with versions of Miles Davis's work: "'Round Midnight," "Now's the Time," "Tempus Fugit," "Summertime," "My Funny Valentine," "Nefertiti," "Portia."

Adina remembered an evening years ago, in this same nightclub, when it was the top jazz spot in town. Miles Davis played here and often sat in the audience to listen to others. She'd sat one table away from him that night, breathed in the smoky scent of his sweet dark skin and wondered at making him one of them.

She laughed softly to herself, making her tablemate turn and look.

"Sorry," she said, shrugging. Not that it would have been easy to get to Miles. He was never at the club alone. It was a challenge she'd considered worthwhile. To think, Miles Davis, still making music today.

Rapuluchukwu, leave it in God's hands. Not that she believed in the gods anymore, but she left Miles to his own mechanisms, to the errant hands of time and death. Now these young ones played his music, but without his passion, his focused wildness.

At the end of the next set, the houselights went up. The young man turned to her, lifted his glass in salute and finished his drink.

"As a ghost of this establishment, I don't suppose you could take a walk outside?" he asked.

She considered him for a moment, vibrant and attractive in the way that only the young mortals were with their taut, firm flesh, easy breath flowing through their bodies, unaware of their own mortality. This made them as appetizing to her as those at the ends of their lives, the other end of the spectrum, so unwilling to leave, so desperate to hold on to one last breath.

"Not tonight," she said, crossing her legs and leaning back in her seat.

"Maybe another night?" he asked.

"Maybe," she said.

"My name is Michael," he said, holding out his hand.

"Adina," she said, taking his hand.

"A strong handshake, for a strong ghost," he said, kissing the back of her hand.

She simply smiled and watched him leave.

Whatever he wanted from her, he was willing to wait. His need for her was as clear in his eyes as his death. And there was something else, a flicker of desperation, a kind of hunger.

For a moment she imagined him nude, his strong body covered in bite marks, the blood trickling like dark juice over his cinnamon-brown skin. She shoved the image away. The idea of gorging on him as full as she was now was almost as satisfying as doing it.

If their paths crossed again he would become a meal. After she played with him. Adina would show him what a real vampire could do, not like the weak Remade he had captured earlier. She licked her lips. He would be delicious. The words of the Whisper would settle nicely in his sweet body, his warm blood. Maybe she would take him to her place and bathe in his blood. She shuddered in anticipation.

She stood and stretched. This night was filled with surprises and there were still clubs and bars open to visit.

The next morning Chun worked out in the basement. These attacks always made his energy bunch and gather in knots. He went through two forms of Tai Chi, very slowly, leveling the energy in his body. Feeling more centered, he walked through his sword form, first with the light wood sword and then the steel sword. Finishing the form, a fine sheen of sweat on his face, Chun finally felt ready for the day and, more importantly, the evening.

"How about a walk before we go to work, Ping?" he asked the

dog, who was sitting patiently at the doorway of the dining room. Ping ran to the front door and waited to have her leash snapped on.

While they walked, Chun listened to voice mail on his cell phone. A new client wanted an interview this afternoon. Chun returned the call. The nervous man didn't want to meet at his office, so they settled on a restaurant near the man's job. He wanted to talk to Chun about a missing person.

Chun made his money as a private investigator, finding lost things and people. He was very good at it, another side effect of the vampire infection. This day work supported his night job.

Back at the house, Chun showered and dressed in better clothes.

"Let's go to work, girl."

He placed his steel sword in its leather case and carried it to his car, followed by Ping. It didn't take long to drive to meet his new client.

Jim Piper was in his early forties. Ron, his sixteen-year-old son, was missing. Piper had gone to the police, but since the boy had run away before, he felt they wouldn't aggressively look for him. The father was convinced his son was in danger and wanted him found quickly. Chun was inclined to think this was another runaway incident, but knowing the streets as well as he did, he also knew there was real danger there.

Piper gave Chun a picture and, more importantly, a watch that belonged to Ron. Chun told the man he would call when he had something.

Chun put the boy's watch on and started at the bus terminal, then went to the train station, waiting for a sense of him, more than his face in the crowd. He drove to the usual places teenagers hung out, uptown and downtown, the Tombs, Gramercy Park and Washington Square Park, taking Ping for a walk around each area. It was Ping's job to stay alert to their surroundings, since these searches were distracting for Chun.

A bolt of energy, like electricity, danced on his wrist near the South Street Seaport.

From an outside deck of the shopping mall he could see a group of teenagers skateboarding below on the side steps. Ping lay down at his feet while Chun closed his eyes and reached out with his inner sight. Taking slow breaths, he focused on the tingling around his wrist, and felt the surrounding air for its source.

The boy had been there hours ago; his imprint was clear. There was no sense of which way he may have gone. He looked at the boy's watch—4:30 PM—a half hour of daylight left. He'd come back to the Seaport early tomorrow; hopefully the boy would return. The night would come soon and he would have to get back to his other job. He waited on the deck, slowly sipping coffee, watching the sun set. He'd forgotten there was beauty in the ending of a day. For him it heralded the nightly hunt, not a time to rest.

Adina moaned in torpor, the semiconscious state that vampires lay in while waiting for the night to come. The Whisper sang in her head, in images, sprinkled with words.

. . . bodies torn open, a chaotic field of human remains, heads, arm, legs, hands, fingers . . .

. . . her naked, floating in a sea of warm blood, weightless and sated . . . *Fumiya,* suffering.

. . . a wave of blood covers her, she is dragged down in the warmth, not suffocating, but drawing the blood into her lungs, her mouth . . . the blood is alive, squirming into her ears, between her legs, into every opening of her body, her back arches in orgasmic pleasure, her skin is stretched as the blood bloats her, filling her out like a balloon . . . she is going to explode . . .

Ayzie, let it come.

Adina jerked up out of the bed, her eyes searching the dark. For what? She shook her head. Every night she woke to some phantom in the room. No one was ever there, just memories of the Whisper from her dreams, nightmares of torpor.

"Fumiya ayzie," she whispered, a burning surge dancing along her spine. She closed her eyes and moaned from the pain. She hadn't expected the Whisper to call her out so soon. Hunger stirred inside. She didn't usually feed two nights in a row. This happened if she spent time near another First. Maybe it was the influence of that creature from the alley last night.

She dismissed a fleeting thought of holding off. She'd tried that before and could not control the maddening hunger and pain that came from denying the Whisper its place. She shook her head. No point in going through that again.

She didn't know why no First lived long without the ritual. It was woven into the fabric of their extended existence. To deliver the words into the almost-dead body of the victim, to drink his blood, to live. She smiled. Although people thought of vampires as the undead, she believed their lives were on another evolutionary level that unmade humans didn't comprehend.

Uwaezuoke, the world was imperfect; that was all she needed to understand. Whatever the reason, she would have to feed again tonight.

She dressed for the evening. Tonight she didn't feel like wearing black. The dark red leather bodysuit, with its deep V-neck and slit legs, matching boots and jacket and the sunglasses from last night would do.

She considered taking the human she held in her basement, but changed her mind. Something fresh would be better for the ritual. She didn't want to rush feeding on that one.

Chun sat on the deck of the Seaport a few moments after the setting sun painted the sky in bands of purple, red and pink. On the lower deck the teenagers slowly dispersed. The missing boy hadn't shown up. Chun removed Ron's watch and put it in the leather pouch at his waist. The threads of Ron's energy detached as soon as Chun was no longer in physical contact with the watch. He couldn't afford to be diverted by the search while following the vampire.

Chun stood and stretched. He would come back earlier tomorrow to see if the boy returned. Ping stood up and yawned.

"Let's go, girl," Chun said to Ping. He drove home and fed Ping, leaving her to guard the house.

Fortunately, it was a quick drive to Adina's house. He parked his car a couple of blocks away. With his sword strapped to his back, hidden under his large overcoat, he found a good spot in the alley across the street to watch her house with binoculars.

She didn't waste any time once the sun set. As in the past days, the vampire left her house not long after the sky darkened, hailed a taxi and sped away.

Chun waited fifteen minutes, making sure she didn't return before he entered the private courtyard. The gated fence between the house and street wasn't locked. He stood in the shadow of the large tree inside the fence. Weeds and wild roses overgrew the small yard, and ivy covered much of the walls of the house. His heart raced. He willed himself to calm down. He needed to focus. Was there a way into her house?

He closed his eyes and reached out. His augmented sight worked from the inside out, like three-dimensional waves in water. Every movement of the objects within the boundaries of his widening circle—insects, wind through leaves, birds, people in the street, and the surrounding buildings—caused ripples.

He took a deep breath and pushed to direct his attention on her house. There were no vibrations or the hum of an alarm system. He pushed deeper into the house. There was someone in the basement. A heartbeat pulsed, making subtle waves in the air. It wasn't another vampire. A vampire's heartbeat was slow, just fast enough to pump the mix of poisoned blood and the blood of their latest victim through the body.

Chun released his concentration. Why was she confident enough to leave the house with someone inside? He frowned. This didn't feel right. He had to keep his mind on his objective, to see if there was a way into her house. He hadn't come here to rescue anyone.

He moved to the side of the house, trying to avoid the wild roses that twisted around the edges of the yard. The windows were barred on the outside and shuttered on the inside. The shutters seemed metallic. He shook his head. This wasn't good. He worked around the outside of the house, but every entrance was barricaded. Even the windows to the basement had been sealed with bricks. He pressed his ear against the wall. Nothing. No doubt the house was soundproofed—vampires liked to play with their victims.

He put his hands on the bricked window and reached out again with his senses. Someone was definitely inside. A steady heartbeat thumped, and Chun could hear the slow whoosh of air moving in and out of that person's lungs. Whoever it was wasn't moving much; perhaps the victim was bound in some way or unconscious. He crouched against the house, hands tightened into fists.

He pounded his fists against his thighs, remembering the ultimate goal, the greater good. Besides, what could he do, dig into the earth and break through the walls to save one person? He stood. What if—? He took the missing boy's watch out of the pouch and held it. No. It wasn't him; none of his energy spiked near the house, inside or out. Chun took a deep breath and placed the watch back in the pouch.

"I'm sorry," he whispered, patting the bricked window. He reminded himself of one of the Noble Truths of Buddhism: we all experience suffering. If he took care of the vampire tonight, he could return, and perhaps aid the unfortunate person in the basement.

Chun left the house. He didn't need a personal item to sense a vampire, especially a First. Her energy signature danced in the air, sharp-edged and bitter. Adina was hungry again. He frowned. This was unusual. Two days in a row. It was going to be a long night.

Adina walked the streets, savoring the movement of humans around her. As the sidewalks filled for a Friday evening, painful hunger accelerated up and down her bones. Hundreds of years ago she'd satisfied herself early in the evening, wanting the burning to stop. But she learned to savor the sensation. Pain or pleasure, it was all one feeling. The longer she waited, the more violent the feeding, the greater the pleasure.

Each step sent a fiery wave up her spine, joining the growing hunger in her stomach. Each person she passed on the street, every woman, man and child, was the answer to her pain, the relief she needed. She could barely wait for lights to change at street crossings with people standing near her. Images tantalized her: tearing into flesh, blood flowing through passersby splashing on her. At one corner, she bit her own lip. Thick blood leaked in a bitter trickle into her mouth.

The nightclub she met Michael in last night was near. If she went in and saw him, she didn't think she could sit and listen to music with this hunger growing inside. As much as she wanted to consume him, she didn't want it to be fast. A cramp gripped her stomach. She grabbed a lamppost.

"Are you alright, miss?" a man in a suit asked. He put his hand on her arm.

The blood surging through his body sang to her, as if it begged to be allowed to put an end to her pain. She suppressed a growl.

"I'll be okay." He would do.

A woman came up to them. She was clearly with the man. "Can we take you to a hospital?" she asked.

Damn. "No, it's okay. I'll be fine, I just need to eat something." Adina pulled away from him and walked around the corner. Some of the sidewalk cafés of Greenwich Village still had tables outside, even though the evening air was cool.

Someone was in the alley behind her. One person.

She ducked into the alley. The narrow passageway ran through the middle of the block, winding along the backs of buildings and fenced-in gardens. The human was deep in the middle of the block, sitting against a pile of boxes, smoking a joint. He was young and healthy. Though his long blond hair hid his face, she could tell by his clothes and smell that he was probably living on the street. Perhaps a runaway. Even better— no one would be expecting him home tonight. She smiled and watched him, the burning and hunger intensifying.

Chun picked up her trail in the same neighborhood she had been in the night before. Odd for her to hunt so close to her last killing. She was getting sloppy, good thing for him. He stood in front of a leather shop, pretending to window-shop so he could track which way she had gone. He followed her trail through brightly lit streets to an alley. Ducking into the darkness, he removed his sword from under his coat and carried it in his right hand, against the side of his body.

He sensed another person in the alley. Human. No doubt her next victim. His only chance was to catch her feeding. She would be too occupied to be fully aware of his approach.

Adina closed her eyes and let the sound and smell of the boy's body fill her senses until he was no longer a human being but a web of blood circuits, veins pulsing with sweet fluid, stomach gurgling, heart pounding.

She growled. He looked up, his eyes dazed by the drugs. She walked slowly toward him, stumbling a little.

"Hey, girl . . ." he said, standing.

She easily pushed him to the ground and slid next to him, her hand still on his shoulder.

"Don't get up for me," she said, smiling slightly.

"I was just—"

"Yes, I can see you were just getting high," Adina said. "I don't have a problem with that."

"You're not going to bust me?" he asked.

"Not at all." She sat closer to him, the swish of blood rushing through his body echoed in her ears. Feverish, the blood hunger churned in her veins.

"Hey, do you want some? I think I have another joint in here." He rummaged through his backpack.

"Want some? Yes, but not that." She shoved the backpack away and pulled him across her lap.

"What—" he started to say, but stopped when he saw her sharpened teeth catch the moonlight.

"You look scared. Don't be. This can be very pleasurable. Well, at least for me."

He tried to pull away and scream, but she handled him like a doll, putting her hand over his mouth and holding him down.

Chun stared in horror. For a moment he thought she had Ron, the missing boy, but the moonlight revealed her new victim was another teenager. As much as Chun wanted the words from her, he wasn't sure he could watch her kill the boy. He centered himself and gripped the sword in both hands.

He heard a sound behind him too late. A hard object smashed into the back of his head and everything went black.

Adina jumped to her feet, releasing the boy, who scurried down the alley as quickly as he could. Michael, the writer from the jazz club, stood over the body of a man, a piece of bloodied wood in his gloved hands.

"Well, looks like I got here just in time," he said, tossing the piece of wood aside.

"You're following me?" she said.

"I would say we were both following you. I suspect for different reasons," Michael said, kicking at the sword.

She looked down the alley to where the boy had run, then back at Michael.

"You won't need him," he said. He walked up to her, took her in his arms and kissed her. She started to push him away but instead drank in his obvious desire. Then she bit his lip.

He jerked but didn't pull away. She licked his lip, the drops of blood intensifying her hunger.

"You know what I am?" she asked.

"Yes, Adina. I know."

He kissed her again, wrapping his arms around her tightly. "It took me a while to find out your kind were real. It's surprising how much information is on the Internet and the streets if you take the time."

Adina pushed him away from her. "I imagine you did more than that."

"Yes, I would do anything to find you," he said.

The moonlight flowed over his face. His pea jacket was open, the white shirt unbuttoned; smooth brown skin invited her bite. He was beautiful. She ran her hands over his chest. His heart beat strongly, his body firm and obviously aroused.

"You've gone through a lot to find me. Why?" she asked.

"I needed to find a way to meet you, let you see I wasn't a threat. I'm dying. I know I don't look sick, but inside I am." He touched his head. "A tumor. The doctors say I might live one or two more years."

"What do you want?" she asked, even though she could guess.

"To be like you, to be Remade," he said.

"Indeed." She considered him. It had been hundreds of years

since she had changed a human into a vampire. "I think we should get out of here. The young one might call the police."

Michael walked over to Chun and went through his pockets and found car keys. "He has a car. If we could find it—"

"I won't have any problem following the trail of his crude scent back to it," she said.

"Your place or mine?" he asked.

"Mine." She prodded Chun with her leather boots. "Let's bring him and his sword."

They had no trouble dragging Chun between them, like a drunk friend, to his car. They slipped him into the trunk and drove to Adina's house.

Chun came to tied to a chair. The back of his head hurt like hell. Adina had her back to him and was straddling a shirtless man on a chair. He thought at first the man was tied also, but could quickly see that wasn't the case. They were kissing. He closed his eyes and gently tried the bonds on his arms and legs. They were tight enough to keep him secure, but not so tight as to cut off his circulation.

"He's awake," Adina said. "You might as well open your eyes, Chun. I can feel you're conscious."

He opened his eyes. "What did you do with the boy?"

"The boy? You mean in the alley?" she asked, standing. She picked up his sword and leaned on it.

Chun nodded.

"He got away," the man said. "A fair trade. We have you."

"Who the hell are you?" asked Chun.

"Where are my manners?" Adina said. She picked Chun's wallet up from the floor and read his name. "Chun Zhang, meet Michael Simon."

Michael stood and bowed slightly.

"I'm guessing I can thank you for my headache?" Chun asked.

"That's right. Couldn't have you hurting my Maker," Michael

said, sitting on the black leather couch opposite Chun, drops of blood seeping from small wounds Adina had made on his chest.

"Maker?" Chun asked. "You *want* her to change you into a vampire?"

"Remade into something stronger than human, yes. Into something that can live forever—absolutely," Michael said.

"Why?" Chun asked, trying to buy time.

"*Glioblastoma multiforme.* A fancy name for inoperable brain tumor that's aggressively killing me. I have no interest in dying in a painful drugged haze. Why not live forever?"

"But—" Chun started to say, but Adina put her finger to his lips.

"Now, now, don't try to talk him out of this. He's very determined. You have no idea how determined." She turned to smile at Michael.

Chun felt a sudden surge of hunger. Heat radiated from his groin, up his chest to his neck. He stared at her. Somehow he was picking up her feelings, sharing her reactions.

Adina dipped her nail into the bleeding wound at the back of Chun's head and licked the blood. She frowned. "Your blood doesn't taste right. You're only the latest hunter to follow me, but you're not quite human, are you?"

"It doesn't matter what I am," Chun said.

"Oh, but I think it does. I'd like to know before I kill you," she said.

Michael stood. "You said I could feed on him, after you Remade me."

"That's true, I did." She pointed the sword at Chun and winked.

Chun had a sinking feeling in his stomach. "You can't trust her, you can't trust any of them. She's going to kill you."

"You don't listen very well, do you? The tumor is already killing me. At least this dying is part of the transition to a different life. Besides, who should I trust—you?" Michael said. "I think you would say anything to destroy her. That's not going to happen." He walked over and slapped Chun hard.

Adina caught Michael's hand before he could slap Chun again. "No need for that. Not yet."

She put her face next to Chun and sniffed him. "Definitely not all human." She looked into his eyes, holding his chin. "But you're not vampire. You have the blood of a First in you, don't you?"

Chun tried to jerk out of her grip.

"Yes. I see. Not very talkative. You hunters are quite stubborn, but I can be persuasive." She brought his sword down, embedding it in the floor before him. Her face contorting in pain, she grabbed her stomach.

Chun winced, lurching in the chair. Pangs of hunger tore at his gut.

"You feel it also?" Adina asked. She caressed his face with a finger. "I taste an echo of my blood hunger in you."

He didn't want to feel what she felt. This had never happened before. Maybe he had connected to her while he was unconscious. Whatever the reason, he wanted the hunger to stop.

"This will be very interesting for both of us," she said. "I'll bet you've never been this close when we Remade one of you, other than the time you were changed."

Adina spun toward Michael and pushed him onto the couch.

Chun tried to stay calm and centered, but squirmed in the chair in spite of himself, her craving pouring into him. He wanted blood. He'd never wanted blood before, but he'd never been this close to a First for so long.

"Watch and learn, hunter," she said, smiling at Chun.

"Is it time?" Michael asked.

"Yes," she said, caressing Michael's bare chest. "Past time."

She worked over Michael for the next hour. After half an hour, he started screaming. She quickly ripped out his vocal cords, collapsed one lung. After that, the sounds Michael made were muted, more guttural.

Chun was disgusted by the sight but couldn't look away. Adina's yearning pulled him into the unfolding violence. The more she ravaged Michael's body, the deeper her satisfaction reflected in Chun. Her passion built into an indescribable wave of lust. Chun couldn't control the reactions from deep inside his body. The tainted blood wouldn't let him. Thoughts left him as everything became animal sensation. Her tongue against his skin, the thick warm blood sliding down her throat, blood slippery and slick under her hands. Chun's heart raced, his breath quickened, adrenaline flooded his body. Adina's desire dragged him to the brink of orgasm.

Near the end, Michael turned toward Chun.

Chun could see terror in his eyes. Adina looked at Chun, smiled and turned Michael's face toward her. "Pay attention," she growled. "I have something to tell you."

She whispered, *"Fumiya ayzie, kambui sipo,"* and ripped into his throat.

Chun tried to push away the sounds of her feeding but the contact with her remained strong. As Adina filled, he was engulfed in the same orgasmic high she floated in. A shiver ran through him as release came to both of them.

She was suddenly beside him. She ran her nail along the side of his face. Chun jumped.

"Don't tell me you didn't enjoy that, half-made," Adina said. She laughed, Michael's blood splattered over her arms and neck. She walked into another room and came out with a wet towel, wiping the blood off.

Holding the blood-soaked towel near his face, she asked. "Want a lick?"

He turned away.

She laughed. "So, you don't drink." She sat down next to Michael's body and patted his thigh. "He really wanted it, you know. He believed I'd Remake him. It would have been a great disappointment for him to discover he wasn't going to live forever. The Remade can't. You have to agree I've done him a favor." She stretched and leaned forward, her elbows on her knees. "What to do with you? Perhaps make you part of my collection. I'm curious how you came about."

She untied some of the knots, releasing him from the chair, but leaving his feet and hands tightly bound. She threw him over her shoulder, grabbed his sword and carried him to the basement.

Adina dropped him to the dirt floor. A pervasive smell of death permeated the walls and floor. Many people had died in this place.

"You probably don't need the light, but not everyone here is special like you and me," she said, flipping on an overhead light.

There were four large trunks with grates on the sides in the center of the room. Chun sensed life in one; the other three were empty.

"You know which one has my other guest, yes?" She waved her hand in the air. "Your sensing is crude, you know. It fills the air like the scent of rotten fish." Adina laughed again, her cheeks flush with Michael's life. She stumbled a little, as if high.

She unlatched the trunk and pulled an unconscious body out. It was Nisi.

Chun squirmed backward. "No."

"You know her?" Adina asked, propping the bound woman up against the trunk and sitting on the trunk next to her. She caressed Nisi's dreadlocks. "Do you have a vampire hunters' club, meet for drinks, give out assignments?"

Chun stared in horror. Nisi was bruised and marked with puncture wounds, her torn clothes streaked with blood. She must have put up a good fight, but her skill hadn't stopped Adina from taking her captive and, worse, feeding on her. Nausea rose in his stomach. He vomited on the floor.

"I'm sure she'd appreciate your gesture of disgust if she were conscious," Adina said. "She's lasted quite a while, although I don't think she'll be with us much longer." She released Nisi's head from her hold. Nisi slid sideways and moaned; her eyes fluttered open for a moment. She looked at him, shook her head and passed out.

"Nisi," Chun said. He closed his eyes to concentrate. Her heart was still beating. She was alive. For now.

Adina lifted him from the floor to a standing position. "Why can you do that?"

"If you let her go, I'll tell you everything," Chun said.

She laughed in his face, dropping him to the floor. He couldn't keep his balance with his ankles tied. He fell to his knees. She stooped down, tipped his head up with a nail under his chin.

"Why would I let someone go whose life is dedicated to destroying me?" she asked. "Maybe I should Remake her. What do you think? How would she feel about changing sides?" Adina laughed. "But let's forget about her and talk about you. You have the blood of a First in you. I can taste that much."

She ripped his shirt open to examine his chest and neck. She traced the scars with a finger, her eyes closed. "Hmmmm, let's see. You were attacked by a First and somehow survived. Now you live with his blood mixed in with yours. The blood changed you: you run faster, hear better, see in the dark, feel around with your clumsy perception. Is that close enough?"

"Yes," he said. His mind scrambled for a way to get himself and Nisi out of this alive. He flexed hopelessly against the rope around his arms.

"I wondered what was following me. I've never heard of anyone like you before." She released Chun and sat on the trunk. "Still, the question is what to do with you? Unfortunately, I don't like the taste of your blood. It doesn't have the full body and sweetness of normal blood. You're not a very good conversationalist. None of you hunters are." She prodded Nisi with her boot. "You might be fun to play with. Maybe I could urge you to be more open. Or just open you up." She giggled, still high on Michael's blood.

"Now I see why the hunger came again. Your mixed blood called it out in me. Connects us now," she said. "I don't think it would do to leave you around for long."

Adina picked up Chun's sword and swung it through the air with one hand, the seven-folded steel singing over him. The sound reverberated up and down his spine. Vibrations, sound, the blood of a First. If he was affected, how would a First react to the words he had collected?

"*Adiilch'il*," he said in Navajo. Be a crash of lightning. The beginning words from an effective section of the secret he had compiled in his notes.

She stumbled forward, letting the sword go. It clanged into the corner of the room.

Chun felt a surge of stinging pleasure through his wrists and feet. A stronger echo of the sensation snapped back at him from Adina. His heart skipped a beat; the words did affect her.

"What . . . what did you say?" She stumbled to him, went to her knees and grabbed him by the throat.

He repeated the phrase.

Holding him with one hand, she covered her eyes with the other. A shudder shook both of them.

"Where did you hear that?" she growled. "Did the First who attacked you say those words to you?"

"I have his words and others," Chun said.

Her eyes narrowed and she shook him. "How many words?"

"More than I can remember. I keep them in a notebook at my place, here in the city."

"What else do you know?" she asked.

"I know you need to use certain words when you feed, like tonight, they are part of the blood hunger. They are also part of the secret that makes you different than the Remade."

She released him. Chun fell onto his back. Adina walked to the corner to retrieve the sword. She held the blade to his neck.

"Kill me and others will know the words. I've made arrangements for someone else to get the book," he said, looking her in the eyes. "You know there's power in these words. Do you want to take the chance of another having this power?"

"What do you propose?" she asked, lifting the blade off his neck.

"We go to my place, I'll give you the notebook and walk away from all of this. Give up hunting. This mix of blood has given me more than extra abilities. It has made me sick inside. I'm tired of all the death." Tears filled his eyes as he looked at Nisi.

"Yes, I believe you are," Adina said.

It was true. At that moment, Chun wanted nothing more to do with this mission.

She turned her back to him and walked over to Nisi with the sword.

Chun held his breath.

Adina dropped the sword, picked Nisi up and locked her back into the trunk.

"Don't think I trust you, but I want that notebook." Adina lifted Chun to his feet. "I don't care what you do with the rest of your life, as long as you give the book to me, leave this city and make sure our paths never cross again."

He nodded.

She carried him to the car and put him in the trunk. It was a fast ride to his house.

Chun rolled around in the dark trunk so his hands could reach a backup weapon he kept under the spare tire. He barely had time to slip the small knife in the side of his work boots before the car stopped.

She untied his arms and feet before taking him out of the trunk.

"We should go in the side entrance," he said.

"No matter how you've been changed, you're not stronger than me. There are many bones to break in the human body. You've seen how imaginative I can be in giving pain. Do I have to say what I'll do to you if you try anything?" she asked.

He shook his head.

He rubbed his wrists to get the circulation moving again as they walked to his house. She kept her hand wrapped around the back of his neck. He had no doubt she could easily crush his vertebrae with one hand. His gait was shaky from nerves as much as from having had his legs tied. The memory of Nisi in Adina's basement flashed in his mind. If there was any chance of saving Nisi, he had to stop thinking about her and be in the present moment.

He unlocked the door. Ping barked from behind the door.

"Just a minute," he said to Adina.

"You make sure it's under control or I will," she said.

"Okay." He opened the door a couple of inches. "Go to the basement, Ping."

She pressed her nose at the opening and barked louder, toenails scraping against the metal door. "Stop, Ping. Go to the basement," he said.

Ping whimpered but padded away from the door. Chun waited a minute before opening the door.

"I need to lock the basement door so she won't come back up," Chun said, when Adina held him back. He pointed to the open door on the other side of the kitchen.

Adina walked with him across the room. Chun looked down the stairs and could see Ping's eyes reflected in the kitchen light.

"Good girl. Go to the box," Chun said, knowing Ping would obey their code word.

Ping growled low and walked away from the steps into the darkness of the basement. Chun locked the door.

"Okay, where's the notebook?" Adina said, shoving him against the door.

He pointed to the dining room. She looked away for a moment. Chun stumbled to his knees, snatching out the small knife hidden in his boot. As she reached down to grab him, Chun swung his arm up and down. The knife slashed through one wrist, then the other.

Blood spurted out. Having fed two nights in a row, Adina's body was rich with blood. The mix flowed thinner than her blood alone would have. Chun had hoped this would happen. Every drop of blood she lost was an advantage for him, and he needed all the advantages he could get right now. Not surprisingly, he felt a stinging at his wrists. The connection between them was still strong.

She reached for him again, but Chun scrambled across the floor. He clawed under the small kitchen table and pulled loose a sword, half the length of the one lost at her house. He turned and pointed it at her.

Adina didn't pay attention to the wrist wounds, letting the blood spill to the floor. She laughed. "You can't be serious." She ran toward him.

He quickly turned and rolled out of her way, the short sword cutting across her thighs. Blood leaked from the gashes. His thighs burned, echoing her wounds.

"You'll never bleed me out through these little cuts," she growled. She threw the table at him. He ducked, the table slamming into his shoulder, throwing him against the wall. She rushed him, but Chun kicked the table at her and ran into the dining room.

She turned to chase him, almost losing her footing. The floor was slippery with blood, giving Chun time to get around the dining room table and grab another short sword from behind a cabinet. He stood in a low stance with a sword in each hand. She vaulted the table, expecting to land on him, but he ducked more quickly than a human could have and slid under the table to the other side.

"You do move fast," she said, gripping the end of the dining room table. "Don't tell me you don't enjoy some of the side effects of First blood in your body."

He inched along the wall toward the doorway to the living room.

"Still not talking? I will hear you scream tonight." She picked the table up and flung it at him. It shattered against the wall, but he was already through the doorway.

He jumped over the low couch to the middle of the room and took deep breaths to gather his energy. She was through the doorway in two steps and shoved the couch aside. Only the trunk coffee table stood between them. Chun stood crouched, holding the two swords in front, pointed at Adina.

"Tell me where the notebook is and I'll kill you quickly," she said.

Suddenly Ping charged her from the hallway behind Chun. The dog had crawled from the basement through the hidden passageway as trained. She jumped into the air and landed on Adina, her strong jaws clamped on the vampire's neck.

The First tripped backward to the floor and punched at Ping's head. The dog yapped in pain, unlocking her jaws. Adina flung Ping across the room over Chun's head. She landed against the wall and slid to the floor. She didn't move. Chun could hear her heart still beating. She wasn't dead.

"Not dead . . . yet, but she will be," Adina said, getting to her feet. Blood dripped from her neck. "After I kill you." She coughed and put her hand to her neck.

Chun coughed, and started to reach for his neck. Spikes of pain itched at a wound he didn't have.

"What will it be like to experience your death, I wonder. Let's find out," she said, taking a step toward Chun.

"*Niyiilkaah doo i ii aah,*" he said in Navajo.

The words sent waves of pain and pleasure along his spine, and his fingers and toes tingled. The effect on Adina was more intense. She flung her arms out to the side and screamed.

Chun sprang into the air. He landed with his feet on her chest, knocking her to the floor. Still in the grip of the words, she bucked to throw him off.

He repeated the words again. She growled and arched up, her hands reaching for his neck. Chun swiped outward with the two swords, cutting off her hands. Blood gushed from her wrists.

The swords dropped to the floor. His hands were gone, his wrists throbbed, echoing Adina's pain.

No, not his hands, Adina's hands. He reached down to grab a sword but his hands wouldn't flex.

Adina growled, knocking him off her with her arms, spraying blood across the room. "That didn't work out the way you planned, did it?" she said. She tried to stand but the blood loss was becoming too great. Managing to sit up, she leaned against the living room wall. Blood poured from her wrists onto the wood floor in a widening misshapen circle. She tucked her wrists under her arms in a vain attempt to stop the blood flow. The thick, dark liquid seeped down her sides to the floor.

Chun's energy dissipated but at a slower pace than Adina's. His hands were still useless.

"You can't kill me," she said. "You would die too."

"It would be worth it," Chun said, crouched on his knees.

"Then who would save your precious Nisi?" she said, closing her eyes. "Ah, yes, Nisi."

He thought she had passed out, but instead she whispered, "Chun, come here."

The connection between them pulled at him, like a thick rope around his neck. He slid back away from her. "No," he said.

"I need you," she said.

He blinked. It wasn't Adina, it was Nisi, blood-covered and begging, with open arms.

"Chun, please."

"Nisi?" he said.

"Yes, come here. I need you."

The tips of his fingers tingled. He leaned toward her. "But—"

"Please," she pleaded.

He had to save Nisi.

He shook his head. Nisi wasn't here.

He blinked.

Adina's eyes wre still closed, her head slumped forward, the lake of blood growing around her.

He blinked and shook his head.

They were home, in the hut he had built for them. Adina was hurt. Someone had hurt her.

"Tacuma, come here," she whispered.

He would do anything for her, be anything. He loved her with every breath of his body. There was something wrong. His body didn't feel right; he was weak. This wasn't his home. Where was he?

"Home, my love, we're home." Adina's voice was barely audible. "Please come to me. I need you."

"Yes," Chun said, looking at her. It was the sweet girl he had married. She hadn't changed, still beautiful with a smile that pulled him into her eyes. Dark brown eyes that hid much, said everything.

Blood.

There was so much blood.

He slowly crawled toward her, aching for her, so hungry.

Nothing mattered except keeping her safe.

His hands felt strange, tingly, as if waking from a dream.

Why was there so much blood?

"Don't worry about anything, just come to me," she whispered. "Need you, hungry for you."

There were two swords between him and Adina. His hands curled around the hilts, and he dragged them with him as he crawled.

Someone had hurt his wife and they would pay.

Blood.

A dog barked. Ping?

Blood.

His wife was dead.

Chun shook his head, took a deep breath and pushed out with all the psychic energy he possessed. The connection between him and Adina collapsed and the room came into sharp focus.

"No," Adina said, looking up.

Chun dove to her and, in a quick scissor action, cut off her head. He rolled off her body. Her head lay on the side, eyes open, staring at him as her body twitched.

Ping whimpered. Chun laid the swords on the couch and went to Ping. "Steady, girl," he said as she started to stand. Quickly checking the dog for broken bones, Chun ran his hands over her body. There was no serious damage.

"You're going to be okay," he said, giving her a hug.

Chun picked up Adina's head by the hair and carried it, dripping blood, to the basement. Ping followed him, limping. He threw Adina's head into the refurbished wood-burning furnace, turned up the heat and watched it catch fire and burn. Ping rubbed against his leg.

"Good girl. It's alright now," he said, scratching behind her ears, his bloodied fingers leaving pink traces in Ping's gray fur.

He looked at his hands. Her blood covered them. The blood. The answer was in the words: the patterns of sounds and the blood of a First. He ran back upstairs, grabbed a jar from the kitchen, went in the living room and scooped as much of her blood into the jar as he could. He went through her pockets until he found the keys to her house.

Ping followed him and stood at the doorway of the living room, sniffing at the blood soaking into the area rug near her paws.

"Back girl," he said, pointing to the kitchen.

He quickly rinsed his face and hands in the kitchen sink, and threw on a black sweatshirt hanging on the back of the kitchen door. Hopefully the blood on his black jeans wouldn't be too obvious if someone saw him on the street. He had to get back to Nisi first. Then he'd come back to clean up the rest of the body.

He looked at the jar of blood on the kitchen table and picked it up.

"Let's go get Nisi," Chun said to the dog.

With Ping in the front and the jar of blood in the backseat, Chun drove back to Adina's house.

He ran to the basement, carrying the jar, followed by Ping and used his discarded sword to break the lock on the trunk. Carefully lifting Nisi out, Chun put her on the floor.

She was still breathing, but her heartbeat was weakening. She was fading fast. He wasn't going to make it to a hospital in time.

Nisi opened her eyes. "Chun."

He caressed her forehead. "Don't say anything, save your strength."

"Too late," she said.

Chun looked at the jar of blood next to the trunk. He picked it up.

"No, it's not. This is First blood," he said. "It could save you."

"No," she said, trying to lift her hand to push it away.

"You can't die, Nisi. I can't do this without you."

Her eyes closed. She went limp. He could feel the life seeping away from her. He laid her down and opened the jar.

"Please forgive me," he said and poured the blood over her open wounds.

He whispered, *"Fumiya ayzie, kambui sipo."*

The blood moved as if alive, pushing itself into her wounds and mouth. Tears poured from his eyes. This had to work.

Chun sat for what felt like an eternity, watching her prone body.

Ping whimpered nearby.

Finally, with a gasp, Nisi opened her eyes.

The Touch

DONNA HILL

Prologue: July 1804, New Orleans

Her silhouette casts a long, lean shadow against the stark white of the full moon. Perfect in every way. From her vantage point upon the rooftop of her palatial home in the Saint John's Parish of New Orleans, the city and all its inhabitants are there for the taking. That pleases her greatly.

Her hair lifts lightly from her shoulders, blown by the humid summer breeze. If only the wind could cool the fire that rages in her veins and pounds through her skull.

She digs her long nails deep into the soft flesh of her palms until the tiny punctures send a jolt through her vibrating body. She closes her eyes and shivers before bringing the wounded palms to her mouth and sucking until the tiny wounds seal shut.

A low growl rumbles deep in her throat. For an instant the fire dies down, but she knows it will not last. As much as she relishes her life of eternity, her silent wish is that she will not spend forever alone.

July 2004

The newscasters have proclaimed today the hottest day on record in the past one hundred years. People are falling out on the streets of New York City. Dropping like flies. *Easy prey.* The citizens are advised to stay indoors, drink plenty of fluids. *Yes. Fluids.*

Selena LeBeau stands in front of her dresser and slowly brushes her ink-black, shoulder-length hair. Men and even women often comment on the beauty of her tresses. It has the weight of the Orient, the sleekness of the Indian and the rich color of Mother Africa.

Her features are just as exotic. She can be anyone. Given the right light she can appear Cuban or Ethiopian, Guyanese or Arab. Much of it depends on her mood, the time of day or month or where she decides to call home.

She sets the brush on the gleaming black mahogany dresser and gazes at the naked reflection that only she can see. Her body is a vision of burnished perfection. Breasts that rise to exquisite fullness. Waist that dips seductively, flaring out to firm round hips and down to the legs of a dancer. She is the dream of every man and woman.

Her slim fingers drift across her butter-soft flesh. She cups her throbbing breasts in her palms and gently squeezes them, then licks her red lips in sensual delight.

A glance over her shoulder brings into focus the supine body of a nameless man who she thought could be the one. Again, she is wrong. Wrong and disappointed. She frowns. Her search must continue. One day she will find him.

Selena sighs. So much trouble to get rid of them afterward. She suddenly hovers over the motionless form on her bed. She stretches out her finger and brushes it across the final trickle of blood that seeps from the deep wounds in his neck. She brings her fingertip to her mouth and licks off what remains of his essence.

Joe. She thinks she may have said his name during the final throes of his orgasmic release. Selena smiles. *Yes. Joe.* He was fun while he lasted.

Effortlessly she wraps the heavy body in the blue satin sheet, ties both ends with cord and carries her bundle to the backyard, where she quickly disposes of it alongside the others.

"I must plant another rosebush," she says softly, tossing the last shovelful of dirt onto the mound. The light from the full moon creates eerie shadows of the unworldly work being done in the garden.

She wipes off her hands and returns inside. She must hurry. If she doesn't, she will be late for work.

Even with all the heat she is certain her regular clients will be there for her ministrations. They can't resist—they're addicted like junkies to their drugs. If she is lucky, maybe a new face will grace her establishment on this sinfully hot July evening.

She smiles with anticipation.

•   •   •

The streets of Manhattan barely crawl with life. Only the die-hard few dare to venture out of doors, even though the blazing sun has set.

Selena casually strolls down Sixth Avenue in the West Village, intermittently peeking into slender alleys in the hope that she will come upon an unsuspecting soul to stave off her thirst. Her veins throb. The heat has her blood on fire.

She walks faster. She needs to get indoors. She doesn't want to take another life—to send another person forever into the abyss of darkness, to prowl the nights for all eternity in search of something they will never find. The only relief Selena will get tonight will be through what she does best. It will cool the thirst. Her little secret.

The building is up ahead. Discreet. It looks like any other building on the semi-run-down block. But looks can be deceiving.

Selena walks up the steps of the two-story red brick structure and inserts her key into the battered lock. A cooling breeze greets her when she opens the door and steps inside. She turns on the small shaded lamp that sits in the front window. It's an indication to her customers that she is now open for business.

With an unearthly swiftness she moves from room to room, preparing them for the night's visitors. She lights scented candles and takes out fresh towels and sheets, placing them on the tables along with her array of massage oils. Each one is designed to elicit a variety of sensual pleasures, from soothing to stimulating. Within moments, the heady scents of ylang-ylang, opium and African musk waft through the air.

Selena enters her private dressing room and changes from her street garments to her work attire. Beneath the near sheer, floor-length off-white gauze dress is nothing but her warm, bare flesh. She works best this way.

She pads barefoot across the pristine white wood floors to the small kitchen in the back room. She takes three bottles of chilled white wine and brings them to the reception area, placing them strategically on the three round antique tables.

From the overhead cabinet she removes a tray of crystal glasses and brings them out front. All of her movements are precise, deliberate. She looks around at the flickering lights, inhales the seductive scents, salivates over the bloodred drapes. Ambiance is everything.

The doorbell rings.

Ahhh, yes, and so we begin.

"*Charles*." Her smile is brilliant as she welcomes her first guest of the night.

She'd met Charles six months earlier at a nightclub on the Upper East Side. She'd been in heat, her thirst nearly insatiable for days, her body in desperate need of physical release. She'd been prowling the clubs for hours to find the right one and she'd happened upon him. Charles was an incredible specimen of a man: tall, sleek, muscular, his skin the color of oak. She'd made her way across the floor. His back was to her and she'd brushed her breasts against him. The shock she'd received sent her eyes rolling to the back of her head. She'd bit her lip to keep from crying out. Yes. He was perfect.

"Oh, I'm sorry," she'd said, when he turned to her. "It's so crowded in here." Her eyes had changed colors as she smiled. She'd watched his breathing escalate, the pulse in his neck pick up its beat. She extended her hand. "My name is Selena. Selena LeBeau."

They'd danced for hours and drank until they could drink no more. And then she took him home. He'd been hers ever since. She knew in her heart he was not the one, but he brought her immeasurable pleasure.

She takes his hands and reaches up and kisses each of his cheeks, European style. "Come in. You must be exhausted

from this unbearable heat. I'll bring you something cool right
away."

"As always you're ravishing and looking as cool as an ice-
berg."

She laughs. "Mind over matter," she says, leading him by the
hand to the sitting room. She gets him settled on the red velvet
couch that she'd had imported from France. They say it had once
belonged to a king. She'd known him, too.

"So, how have you been managing in all this heat?" Charles
asks, taking a limp handkerchief from his shirt pocket and mop-
ping his brow.

"Oh, I simply do what they instructed on the radio and tele-
vision—drink plenty of fluids." She pours him a glass of wine
and hands it to him. Her eyes darken. "Drink up."

He raises his glass to her in a toast. "To a lovely evening with
a lovely woman."

The corner of her mouth lifts in a sly grin.

They talk casually for a few moments, as is their custom—it's
all a prelude to what they know is to come. Finally she takes his
hand and pulls him up from the couch.

"Come, let me prepare your shower."

When Charles emerges from the shower, a towel wrapped
around his waist, Selena is waiting for him in the first room.
She glances at the towel and it falls to the floor. Charles
smiles.

"I always wonder how you do that."

"My little secret." She turns her back to him and goes over
the oils and lotions on her table. "Go on, lie down, relax," she instructs. She selects several small bottles, puts them on a tray and
returns to his side. Charles is on his stomach.

For an instant, her eyes flame red, then brilliant yellow as she
gazes hungrily at the rippling muscles of his back.

"I've prepared something very special for you tonight," she

says in a husky whisper. Her nipples harden to peaks, taunted by the fabric of her gown. She shivers.

"Hmmm," he murmurs.

She rubs the oils into her palms and begins at his neck, administering deep, penetrating strokes, then down the contour of his back, fanning out in broad circular motions. She can hardly breathe. The electric current from his body infuses her and she moans softly as she gives as well as gets pleasure.

Selena came to realize decades ago that this selective act of touching the right human form had a magical way of quenching her bloodlust. Through the art of touch she was able to satisfy her carnal needs and spare human souls. Of course, this very sensual pleasure invariably led to hours of scintillating sex that left her and her chosen one weak but sated. An added benefit.

She had an array of select clientele whom she'd sought out all over the world during her nocturnal sojourns. Only they knew of this special place, The Touch, tucked away in a nondescript building in the middle of Manhattan.

Effortlessly she turns Charles onto his back. His lids are heavy from the wine and the soothing massage. Her breathing hitches as her eyes trail along his body and settle on the erection that beats only for her.

Her gown falls from her body to pool around her bare feet. In an instant she hovers over him, holding him captive with her eyes. His mouth opens to speak, but no words come out.

Reflexively his large hands grip the sides of the massage table as she lowers herself onto him, taking in his length and breadth in agonizingly slow measures. He knows he cannot touch her. That is the rule.

The cords of his neck strain as she begins to move in circular motions. Selena groans deep in her throat as she grinds her hips hard and steady against him, building in tempo and momentum. The candle lights dance wildly, casting huge, macabre shadows against the walls.

The beat builds deep in her belly, squeezing him, causing him to tremble uncontrollably. He opens his mouth to cry out, but he cannot. The exquisite torture goes on and on for hours. His life force fills her again and again and again.

She can't seem to get enough tonight, enough to quench her thirst, cool her body. She takes a tiny nip from his shoulder, hoping that it will help. It does not. Her head swims and her body churns as she takes him deeper and deeper inside her internal firestorm, praying that he will be able to put out the blaze. But he cannot.

Hot tears spill from her eyes when she realizes what she must do.

"Good-bye, my sweet Charles," she whispers.

His eyes widen in awe and terror as her mouth opens and her incisors lengthen to deadly peaks.

The sound is no more than a slight pop as her teeth find their mark. Rich, red blood spurts from his neck and she sucks wildly. She feels release rushing through her as she continues to grind her hips against him. Her insides contract violently, capturing the last of his fluids, drawing them into her for all time.

Her body cools as Charles lies limp beneath her. His heart slows . . . then stops.

Tenderly she lays her head on his chest, strokes his cheek and closes his eyes. She will have to plant a very special rosebush for Charles. Yes, a very special one.

Selena makes quick work of preparing Charles's lifeless body. Without straining a muscle, she lifts his deadweight and carries him to the bathroom. Tenderly she places him in the tub of warm water sprinkled with special herbs that will gently evaporate any remaining fluids in his body as well as remove any lingering scents from the flesh. An old trick she'd learned from the ancestors. It will make his body more difficult to find by other hunters who gain pleasure from ravishing human remains.

"You don't deserve that kind of end, dear Charles," she coos as she sponges his limbs.

While she washes him, Selena reflects on what went wrong tonight. It was not supposed to happen. She and Charles should have had many more human years together. She realizes that her lust has been increasing rapidly, her cooling spells growing shorter in duration, her cravings more intense and her ability to be sexually satisfied almost unattainable.

For decades she has been able to control her desires through the art of touch. The feel of her hands against warm, human flesh, the sense of their life force pulsing through veins and sinew beneath her fingertips, had the mysterious power to still the heat that sought to consume her. But no more.

Selena was frightened.

She was frightened that she would be doomed like her many brethren to walk the night earth seeking not pleasure but sustenance to survive this living hell.

She'd heard the stories from others who'd become so desperate that they preyed on animals and small children. She would not come to that end.

Selena lifts Charles from the water and binds him tightly in a sheet. Her next customer will arrive shortly. She hopes he will have better luck than poor Charles.

A tingle begins to run through her veins as she tucks Charles into a large cedar chest until she can bury him later. The tingle begins to grow warm. A slickness seeps from between her thighs.

"Noooo," she cries on a strangled breath as an overpowering rush of desire roars through her, tossing her against the wall with its force.

Her eyes flash a luminous yellow as her fangs graze her bottom lip. "So hot . . . so hot . . ." Tears spill from her eyes.

Selena's quest is imperative now. She must find a man to satisfy her, and quickly.

The doorbell rings.

In a week's time, Selena disposes of a half dozen more male bodies. Her garden is magnificent, but her clientele at The Touch has dwindled to a troublingly low number.

Her lust is almost constant now and she can think of nothing else. Her only relief comes when she sleeps and even then she is plagued with dreams of the hunt. But some nights she doesn't have the dream; she has a vision.

In her vision there is a man. Although she cannot see his face, she can tell he is beautiful. He moves with an easy grace and the power of a panther. He comes to her at night to whisper loving words in her ears, promising to touch her in all the tender places. When she is with him, her heart feels at peace. There is joy in her soul and she can feel herself smile—really smile. They talk and laugh, hold hands in the garden and discuss the future—their future. He makes love to her, a gentle love that fills her in a way she has never been filled before. During these visions, for the first time in her unearthly existence, she feels alive. The heat stays cool in his presence. Her desire to devour is in abeyance. She begs to see his face, for him to step into the light. He simply says, "In time, my sweet Selena. In time."

Selena awakens. She frantically looks around the room, hoping that she can catch a glimpse of him, grab hold of his scent before he vanishes again. But he is gone. In her heart she knows it is more than a dream. It is real. And she understands what she must do.

She will not allow herself to succumb to the eternal darkness. Her gift of touch is all that enables her to walk in daylight among the living and is the only thing that keeps her sane.

There are many of her kind who envy, even hate, her because of it and she knows she must be careful not to be caught in one of their sinister traps. They would love nothing more than to see her like them. Lifeless. Empty. Condemned never to see the light of day.

How many agonizing years had she spent hating what had been done to her, taken from her? Until she finally accepted her fate.

She was only sixteen at the time. A beauty, everyone said. Her wealthy quadroon family doted on her. In the parish of Saint John she was the envy of young girls her age and the desire of every man both young and old.

Her grandmother, Noelle, warned her repeatedly about walking alone at night in the garden. "There are forces that you do not understand that wait for you. Wait to steal your soul," the old woman warned.

"Granny, I will not be afraid to walk in my own garden," Selena replied with the bravado of youth. "I can take care of myself."

Noelle clucked her tongue and shook a long finger at her grandchild.

"They took your mother and father, *chère*. They came in the night," she added in a harsh whisper.

"Mama and Papa drowned! I will not listen to any more of your wicked stories. You always try to frighten me."

"You should be frightened. You must be careful, *chère,* I can't bear to lose you too." She began to weep.

Selena rushed to her grandmother's side and knelt down at her feet. She rested her head on the old woman's lap.

"You won't lose me, Granny. I promise to be with you always."

Noelle dug inside the heavy folds of her dress and removed a cross that hung on a thick gold chain. She pressed it into Selena's hand.

"Wear it always." Her eyes were fierce and intense. "It will protect you." She closed Selena's hand around the cross.

"Protect me from what?"

"From the vile creatures of the night."

Selena chose not to believe the rantings of her grandmother, attributing the old woman's tales to the ancient folklore that was part of New Orleans history and mystique. She'd always heard about the night crawlers, the dark ones. But they were only folk stories told to children to keep them in line.

So with the confidence and the naïveté of youth, Selena continued her nightly strolls through the gardens. Most nights she took the cross with her, even though she told herself she didn't believe her grandmother's stories.

However, on this particularly blistering summer night, she'd unwittingly left the charm in the pocket of another dress.

The house was quiet when she ventured outdoors. Her grandmother and the servants were asleep. This was the time that she enjoyed most, the stillness, the silence, the utter hush of deep twilight. A time when she could think and dream a young girl's dream of one day having a family and a loving husband.

While she sat engaged in her fantasy, something as light as a breeze and as unsubstantial as morning mist brushed her cheek. She looked around but saw nothing more than the movement of shadows against the moonlight.

The unseen thing touched her again along the back of her exposed neck, making her nearly swoon with the electric current that surged through her.

Her lithe, young body began to feel warm all over and an unfamiliar beat pulsed between her thighs. Inexplicably she felt unseen hands begin to gently explore her body.

She moaned softly, both frightened and excited by these new sensations. Her name, spoken in a raw, sensuous whisper, floated in the air.

"Selena . . . Selena . . ."

She thought she must be hallucinating. Or maybe she was experiencing some strange dream. Whatever it was, she didn't want it to end or to awake from its grip.

"Selena . . . Selena . . ."

"Yes," she cried in a strangled voice.

The invisible hands continued to touch, to taunt and to torment her young, untainted body.

Selena trembled in the humid night air. Then, just as suddenly as it had begun, it stopped.

Selena opened her eyes, looking around wildly. Her heart pounded hard in her chest. She caught a glimpse of what looked like the shadow of a man and then nothing. Blackness.

She was too afraid to tell anyone what had happened to her in the rose garden. They would all think she was mad and she certainly couldn't tell her grandmother. But she was totally consumed by the desire to again experience the mysterious touch and she could barely wait for the next nightfall. Her young sexual appetite had been unleashed and it craved fulfillment.

Each night, once she was certain that the household was asleep, she would tiptoe out into the silent garden, awaiting the touch.

Night after night the visits became more provocative, more daring. Her invisible lover was quickly dissatisfied with only whisper-light touches through Selena's clothes. Selena soon found herself sitting on the marble bench, her hands rising to push down her dress, eagerly exposing her young breasts for the seductive but unseen touch.

Selena whimpered each time cool, invisible talons trailed across her tender flesh.

The following night she slipped out of more of her garments until she lay naked and exquisitely open beneath the cool glide of moonlight.

She felt those hands that she could not see part her thighs and bend her knees. Something hot and wet laved a wicked trail across her belly and down through the curls guarding her virgin flesh. She choked out a gasp as the delicious wetness settled on her pulsing clit and sucked. A spasm locked her spine as the suckling continued and built with intensity, sending her into paroxysms of delight.

Night after night, Selena became a slave to her body and the sensations wrung from it by the addictive touch. Her days were spent waiting for night and she listlessly marked the hours between sunrise and sunset. She hardly ate. She barely slept. Her youthful animation drained away, leaving her eyes vacant pools locked into a world that only she could see, a world peopled only by her and the lover who made her arch in ecstasy and cry out in foreign tongues.

Her grandmother became more alarmed as she watched the slow but steady transformation of her beloved granddaughter. Daily Noelle checked Selena's neck and her wrists, looking for signs that one of the living dead had defiled the child, but she could find no telltale signs of such unearthly possession.

A hollow-eyed Selena would simply gaze blankly at her grandmother and drift to her room to patiently wait for dark to fall.

The secret seductions in the garden lasted for three blissful months.

But on the eve of Selena's seventeenth birthday, her life changed forever.

She was in her bedroom, the door to the garden open to catch a glimmer of a breeze, when she was suddenly surrounded by dancing shadows, the scent of rich earth and a soft mist that coated her skin.

"Selena, it is time," the now-familiar voice of her invisible lover said.

"Yes," she muttered, transfixed as for the first time a shadow began to coalesce in front of her and the owner of the touch took form until he stood gloriously before her.

He was a perfect specimen of manhood carved in ebony. Selena tried to make out his face but her eyes refused to focus. Looking at his face was like watching an image through a foggy mirror. No matter how hard she tried to see, his features remained only a shadow, shifting and sliding each time she thought she'd seen his true face.

She felt herself lifted off her feet and placed gently down on her bed. The months of ecstasy were nothing compared to the sensations he dragged from her that night. She was caught up in sexual thrall, panting for release, her eyes glassy with desire as the sexual torture peaked—only to begin again. It went on for hours. Her body was no longer her own and she gave it freely, needing desperately to reach the satiation only he could give her.

Spread-eagled on the bed, her young body throbbing with need, she suddenly felt her insides filled with a force and a heat that was so powerful it hovered on the edge of pain, the pain mixing with the pleasure until she couldn't tell the two sensations apart. Her toes curled and her back snapped up in a taut bow as powerful explosions rippled through her over and over again, leaving her so weak she could do little more than whimper hoarsely.

She felt her hair lifted from her shoulders and tenderly brushed aside, baring the tendons in her neck still pulsing with the rush of blood in the aftermath of orgasm.

"So young," he murmured, his hot breath beating against her skin. "So innocent." He moved deep inside her and she trembled. "I've tried to stay away, Selena, but this is our dark destiny." His yellow eyes held her captive. "I know this is wrong, but I can no longer resist you." A tear of regret slid down his cheek.

"Forgive me," the voice of her lover whispered in her ear before he sank sharp fangs deep into her tender flesh.

Her body arched, a climax catching her up and gripping her with steel talons, tearing through her just as her wild-eyed grandmother burst into the room holding up a huge gold cross.

Her shadow lover howled in agony and was gone.

Now, years and centuries later, Selena knew he was out there somewhere. Roaming the earth as lonely as she, as unfulfilled as she. She prayed that he hunted for her as she hunted for him. They would meet again, of that she was certain. But when . . . when?

Time was running out. She could feel its hot breath upon her neck like a ravening beast as it loped steadily closer. If she did not find surcease soon, the uncontrollable fire within, the overwhelming need for blood, would become stronger even than she. It would control her. It would destroy her.

She must take fate into her own hands she decides, as she awakens once more with the heat curling inside her. Perhaps a change in atmosphere and location is what she needs. It has been a while since she has traveled. She smiles, imagining all the new bodies that can be seduced by her touch.

Throwing back the covers and crossing the cool wood floor of her bedroom she goes to the bookcase and pulls out the encyclopedia and flips open to the map of the world. Her eyes race over the pages searching for the perfect spot to launch her quest.

Ahh, the Caribbean. Perfect.

She conjures up the image of its sandy beaches in her mind's eye, the scantily clad bodies of sun-seeking tourists and cool blue waters. Ahh . . . an endless supply of new flesh.

Willing her mind and body to leave the confines of her present space, images become reality and in the blink of an eye, Selena, garbed in a flowing ankle-length skirt in a cool mint green and a matching tank top, casually walks up to the front desk of the Key Hotel on the island of Saint Thomas. She smiles seductively at the young man behind the counter.

"Good morning," she says in a husky whisper.

The young clerk looks up from his newspaper and his eyes spark with interest at the beautiful woman who seems to have appeared out of thin air.

"How can I help you?" he asks in a lightly accented voice.

Selena leans forward, letting him inhale her alluring scent, knowing it will slowly seduce his senses, rendering him as putty in her hands. She places delicate fingers on the counter, letting them suggestively stroke the hard, marble countertop as the young man fights his growing urge to touch her. A line of perspiration breaks out across his top lip. She stifles a smile at his easy susceptibility.

"I was hoping you could tell me about your health club here in the hotel." She smiles, her teeth sparkling like polished pearls.

"Uh . . . we have a wonderful club, all of the amenities. It is open twenty-four hours. Hot tub, Nautilus, and there is also an aerobics class."

"That sounds wonderful. Do you know if they employ a masseuse?" She takes a breath and her breasts rise alluringly.

"I . . . uh . . . no. The last one we had got pregnant and had to leave. We haven't found a replacement."

Selena's brow rises. "Who would I need to speak with about the position?"

The young man blinks rapidly. "You're a masseuse?"

"A very good one, or so I'm told," she says mockingly.

He swallows at the images her words have evoked in his fevered mind. "You would need to speak to Mr. Mack. He's the hotel manager."

She lightly runs her long nails across the top of his hand, a slow touch to tantalize him but not bring him full arousal. Yet. "You have been so helpful." She leans closer and lifts up the gold name tag on his blue uniform jacket. "Michael," she purrs. "Perhaps you will be my first customer."

His breathing rushes out in an audible rush.

"Where will I find Mr. Mack?"

"He . . . he's in the back office. I'll call him." He quickly reaches for the phone.

Selena places her hand on his, her soft grip causing a tightening in another part of his body. "Why don't I surprise him?" She looks him deep in the eyes, holding him in place. "He won't mind."

"No," he says, transfixed. "He won't mind."

"Where is his office?"

"Down the hall," he says, the words coming out in slow drips.

"Thank you, Michael. You have been very helpful. I won't forget that." She lifts his hand and brings it to her lips, her breath a hot whisper across his palm. Smiling slyly she places his hand back on the desk and walks down the hall.

Michael watches her walk away, his unblinking eyes glued to her undulating hips.

Mr. Mack is a large man with skin the color of burnt sugar. He is a symphony of circles, from the shape of his perfectly round head and bulbous facial features to the rotund shape of his body. His small, dark eyes peer out at the world from behind thick glasses.

Mr. Mack was the boy that never made the team, the one ignored by the girls and tormented by the boys. He turned to books and finding ways to make people pay. Mr. Mack takes great pleasure in making people pay even for the smallest infractions. He runs his tiny hotel like a general, terrorizing his employees with threats and slavelike hours. Turnover at the Key is notoriously high.

Mr. Mack almost falls out of his chair when Selena appears before his desk. He is just finishing a scathing letter of dismissal to the new accountant.

"How did you get in here? Who the hell are you?" he says in a voice like sandpaper.

"I was sure that you wanted to see me," Selena says, smiling beguilingly.

"What?" He adjusts thick glasses that have oddly fogged up. When he finally is able to focus in on her, he eases back in his seat at the sight.

"As I was saying," Selena continues, "I knew you wanted to see me because you have a job for me." She sits on the edge of his desk and casually plays with his desk calendar, flipping the pages faster and faster. Selena watches from the corner of her eye as he slowly slips under her spell.

"I can begin in the morning. You need a masseuse. Your last one left. I can bring new guests to your establishment." She laughs, the sound like tiny bells in the quiet room. She extends her hand, which he hypnotically grasps. "My name is Selena LeBeau."

"Selena," he murmurs, unable to tear his eyes away from her.

"I'm sure you have a room here that I can stay in."

"I have a room here that you can stay in," he echoes obediently.

"Why don't you call the front desk and tell them to reserve a room for Ms. LeBeau? She will be staying indefinitely." She picks up the phone and hands it to him.

Mr. Mack dials the front desk. "Michael, please have a room ready for Ms. LeBeau. She will be staying indefinitely."

"Something on one of the upper floors," she says.

He duly relays her order.

"And let him know that I will be ready for work tonight," she commands.

"Ms. LeBeau will start work as the new masseuse tonight."

"Very good, Mr. Mack." She takes the phone from his hand and hangs it up. "Well, I won't keep you. I know you are a very busy man." She hops down off the desk and is gone as suddenly as she came, leaving him staring at his half-finished dismissal letter with only a vague memory of a very beautiful woman.

● ● ●

Selena takes her time strolling through the hotel, taking in the sights, memorizing all the exits, zeroing in on the guests and deciding which ones are possible customers. The bar is always a good place to meet people, she decides. She smiles at the possibilities.

When she enters the hotel bar, there are only a few patrons, mostly couples. But she does spot several people sitting alone. She finds a secluded seat by the front window, a perfect place to watch the comings and goings unnoticed.

"Can I get you something to drink?" boldly asks a young man wearing tight black pants and a white shirt open almost to his navel, displaying a formidable set of toned abs.

Selena's eyes rake over him until he begins to fidget. She places her hand lightly on his muscular arm.

"Yes, a glass of very red wine," she requests.

He swallows hard. "Right away."

Selena stretches out her long legs, then crosses them. Yes, this place will fill her needs, she thinks, watching the array of men and women walk into the bar. The bare arms and legs, the allure of tender flesh, drive her wild. Her heart races with anticipation.

The handsome, half-dressed waiter returns with her wine.

"Thank you. By the way, do you see that man at the far end of the bar?"

The waiter turns and looks. "Yes."

"Do you know if he's alone?"

"I believe he's by himself."

Selena smiles up at the waiter. "Whatever he's drinking, it's my treat."

"Yes, ma'am. Anything else?"

"Perhaps you might like to stop by the massage parlor later on this evening."

His eyes widen. "Excuse me?"

"Oh . . ." She giggles and extends her hand. "Selena LeBeau.

I'm the new masseuse. I start this evening. And I would love to work some of those kinks out of your body." She watches with fascination as a thin film of perspiration crosses his hairline.

"Uh . . . sure. I don't get off until ten."

Her gaze holds him in place until she's ready to let him go. "Perfect. I'll expect you."

He turns and walks toward the bar, stopping next to the gentleman Selena has pointed out. The man turns his head toward Selena as the waiter speaks to him. She gives him a finger wave and smiles in invitation.

He picks up his drink and walks toward her.

"Mind if I sit down?" he asks, his features even more striking up close.

"I'd like nothing better."

He takes a seat and pulls his chair close to her. "Thank you for the drink." He takes a sip.

Selena's right brow rises. "I can give you much more than a drink," she says.

For a moment, he's taken aback by her bluntness. He laughs nervously. "Can I at least know your name first?"

"Selena LeBeau. And you are?"

"Marcus Hunter."

She takes his hand. "A very strong name." She strokes his knuckles with the tips of her nails and watches his Adam's apple move up and down.

"Are you here on vacation?" he finally asks.

"In a way. But I work here."

"Really." He takes a swallow from his drink.

Selena signals the waiter for another drink for Marcus. "I'm the new masseuse."

"That must be an interesting job."

"Oh, it is." Her eyes flash dark fire.

"What made you decide to become a masseuse?"

"I suppose you could say it was a calling." She laughs lightly. "I'd love to work on your body."

She can feel his heart rate escalate.

Marcus swallows hard. "That might be nice."

"Have you ever had a full-body massage?"

"No."

"Then you're in for a treat. Actually I start tonight."

"Tonight?"

"Yes, in the hotel spa."

The waiter appears with his drink. Marcus quickly takes it and downs the liquid in one long gulp.

"Would you like another?" she asks in a husky whisper.

"I think I've had enough for now," he says slowly, measuring his words.

"Then why don't we go over to the spa and I can demonstrate what I was talking about?" She holds him steady with her gaze.

Unable to help himself, he nods.

Selena takes his hand and eases him to his feet. "Are you here with anyone?" she asks as they leave the bar, needing to know if he will be missed.

"I'm alone."

Not for long.

Marcus follows Selena into the spa. She walks up to the reception desk attended by a young woman.

"Why don't you take a long break?" she says to the young woman. She places her hand on the woman's arm and looks intently into her eyes. "Your services are not needed now."

"I think I will take a break," she says in a stilted voice. She turns off the computer, gathers her purse and heads toward the exit.

"I'll let you know when you are needed again," Selena calls cordially as she watches the woman walk out.

She looks around. The spa is deserted at this early hour, the other guests out frolicking in the bright sun. Perfect, she thinks.

"Come. Let's get started."

She leads Marcus to the private room in back and locks the door. Quickly she assesses the space. She raises her hand and the supply cabinets open. Not the fragrant oils that she would use, but they will suffice. She turns to Marcus.

"Why don't you take a hot shower? I'll prepare it for you and then we can get started." She leads him to the shower and adjusts the water. "There's a robe and towels right there," she says, pointing to a stack of fresh towels and the robe hanging on a hook.

"Thank you."

"I'll be up front." She turns and leaves him.

While Marcus is in the shower, Selena prepares herself. She disrobes and puts on one of the smocks. She grimaces as the rough overwashed fabric brushes against her skin. Not her choice, but she won't have it on for long. She assembles the oils and lotions on the table along with several towels. She checks the linen closet for extra sheets. She may need something to bind him in if things don't go well. Ideally she would like to spare Marcus as long as the passion and the bloodlust don't overtake her.

"I'm done."

Slowly Selena turns. She smiles as Marcus stands before her. She extends her hand toward the massage table. "Lie down. Relax."

Marcus walks over and starts to climb up on the table.

"You won't need the robe." She walks up to him, loosens the belt and hands him a towel. She opens his robe fully, letting it fall to the floor. Her eyes rake over his body, igniting a fire inside his loins. He moans as his erection rises. She inhales his clean human scent and the blood rushes hotly to her head. Her fingertips begin to tingle.

"Lie down," she says in a thickened voice.

As if he has no will of his own, Marcus does as instructed, lying facedown on the table.

Selena momentarily closes her eyes as the heat slowly builds within her. Her eyes spark yellow, then red as she extends her hands toward his bare back. When her fingers connect with his cool flesh, she shudders with excitement. The electricity courses through her. Yes, she is pleased.

Pulling herself together she pours oil into her palms and rubs them together, then begins a slow, sensual caress. She presses her fingertips into the hard lines of his back, along the slope of his spine. Her head begins to swim. Her clit swells and throbs. She opens her smock as the temperature in the room quickly rises. The smock falls to the floor. She presses her naked body closer to his.

He turns his head to look at her. His eyes widen.

Selena slips her hands beneath him and easily turns him onto his back. She looks down into his eyes while her hands massage his chest. She watches his erection rise toward her and she smiles. Yes, he will do just fine.

"You have a beautiful body," she says in a hoarse whisper. She inhales his scent and her breasts brush against him.

Before Marcus can react, Selena has taken him inside her. "Don't speak," she warns, moving in a circular rhythm. "Don't touch."

Marcus grips the sides of the table as something unearthly passes through him. The room becomes dark, as black as a starless night. He is transported. His body is no longer his. He wants to cry out, but is afraid—afraid of what may happen if he does and afraid that the incredible sensations will stop.

Selena is in her own world, relishing the joy that he is giving her body. She wants more, needs more and drains him over and again until he is hanging on to consciousness. Her body is screaming—on fire. His fluids can't put it out. He has no more to give. Selena whimpers. She looks at Marcus. His eyes are glazed. His breath is shallow.

"Look at me," she commands.

With great effort Marcus tries to focus on the face above him. "Help me," he whispers.

"Yes, I will put an end to it all."

Her fangs flash an instant before she sinks them into his neck. His body spasms with an erection that feels like steel covered in velvet.

Release overtakes Selena, sweeping through her in endless waves. Her body finally cools as the last of Marcus's life force flows from him to her.

This was not how the evening was supposed to end. Sated, Selena bathes herself and then wraps Marcus's lifeless body in several sheets. She should have been able to have several days with Marcus before she reached this point. Her needs have grown to unmanageable proportions. And she is only totally satisfied after a kill.

She must find the one who can quench her appetite. Her time is running out, she realizes in something very much like mortal fear.

Selena remained at the resort for a month, searching fruitlessly. Each night she kills five or six men and sometimes even women. She'd lost count of the bodies she'd disposed of in the sandy dunes behind the hotel. Rumors were beginning to buzz about all the hotel guests who were disappearing without a trace. The police had even been called in to investigate. They were pressing to interview the hotel staff, certain the murderer must be among their ranks. Selena knew it was time for her to leave. She must find a new hunting ground.

For the next six months she roams the continent of Europe, then Africa and even the Orient. Her bloodlust is frenzied—totally beyond her control. She has become what she abhors most—a monster.

One morning while sitting in her hotel room in Hong Kong, she opens the paper to read a chilling article about a massive burial ground that has been uncovered near the banks of the river. According to the coroner's report, the bodies had all been drained of blood and each one exhibited bite marks like those from a wild animal.

Using DNA testing to identify and trace the bodies, police had interviewed friends of several of the victims who described them as having been last seen in the company of a beautiful woman. A hefty reward was being posted for the capture of this unknown woman or any information leading to her whereabouts. A rough sketch was included at the bottom of the article—an eerily accurate picture of Selena.

Angrily Selena snapped the paper shut. The hunger had won again, making her become sloppy in her search. It had once more cost her a perfect hunting ground. Now she would be forced to flee or risk her life. There was a disturbing pattern to her life of late. After only a few months in each new place, inevitably newspaper stories would emerge about a mysterious woman and the trail of dead bodies left in her wake. Despite crisscrossing the globe, she was rapidly running out of places to feed.

As a last resort, she could seek refuge with her own kind, deep in the bowels of the cities. But she was not like them. She wasn't!

Selena rested her head on her arms and wept. She was so lonely.

By the time Selena returns to the States, snow and ice cover the black-tarred streets and concrete walks of New York. Her garden is covered in a blanket of white. A chill penetrates her desolate brownstone, the exotic furniture covered in dust cloths. Selena moves from room to room, throwing open the windows, letting in the chilling air, hoping to cool down her already feverish body.

She hugs her arms around her slender frame and stares out at the magnificent skyline. Somewhere out there is her destiny, she muses. Somewhere out there is her dark prince, the one who will forever quell the fire that smolders within her. But where? She's traveled the globe, haunted the alleys, nightclubs and corporate environs of the world. And each day her plight grows more desperate. The touch—her last link to any semblance of a normal life among humans—is weakening. The simple feel of flesh no longer satisfies her cravings. And with each rise and fall of the sun it is becoming more deadly for her to venture out into the daylight. Just lately she's begun to feel the sun's fierce rays sear her soft skin, penetrating even the heavy winter coats she's donned. She is forced to wear dark glasses during the day, even while in the confines of her home, and has steadily grown more and more weary during the daylight hours, sleeping like one drugged. The only saving grace is the shortness of the winter days. But spring is only weeks away. Will she become a prisoner in her own home? Afraid to venture out for fear of being scorched by the sun?

What is the joy of immortality if one cannot enjoy the simple pleasure of walking among the living, inhaling the scent of life?

A flicker of resolve moves through her. Tonight, for the first time in months, she will reopen her salon. Perhaps tonight she will be lucky and not have to kill. Perhaps tonight she will find salvation.

Selena continues her vigil by the open window as a light snow begins to fall. The tiny flakes remind her of miniature diamonds twinkling against the waning light. In her weakened state, she must wait for full night to fall before it is safe for her to go out.

Movement from across the street catches her attention. A van has pulled up and two men jump out and begin to unload. Behind the van a sleek, dark Mercedes-Benz parks and a tall, slender man dressed completely in black steps from the car, his movements lithe and quick despite his muscular build. Selena momentarily believes the figure is an apparition. She looks closely as he directs the moving men. He turns and looks up, as if sensing her presence gazing down on him. A wide-brimmed, black hat shields most of his face, but she is sure she sees him smile, his teeth a brilliant white against ink-black skin.

Her breath races and she presses her hands against the icy glass of the window, willing him to come to her. In a blink he has disappeared.

Selena shakes her head and swallows rapidly. Had she only imagined him? No, it could not be. The car is still there and the workers continue to unload the large van and haul furniture up the steps. In each of the windows of the house across the street, lights illuminate the once empty space, room by room coming to life.

Selena inexplicably feels weak. Grasping furniture, she stumbles across the room and collapses onto the wide, curtained bed. She falls into a deep, dark, dreamless sleep.

When she awakens, the room is shrouded in total darkness. The heavy brocade curtains flap furiously in and out of the open window. Her night vision heightens as she focuses on her surroundings. She rubs her forehead. What has happened? Did she pass out? Then she remembers.

The man! She jumps up from the bed and runs to the window. Dim lights flicker from the windows across the street. She sees movement, nothing more than a shadow moving swiftly from room to room, sometimes appearing to be in two places at once. The van is gone.

As if beckoned, the shadow stills, framed in the window across the street. He is watching her; she can feel his gaze. Suddenly she knows.

•   •   •

A knock on the door makes a catlike smile cross Lucien's face. He strides to the door. "Selena," he greets her, throwing open the portal.

Selena's eyes lock onto his. Her breath catches in her chest.

"I've prepared some refreshment." He bows gallantly and ushers her in with a wide sweep of his hand.

Selena steps inside and in a breath he is next to her.

"My manners are so rusty. It has been centuries since I had a guest. I am Lucien, welcome to my home, let me take your coat." He steps behind her and slips her coat from her shoulders, his warm breath blowing across her neck and sending a shiver down her spine.

"How do you know my name?"

"You already have the answer to that, but you have yet to admit it. But please sit before we begin with the questions," he says in an intriguingly accented voice that is tantalizingly familiar.

Selena does as instructed while Lucien brings a tray of drinks. She takes a glass of red wine and sips.

"Why have you waited so long . . . so long since that night in my bedroom?" Selena asks, recognition swirling through her as the haunting images of their illicit nights take shape in her mind.

The corner of his mouth lifts. "I could not come before now, my sweet Selena. I wanted to, but you must believe me—I could not. You needed to grow, to understand and master your powers."

Her heart pounds. "I've been so lonely. So desperate and now, now I am becoming . . ." Tears fill her eyes.

"*Sssh, sssh,* there is no need for tears. That is why I have come. I could not bear to see you suffer anymore. It is time." In a blink he is sitting next to her, caressing her cheek with one thumb.

She rests her head against his chest, inhaling the unique scent of him that she's missed for so long. "Lucien . . ." She whispers

his name, letting her tongue feel each syllable. "I never knew
your name." And then she realizes she still has not seen his face.

She sits up and leans away to look at him. With each blink of
her eyes, his face and form change, spanning the centuries, taking on the personas of those famous and not so famous from the
ordinary to the extraordinary.

"I am everyone and no one," he says in a rich octave. His voice
vibrates through her.

She reaches up to touch him. "Lucien."

"I am not the one you truly seek, Selena. He is out there. I
have seen him. That is why I have come to help you find him."

"No!" She jumps up and appears on the other side of the
room. "It is you! You I have waited for and searched the globe
for all these years."

He is now in front of her. "That is why you have not been able
to find him. You believed it was me you sought."

"It was," she cries.

"No, my sweet Selena, it was not. Once you find him, you
will find peace, and the loneliness that you have endured all
these centuries will come to an end. Believe me."

"There can be no one else." In her rage she flies to the ceiling
and bares her teeth.

"He will be a human. He will be your greatest challenge. He
will still the fire within you."

In a surreal flash he swoops her from the rafters and plants her
on the floor. As the room recedes, they spin in a macabre dance,
entwined, drawing from each other the bloodlust that fuels
them.

"One last time," he groans.

Selena feels her body filled with his and teeth tenderly nip at
her flesh. She cannot believe that there could be any other for her
in this lifetime or in any other.

When Selena opens her eyes she is back in her room, on her
bed. She grabs her neck and brings away blood on her fingertips.

Frantically she looks around the room. She is alone. She runs to the window. The house across the street is dark. The Mercedes is gone.

"Nooo!"

Like one possessed, Selena combs the streets of the city hunting for Lucien night after night. At times she feels him close enough to touch, only to turn and find herself alone once again. She hears his voice. His scent fills her nostrils. Surely she is going mad.

Finally, after weeks of torment, she makes her way back to the small salon tucked away from prying eyes. Her secret haven. She does not want to believe what Lucien said about there being someone, someone human, but if she is ever to have peace, she must know.

She sets the small lamp in the window to let all who dare to cross the threshold know that she is back and open for business.

By rote she prepares herself and the room. All of her regular clients are buried in her garden. She has been so obsessed in her search that she has not recruited any new clientele. But she will wait. Perhaps some unlucky man or woman will wander by.

Hours pass and just as she is about to give up, the doorbell rings.

She opens the door.

"Hi, I, uh . . . hope this is the right place." He looks down at a small black-and-white business card, then at Selena. "Is this The Touch?"

"Yes," she says without her usual animation, oddly taken by this stranger's open face. She doesn't recall giving out any cards. "Please, come in." She steps aside as he walks past her. His scent goes to her head. She feels momentarily weak.

"Can I offer you some wine?"

"I'd like that." He takes off his jacket and walks around the intimate sitting room. "I see you travel a great deal," he says admiringly, examining the many photographs taken from differ-ent parts of the globe, festivals in Bahia, feasts in the mountains of Haiti.

"My work requires that I move around often," Selena says with a sad smile.

He turns toward her. "A traveling masseuse. How interest-ing."

She hands him a glass of wine. "It can be. What do you do?" She sits on the couch.

He sits beside her, but not too close, she notices.

"I'm a photographer. And I'm very impressed with your pho-tography skills."

"That's the least of my talents."

He tosses his head back in laughter. "I can only imagine. So tell me, how did you get started?"

"At what?"

"This job." He glances around. "You don't have a staff. Don't you worry, being a woman alone in this neighborhood?"

"Not at all. I can take care of myself."

He looks at her for a long moment as if committing her fea-tures to memory. "So tell me then, how did you get started?"

Selena inhales deeply, then tucks her long legs beneath her on the sofa. Slowly she begins to tell him the fabricated story of her life, the lies of where she went to school, tales about her parents, funny anecdotes of close friends and family. All the things she'd lost long ago.

They talk for hours, sharing stories, laughter and wine. Be-fore long the sky begins to turn a rosy pink, heralding the com-ing dawn. Panic fills Selena. She jumps up from the couch.

"I must close up now." Her voice is desperate.

He looks at her, alarmed by her sudden change in demeanor. "Are you alright?"

"Yes, but you need to go. Now!"

"I . . ."

"Please." She touches his arm and a current more potent than any she's ever felt shoots up her arm, streaking through her body with the force of lightning. Her eyes roll to the back of her head and she loses consciousness.

He is stunned but catches her falling figure an instant before she hits the floor.

He lifts her and carries her to the nearby couch.

"Close the curtains," she says, coming to as he lays her down. "Hurry."

He does as she asks and quickly returns to her side. "Let me get you some water."

"No . . . wine . . . red."

He looks at her oddly, but gets a glass of wine. He holds up her head as she sips greedily.

"Easy."

She looks into his eyes and sees a tenderness there that oddly stirs her heart. "Thank you."

"Migraine?"

"What?"

"Do you have a migraine? I heard they can suddenly make you feel weak and sensitive to light."

"Yes, yes," she says, happy to grab an answer.

"Well, just rest. I can stay with you if you like. Or is there someone you want to call? Husband, boyfriend?"

"No, there's no one. I'll be fine. I just need to rest for a while."

He checks his watch. "Wow, five-thirty." He chuckles lightly. "I better go home. I have an early photo shoot." He gets up from the couch. "Guess I'll have to take a rain check on that massage."

"Whenever you're ready."

"I never asked your name."

"Selena."

"Beautiful. It fits you. My name is Vincent."

"I hope to see you again, Vincent."

"You will. I promise."

•   •   •

Days pass but Vincent does not return. Selena finds herself un-
willingly thinking of him and dares to go out haunting the
street in search of him.

Not since her early beginnings with Lucien has she felt so
drawn to anyone or had a man treat her with such transparent
kindness, asking nothing in return but her company. For the
few hours that she'd spent with Vincent she'd felt an ease move
through her. A sense of peace that had kept the urgent rage
abated. The hunger was tempered in his presence.

But now three weeks had passed with no sign of him. And the
fire was building once again. Since that night, she had not had
the desire for blood. Her lust had been once again temporarily
filled through the art of massage, the touch returning to her like
an old and beloved friend. She'd slowly begun to rebuild her
clientele, relieving her hunger through the long deep strokes of
warm human flesh. She entertained nightly, serving as many as
eight to ten men per night, taking and giving pleasure in many
ways, both carnal and platonic.

Tonight, Selena finishes with the man who is her last customer for the evening, a nice young man—an athlete who truly
enjoyed her ministrations.

"I'll see you next week," he says, slipping on his jacket in
preparation for leaving. "You're like an addiction. I can't seem
to get enough."

Selena laughs. He's young, handsome, in excellent physical
health. Under other circumstances she might consider turning
him. But she knows she could never endure eternity with him
at her side. He simply does not have the power to stimulate her
that way.

"Well, as long as you keep visiting me, I'll be sure to give you
just what you need." She walks him to the door. "Good night."

"Good night, Selena." He pauses. "I was wondering, maybe

one Sunday afternoon if you're not busy, I thought perhaps I could take you to brunch."

"Thank you for asking, but it's really against my policy to go out with my customers. I'm sure you understand."

He looks crestfallen. "Sure."

Selena opens the door for him and sees Vincent waiting on the other side, his hand poised to knock. She barely stops herself from leaping into his arms.

The young man looks Vincent over. "Another customer," he says with a hint of jealousy in his tone.

"I'll see you next week."

He walks out and Vincent steps inside.

Selena smiles. "I thought you'd forgotten all about me," she says, keeping her voice light even as her heart beats wildly in her chest.

"I've been out of town on a photo shoot." He takes off his hat and looks at her. "I don't think I realized how much I missed seeing you until now." He lowers his head. "I shouldn't have said that. I bet you get that from your male customers all the time."

She looks into his eyes. "No, it's alright, I feel the same way." She takes his hand as they walk into the living room. "What can I get you?"

"How about some of your fabulous red wine?"

Selena laughs. "Make yourself comfortable." She fixes his drink and joins him on the couch. "So tell me about your trip. Where did you go?"

"I was in New Orleans," he says before taking a sip of his wine.

Selena's breath catches in her chest. "Really? It's been so long since I've been home." She clasps his hands. "Tell me all about it. What did you see? What is the city like now?" she asks, excitement hitching her voice.

Vincent leans back and tells her of his travels, the crew who accompanied him and the wild nights on the streets of the French Quarter.

"Maybe one day I will return," she says wistfully.

"Is your family still there?"

"No. There is no one left." That much was true.

"I'm sorry. I come from such a big family. I can't imagine what it's like to be alone in the world."

"You get used to it. Find ways to fill the holes in your life."

"Tell me how you've been. Are you feeling alright? No more of those headaches?"

"I've been fine. Really."

Vincent reaches out and touches her cheek. "I thought of you while I was gone. I wanted to call but . . ."

"But . . . ?"

"I wasn't sure if I should."

"Let's make a pact."

"Okay. What is it?"

"You can call me anytime."

"I think I might like that."

They clink their glasses in a toast.

"Ready for your long overdue massage?"

"Absolutely."

"I'll prepare your shower." She leaves him and goes into the bath, adjusts the water and sets out the towels and robe. "Whenever you're ready," she says upon returning to the front room.

"Lead the way."

While Vincent is in the shower, Selena prepares her oils and changes her clothing. She feels a giddy excitement at the thought of touching him for the very first time. Her imagination runs wild at the thought of seeing his flesh, of pressing her fingertips into his muscles.

Vincent is special. She feels it as surely as she draws a breath.

She doesn't want to hurt him and silently prays that the blood-lust will stay in abeyance while she is with him.

"All done," Vincent says, stepping back into the massage room.

Selena turns and bites down on her lip at the sight of him. Her breathing escalates and her fingertips begin to tingle.

Struggling for air in her lungs, she instructs him to lie down on the table. She carries the small tray with the oils and lotions and puts it on a stand next to the table.

"I've really been looking forward to this," he says, resting his head on his folded arms.

"So have I," she murmurs. She pours a combination of two of her special oils into her palms and rubs her hands together before applying pressure to his back.

"Hmmm, that's nice," Vincent says as Selena's strong, trained fingers find all of the tension in his back and release it with her touch.

As she works on him, applying more pressure and exploring the rest of his body, a sensual wave of release passes through her. Her head feels light and her body weightless as she touches him, transferring their energies back and forth through her finger-tips.

Her sudden climax catches her unaware, the sweet throbbing just as satisfying as full penetration. And more amazing still, she has only touched him, not daring to take him inside her in case the hunger returned.

"Are you okay?" Vincent asks, looking up into her eyes as she stills.

Slowly Selena brings Vincent into focus. She feels joyful. A satiated smile creeps across her face. "Yes." She rubs his chest tenderly. "I suppose you could say that I really get into my work."

"So I see. You're quite incredible. I don't think I've ever had anyone touch me the way you do. I felt . . ."

"Yes?"

He gazes into her eyes. "I felt like we were one person, like you were touching inside me somehow."

Selena caresses his cheek. "I know." Reluctantly she moves away and turns her back. "You can get dressed now. I'll pour some wine and put out a light snack. I'll clean up here and meet you up front."

Vincent tosses his legs over the side of the table and sits up. "Please don't hide it; something is happening between us, Selena. I felt it the moment we met."

She turns and looks at him. "What do you think it is?" she asks in a husky whisper.

"I'm not sure, but I want to find out. I want to see where things can go between us—outside of work."

"Like a real relationship—dates, dinner, and dancing?" She feels giddy with excitement.

"Yeah, all that and more." He stretches out his hand to her. She walks to him and gives him her hand. He pulls her between his bare thighs, the white towel rising up to his hips. He rakes his fingers through her mass of silky hair. "You're beautiful," he whispers, gazing at her as if seeing her for the very first time. "Is it against your policy to date your clients?"

"I find it works better to keep the two worlds separate," she says.

"Then we have some decisions to make."

She grins. "Such as?"

"Either you break your rules or I stop coming here to see you and we see each other at my place or yours."

She angles her head to the side. "Hmmm. Then at your place or mine, I could do with you as I choose—since you wouldn't technically be a client anymore."

"Will I still get the pleasure of your touch?"

"Yes, that and much more."

Vincent clasps the back of her head in his palm and pulls her to him. Tentatively he kisses her, slowly and with heartbreaking tenderness.

Selena feels tears spring to her eyes as joy and a dreadful realization well within her. *Vincent is the one.* But in order for them to share eternity he must become like her; he must give up his human life.

All in good time, she consoles herself. First she must bind him to her, turn his mind and his heart, before she turns his body.

Selena is happier than she has been in a century. The time that she is able to spend in daylight is beginning to grow again. Spring brings with it new blooms in her garden and her spirit feels refreshed. Vincent, as promised, spends all his free time with her when he is not out of town on a photo shoot. They spend their days in her apartment or his and he readily accepts her explanation that too much sunlight brings on sudden headaches. Vincent is simply content to have Selena in his presence. Their evenings are spent wandering the streets of Manhattan, visiting the array of eclectic shops and cafés. Late into the midnight hour they curl up on the couch and watch old movies, drink red wine and nibble popcorn. Selena feels almost human.

"Lena," Vincent says, calling her by his pet name for her.

She snuggles closer to him on the couch.

"I want to be patient and give you time to get to know me, really see if being with me is what you want . . ."

"Yes?"

"I already know what I want."

She turns to look at him. "Do you?"

"I want you. All of you. I want to know what it's like to be a part of you."

"Are you sure?"

"I've never been more certain of anything in my life."

Her eyes hold his for a moment. "Kiss me, Vincent."

"With pleasure."

This kiss is different. Selena succumbs to the soft seduction of his lips, pressing herself closer to the warmth of his body, needing to feel the beat of his heart next to hers.

"Let me touch you, Selena," he murmurs against her mouth even as he begins an erotic exploration of her body.

Vincent eases her back onto the couch and one by one unfastens the buttons of her sheer black blouse, easing it to the sides to expose her warm, cinnamon-toned skin. As if hypnotized, he reaches out to touch the rise of her breasts and relishes the soft sigh that escapes her lips.

He takes his time, paying homage to every inch of her as he discards her clothing one item at a time.

Selena writhes beneath the touch of his fingertips, restraining herself from capturing him between her powerful thighs and sucking him dry.

"You are exquisite," he says in awe, rising to look down upon her nude body. He reaches out to take her hand. "Come, let's do this right." She takes his hand and he leads her into his bedroom.

Like teenagers they tumble onto the bed, laughing and entwining their arms and legs, searching for tender flesh to nibble and kiss.

But after weeks of waiting, teasing and taunting each other, the feel of her wet sex against his stiff erection is soon more than either can endure.

For the briefest of moments, perhaps only a heartbeat of time, they focus solely on each other, allowing the world to recede into the background. Vincent lowers himself upon her and raises her legs around his waist.

"This is how I feel," he whispers the instant before his body joins hers.

They both gasp with surprise and sublime pleasure at their

union. The waves of pleasure transport them to a netherworld of images, sounds and feelings that are inexplicable, beyond the imaginations or experiences of mere earthly beings. Vincent is both frightened and compelled to continue the journey, his body no longer his or under his control.

Selena draws him deeper, her wet walls gripping and releasing him, tormenting him with pleasure. This is what she has waited for. This man, this time, this now. Lucien was right, she realizes, through a haze of ecstasy. Vincent is the one. Against her will, but what came naturally to her kind, her fangs lengthen as the bloodlust boils like an overheated cauldron. Her nails extend as her fingers claw his back and her hips rise in wild abandon. For an instant her eyes flash an eerie yellow, then fiery red as her climax reaches its apex and she cries out in release. Vincent shudders, then empties the very essence of himself within her.

For long hours they love each other, on the bed, on the floor, on the couch and lastly in a tub of hot water. They make love until the sun begins to peek above the horizon and slip through the slats of the thin blinds. But, today, Selena no longer fears the daylight. She has been reborn. Life is good once again.

As she turns the soil in her garden, Selena realizes that she hasn't added more "fertilizer" to the soil in months. Since she has been with Vincent her hunger has been held in check and the longing for liquid nourishment has been kept at bay. But lately the old desires have begun to resurface. She feels a trickle of the old heat stirring in her blood.

She turns the soil more quickly as her mind races. Somehow, she will have to escape Vincent's watchful eye in order to make her kill. He is scheduled to go out of town on a shoot, he's told her. He will be gone for the week. The night before they'd had frenzied sex, as if they might never see each other again.

"When I get back," Vincent had said as he lay spooned against her, "I want us to talk about making this relationship permanent."

She turned to face him. "What do you mean?"

"I don't want you to be the one that got away. I want to be the only man in your life—forever."

"Oh, Vincent. Do you understand what you're saying?"

"I've never been more certain of anything in my life, Lena." Tenderly he'd kissed her. "I've got to go on this assignment but we'll talk when I get back."

He'd gotten up from the bed and she'd watched him as he moved around the room, collecting his clothes. The ripple of muscle in his arms and legs, the way his warm chocolate skin looked in the early morning light, filled her heart and soul. She wanted to say yes with all her heart, but Vincent had no idea what forever really meant. He didn't know that her kind lived for eternity.

Tonight will be the night, she decides now as she pats down a patch of damp, rich earth, ready for planting. She will quickly quench her thirst with some faceless man while Vincent is away and spare him a life of eternal darkness and hunger. But for how long can she keep her secret?

She brushes dirt from her hands. As she rises from her knees, she's stunned to see Lucien standing in front of her.

"Lucien."

"Beautiful as always, my dear Selena."

"Why did you leave me like that?" She tosses the hoe onto the ground like a temperamental child.

"So that you could find him. I sent him to you, you know." He strolls casually among the rosebushes.

"You?"

He laughs. "I met Vincent while he was working in Marseille. And I knew immediately that he was the one for you. I gave him 'your card.' "

"He never said anything about meeting you."

"He has no memory of meeting me." He looks into her eyes. "Tell me, Selena, are you happy?"

Briefly she lowers her head, suddenly ashamed to have to admit that Lucien was right, that it was not him she sought all these years—but Vincent. And if that were true, then what was it that she felt for Lucien?

"Yes," she says softly.

He nods his head. "I'm happy for you, Selena."

"Are you?" she asks, needing to know his true feelings.

"A part of me selfishly wished that you would be my queen. But I knew it was not to be and that I had to relinquish that foolish notion and allow you to find some form of happiness." He paused. "He will eventually grow old, Selena. His hair will gray and his shoulders will stoop and he will wonder how it is that you do not age as well. The time will come, Selena, and you will have to make a decision. But he must agree. He must understand what it is that you will offer him."

"I know." She sighs deeply. "But I don't know if I can. What if he refuses, what if he is sickened by me and what I am? I don't think I could bear that."

"That is the decision you will have to make. Tell him or let him go. But I believe that he will surprise you. Vincent is a unique human. It is why he was chosen."

He reaches out and touches her face. She clasps his hand against her cheek and closes her eyes, remembering. And when she opens her eyes, Lucien is gone.

Selena prepares for her last customer of the night, a young, virile man whom she'd been working with for several weeks. Of all the potential prey, he was most suitable. He might be missed, but no one would ever connect him to her. They had never been seen together and he only came to her shop late at night.

"Your bath is ready," she says, entering the sitting room with an armful of clean towels. She smiles. The poor boy had absolutely no clue what lay in store for him. Too bad he'd made the fatal error of thinking that he could touch her inappropriately on his last visit, ignoring her subtle hints that she was seeing someone. She'd considered taking a bite then but held back. Tonight is a different story. She has no qualms. What she has is need.

"I'll be waiting for you in the massage room when you're done." She hands him the towels.

"I'll be right out." He winks at her—another dangerous mistake.

While he is in the bath, Selena prepares and awaits his arrival. Her fingertips tingle and she can feel the warmth begin to build. Her blood runs hot and a growl threatens to slip from her throat. She slides out of her clothes and puts on a sheer dressing gown open almost to her navel. She dabs a drop of Egyptian musk behind each ear and at her wrists. She smiles with anticipation as she hears his approach.

"All ready, sugar."

Selena turns. "Then lie down on your stomach and let's get started," she says in a deliberate monotone.

"How about if I start out on my back? I like to watch you while you work."

The corner of her mouth lifts slightly. "Whatever the customer wants." She slowly approaches the table and places her palms on his bare chest.

"Hmm, that feels good already," he murmurs.

"This is only the beginning." She adds oils to her hands and runs them across his skin, pressing tentatively at first and then with more pressure, drawing pleasure from the sounds of his breathing and soft moans.

Selena inhales deeply and her eyelids flutter closed. Then, as if a door or window were suddenly thrown open, a gust of wind spirals through the room. The flames from the candles flap madly. Selena hovers above him as the room darkens and her eyes turn a brilliant yellow-gold. All the while she strokes him, caresses him, lulling him into submission.

She rips away his towel, exposing his swollen genitals. She growls deep in her throat, incisors appearing as she prepares to impale herself upon him.

He looks up at her and terror suddenly registers in his eyes. He opens his mouth to scream the instant she eases down on him, capturing his length, and the cry locks in his throat. Selena tosses her head back in pure carnal delight, giving him a few moments of unforgettable pleasure before she begins to drain him dry.

Every nerve ending in her body is on fire; her skin vibrates from a tension hot enough to ignite. Her cry for deliverance is animal-like as she lifts her prey's head, bares her teeth and sinks them deep into his neck. His body convulses, once, twice as his life spurts out of him and into her.

Selena is frenzied now. The blood, the hot sap is not enough to put out the flames. She sinks her teeth deeper, hitting bone, ripping flesh and tearing it away.

"Oh my God!"

Selena snaps her head in the direction of the voice. Blood and torn skin drip from her mouth.

Horrified, Vincent turns and stumbles out the door. He runs for his car as a wave of nausea overwhelms him, spinning his head and clouding his vision. He drops his car keys three times before he can get his fingers to open the door. Hurry . . . hurry . . . beats his heart. He doesn't want to be the next victim to be pounced upon by that thing . . . that creature . . . that . . . Selena.

He can't wrap his mind around it. It must have been an apparition, someone that looked like her, he frantically tells himself, finally getting his shaking fingers to hold still long enough to fit the key into the lock. His lovely Selena isn't some vile animal with fangs and yellow eyes, the thing nightmares are made of.

But it is her. Deep down in his gut he knows it is her. He climbs into the car and tears away from the curb, tires squealing as he races down the darkened streets of Manhattan. He'd slept with her, been inside her body, tasted her. Oh God. Oh God.

Breathing hard Selena relinquishes her victim, dropping his lifeless body back onto the table. His limp arm falls off the side. She looks at what she has done with an overwhelming feeling of disgust. Though she feels nothing for her lifeless victim, she is devastated that Vincent has seen her. She must find him—quickly—before his fears force him to reveal what he has seen to others.

With unnatural speed she wraps the body and stores him in the cedar chest. There is no time to bathe and prepare the corpse. Selena cleans herself and changes clothes, turns off the lamp in the window and locks the doors. Where would he go? Was he still in the city? She knew she would have to call upon all her powers to locate him. Stop him. Explain.

She searches from on high, soaring above the spires of the towering buildings and alleys, appearing in local clubs and bars only to vanish in the blink of an eye. She takes on many forms during her quest, shape-shifting to blend unnoticed by those around her. Finally her heightened senses pick up his scent.

Shaken, Vincent pulls into the parking lot of Kennedy Airport, quickly takes his bags from the trunk and hurries to the airport entrance. His only thought is to get away. Bone-chilling terror runs rampant through his veins. His hands tremble as he searches for his identification, but his heart stills when he looks up to find Selena in front of him.

"We need to talk, Vincent," she says quietly. Her voice is a gentle command.

"Stay. Away. From. Me," he bites out, backing away from her. Her eyes lock onto his. "You don't mean that. You're just upset. I can explain. Let me explain, please, Vincent." She reaches out and touches his arm, sealing their connection. She feels his resistance weaken. Selena knows she only has a few minutes before the hypnotic trance is broken. She must convince him of her love, convince him of the life they can have together. "Come, let's find someplace quiet."

Against his instincts, he follows her and suddenly finds himself in her house. His head is so full of spinning thoughts and his emotions in such a state of shock, even this fantastic event cannot shake him.

"I know you are afraid of what you saw, what you unfortunately walked in on today in the salon," she says while pouring them each a glass of wine. She hands him a glass and he greedily empties it in one long swallow. "But I need you to listen carefully to what I am going to reveal to you. This is the real truth. I swear it."

She sits next to him on the couch and begins the tale of her life back to her childhood in Baton Rouge, telling him things she has never told another living soul. She unflinchingly details her youthful rebellion and its lifelong consequences, frankly admitting her years of searching and the terrible bloodlust. Hours later, with tears of trepidation running down her cheeks, she looks into his eyes.

"We were destined to meet, you and I. Lucien told me that if I ever found the one, I would finally have peace. I don't want to go through eternity being the beast that you saw tonight. I don't want to roam the world endlessly—alone and lonely. *You* can save me, Vincent. Only you." She feels the control slipping. His gaze is beginning to clear. She's lost and her heart breaks into bitter pieces.

"How? Tell me how," he asks, his tone thready and hesitant.

Selena's breath catches in her throat. Hope lifts her heart and voice. "By truly becoming one with me, by loving me totally the way that I love you. We can share forever together, Vincent. I will never have to prey on humans again. My destiny is in your hands."

"I . . ." he stammers before taking a deep breath. "I came to you tonight because I had something I wanted to give you." He reaches inside his jacket pocket and pulls out a tiny velvet box. He opens it and a beautiful diamond ring sits splendidly in its center. "I love you, Selena. As much as I was sickened by what I saw, there is a part of me that has to believe it wasn't really you, but something or someone else that took you over. It couldn't be the woman I fell in love with. If I don't believe that, I'll go mad. I can't imagine my life without you in it. I believe that nothing is so terrible that we can't conquer it together. Even . . ." He swallows hard and looks into her eyes. "Even what you are."

"Do you truly understand what is being asked of you? This mortal life you now lead will be no more. We will travel the earth together. There will be those who may discover our secret and attempt to hunt us down. You would always live in fear. But we would be together."

"Yes, I understand," he says, slipping the top of her dress from her shoulder to caress her there. "Show me my new life."

Selena looks deep into his eyes and strokes his cheek. How long had she searched for him, this time, this moment? Lucien was right. Finally her quest has ended and she wouldn't spend forever alone. She leans closer and tenderly kisses his lips, his eyes, as her fingers trail across his neck. She must be careful, taking only enough of his blood to turn him—not kill him. She will teach him all that she knows, perhaps even the ancient art of the touch. She smiles as she bares sharp fangs.

"Don't be afraid," she whispers an instant before biting into his succulent flesh. In that instant she knows without a doubt that her nights of hunting have finally come to an end.

A sublime rush flows through Vincent, a feeling of total euphoria, an incredible high. Light and darkness merge and his head spins. His body momentarily spasms and the most incredible climax he has ever experienced takes over his body.

Tenderly, Selena lays him down. "In time you will learn to give me that same pleasure," she says as he drifts off into the sleep of the living dead.

Rumor, folklore or just plain gossip—no one knows for certain. But there are stories about a certain golden couple who seem to never age. They are always together, enjoying the best things in life in the most beautiful places of the globe. Some say they resemble people that they know and met decades ago, others say they're just what they seem—a young couple in love and unashamed to show it.

The only ones who know the truth are Selena, Vincent and Lucien—and they'll never tell.

The Family Business

KEVIN S. BROCKENBROUGH

This is a story about monsters. And blood. Monsters. And being black. Monsters. And fighting back.

Let me introduce y'all to Shelly Brown.

She's the sista over there with the bruises on her face and the large sunglasses covering two black eyes. She's been in this hospital so much, most of the nurses know her by name. She's only in her late thirties but she's spent the last seven years of her life living with a monster.

Yesterday, Ricky Brown, her only son, made the mistake of trying to kill the monster. Ricky's just two weeks shy of turning sixteen, but he decided four years ago that he was tired of seeing his mom get beat up. And getting his own ass beat "just because."

For the last six months, he's been saving up his lunch money. To buy a gun. Unfortunately, the monster had one, too. Ricky's gun jammed. The monster's didn't.

So now Shelly sits in her son's hospital room. Praying to a God she's not quite sure is listening. To save the life of a son who took a bullet in his chest from a man only a paternity test would call a father.

God, I know I got no right to ask you this, but please don't take my baby. Please, Lord. Please.

She's praying so hard, she doesn't even hear the monster she calls husband walk in. Probably 'cause her tears were aimed at heaven and the brother walking in came from somewhere much hotter.

Meet Lou Brown, Shelly's husband. An ex–Golden Gloves boxer clad in a red leather suit, the all-too-accurate wife-beater shirt and single gold hoop earring.

The detectives working Narcotics call Lou one of Philly's most successful drug pushers. Other dealers call him a psycho. Shelly calls him a monster. Each one's right.

Lou leans in and gently kisses Ricky on the forehead: "How's he doing?" Lou asks. "Yo! Rick? Ricky-Rick?"

Ricky's connected to IV tubes of blood plasma and pain-killers. He's also connected by blood to a monster. The fact that the boy's lying there unconscious doesn't stop Lou from flashing the gifts he's brought. He holds up a new box of basketball shoes and an NBA throwback jersey as if Ricky's swollen eyes could open wide enough to see them.

"Check it out: this gear is hot, right?" Lou says, like a loving parent on Christmas morning. Not like the psycho who pistol-whipped his son first, then shot the kid just to scare off anyone else crazy enough to test Lou's heart.

"Yeah, yeah. I'm a leave 'em right here, so it's the first thing you see when . . ." Lou coos.

"You almost killed him," Shelly says. Rattlesnake quick, Lou grabs Shelly by the collar, lifting her out of the chair at Ricky's bedside so that they're face-to-face. She'd scream if she could get enough air down her throat.

"I almost what?" Lou whispers in her ear. "He was playing

ball and got caught in a crossfire. Probably some gangbangers. Right? Right? Say it!"

Lou loosens his grip just enough for her to breathe. "He's your son!" she gasps.

"The motherfucker pulled a gun on me!" Lou snarls. "What was I supposed to do? Stand there and let him shoot me?"

And this is the part that makes you wonder if the Man Upstairs has jokes. 'Cause at that precise moment, Ricky regains consciousness.

"Mom?" Ricky breathes, turning his head blindly. Eyes swollen shut, remember? Still both parents scramble to be the first one he "sees."

"I'm here, baby," Shelly whispers, wrenching herself from Lou's grip. "Momma's here."

"I'm sorry . . ." Ricky exhales.

"It's okay. You just rest," Shelly says, instinctively placing her body between Ricky and Lou.

"No . . . I'm sorry I didn't kill him," exhaling the words, but not the hate. "I'll get him next time." And just as Lou's jaw drops, Ricky slips back into unconsciousness.

"Did you hear that shit?" Lou roars, moving in close enough for Shelly to smell the alcohol still on his breath. "You turned my own son against me. That's fucked up. Come here."

Shelly tries to run, but Lou grabs her by her long hair and slams her face-first into the wall. She thinks she feels something break, but she's taken so many lumps over the years there's no way to tell if it's something old or something new.

Lou would probably still be kicking her to this day if he hadn't felt the barrel of a gun put at the back of his head. Holding the gun is J. T. "Quick" James, a black patrolman whose shaved head, muscular frame and aviator sunglasses evoke images of a mix of Dirty Harry and Mr. T. The nickname is short for "quick tempered."

"Yo, Sis? You okay?" Quick asks.

"She slipped," Lou lies. "You know she all clumsy and shit. I was just getting ready to—"

The sharp thud of a nightstick cuts off the rest of whatever bullshit he was about to say. After getting smacked upside the head a good six or seven times, Lou curls up like a ball, hoping to outlast Quick's anger.

See, Quick doesn't own a pet. But he does own a nightstick. And he walks it daily. Ever see Bruce Lee use a pair of nunchucks? That's the way Quick is with a nightstick. Fluid. Savage. Jacking people up. And looking pretty doing it.

"Why all you tough guys like hitting women, huh? Huh?" Quick asks. "How 'bout I give you some? Huh? You like that? Here, have some more."

Each word out of Quick's mouth comes with at least two blows from that nightstick.

"Let him up," comes a low growl from the doorway. Softly closing the door behind him is the one man in this world Quick is afraid of: Smokey James. This is Quick and Shelly's father, a sixty-year-old barber with the hard body of a twenty-four-year-old bricklayer. He has on a somber black suit and a white shirt as if coming fresh from church—or a funeral. He's sent plenty of folks to both.

Quick delivers one last savage blow and steps away from Lou as Smokey helps his daughter to her feet and into a chair. Lou struggles to his feet and staggers toward the door. He knows that while Quick likes to carry a nightstick, Smokey travels with a straight razor so sharp it could cut glass.

"Lou?" Smokey says, never looking at the man, but still close enough in the small hospital room to feel Lou inching away.

"What?" Lou answers, one foot already out the door.

"You know, seven years ago your wife begged me not to get in her business. But the next time you touch either her or Ricky, me and my boys gonna pay you a visit. And trust me, you don't want that. You hearing me, boy?"

"I hear you," Lou says respectfully, "But this don't involve you. What's going on here is between me and her. That's all I gots to say. We might disagree sometimes, but she knows I love her. Ain't that right, baby? Shelly? Shelly?"

But the pain whooshes out of her like a punctured tire until all that's left of her rage is a whisper: "Go away! Just . . . go."

"Bitch! Who you think you talking to?" Lou says. He takes half a step toward Shelly, but Quick jumps in front of her, waving that damn nightstick again.

"My arm look tired to you, nigga?" he growls.

Lou spits blood into a wastebasket, glares at Shelly but leaves quietly.

Smokey picks Shelly's sunglasses off the floor and hands them to her. She pops them back on without saying a word.

Here it comes, she thinks.

"What happened this time?" Smokey asks, as he walks over to the door Lou just slithered out of and locks it. Smokey ain't never been eager to have folks all up in his business. "I'm listening," he says.

"Well, let's see," Quick begins. "I'd say we got two black eyes, possibly a broken nose, and the way she's breathing all hard, maybe even a broken rib . . ."

"Well, maybe if you'd lock his ass up—" Shelly snaps.

"Oh, no! Don't put that shit on me," her brother fires back. "And whatever happened to that restraining order you was gonna get?"

"A little piece of paper ain't gonna stop that fool," Shelly sneers.

"So, what do you want to do?" Smokey asks, a hard look in his eyes. Silence. Quick looks away, Shelly looks down at the hospital floor that some lazy janitor needs to clean.

"Isn't it a full moon this week?" whispers Shelly at last.

There, she said it. And don't act like you haven't been waiting to hear it.

She rises and walks over to her still-unconscious son. Nobody says a word. The only sound is Quick, tap-tap-tapping his nightstick gently against his leg.

"You sure?" Smokey says.

Shelly picks up Ricky's limp hand. Nods. "I can't live like this," she says, kissing that precious hand. "We can't live like this."

"It's about time, that's all I got to say," Quick mutters.

But the most dangerous person in the room doesn't say a word. Smokey just pours himself some water into a small paper cup and takes four aspirin. For the headache he has—and the one he sees coming.

To know monsters, you got to know the streets where they live. Like the streets of West Philly, where you always hear police sirens in the distance. And people arguing over all kinds of shit. And don't let it be hot and muggy. 'Cause then you got a place with too many people, too fired up, on a night that's just too damn hot. That's when the monsters come out.

Just ask my man Mace, an ex–football player who beats people up for a living. He's the one over there all smashed up against the Lincoln Navigator with a gun pressed to his forehead.

See, Mace told a joke about a monster. And somehow the joke got back to the monster. And the monster ain't laughing.

"Heard your big ass got jokes," Lou said. "Jokes 'bout me. That true?"

"Yo, I don't even know what you talking about, yo," Mace stammers. "Lou! We been cool for years. Come on now!"

"Who told him then?" Lou snaps, jamming the gun even harder into Mace's forehead.

"I don't know! I swear!" Mace says. "I ain't even seen Ricky in days, man. Serious, man. You need to get with Ugly Nikki. Maybe he done blabbed your shit. You know how faggots do."

With his free hand, Lou gives Mace a punch to the gut that makes the big man's knees buckle and flips on Mace's asthma. Gently placing the barrel of his .45 right between Mace's eyes, Lou asks softly, "Did you just call me a faggot?"

"No! I ain't say that!" Mace wheezes. "All I'm trying to—"

"Well, if I'm not a faggot, then how do I know how they do?" Lou says. "Explain."

But before Mace can decide between thinking up a good lie and the best way to breathe, Lou decks him with a quick left hook.

Maybe if I just lay here, he'll just beat my ass instead of shooting me, Mace reasons through a haze of pain.

"Time's up, nigga. I'm thinking the best way to help you with that asthma is to give your big ass more ventilation," drawls Lou. He steps back. Aims. Fires.

By the time he walks away, Mace is already slumped against his new Lincoln Navigator, trying desperately to hold on to life as his blood spit-shines the pavement.

But don't think nobody gives a damn in the 'hood. See help is already heading his way and it's wearing the cutest little Diana Ross–style bob wig and a beautiful beaded minidress like you'd expect to find on Cher. In Vegas. But Cher never made All-City in high school playing linebacker. This is Ugly Nikki. But don't call him that to his face. He's sensitive and plenty big enough to kick both you and your momma's ass.

The cross-dressing Nikki tenderly strokes Mace's face, singing, " 'My world is empty, without you, babe!' "

"Hi, Mace." He smiles. "Tummy ache?"

"Call . . . nine-one-one . . . hurry . . ." begs Mace.

"Sorry, baby. Nikki hungry," he says. Ugly Nikki opens his

big mouth with the lipstick-covered lips. Ugly Nikki has big, ugly teeth. Ugly Nikki also has vampire fangs.

Mace screams one of those loud-ass grade-B horror movie joints, the kind that seems to echo forever. But unfortunately for him, this is the ghetto, where niggas scream all the time. The next day, no one will even admit to hearing anything.

You know how we do.

Gunfire and screams on the streets of West Philly are old news to Shelly but she goes to her apartment window anyway, looking out at a night alive with monsters. Shelly can see Lou stepping out of the alley, crossing the street and heading her way, but it's too dark for her to see Ugly Nikki making a meal out of what used to be Lou's boy Mace.

Shelly goes back to throwing clothes into an overnight carry-all. There ain't shit in her and Lou's apartment worth much, unless you count his stuff, but she'll be damned if she'll leave Lou with only the clothes on her back. She stops for a minute to take one last look around, her eyes stopping on a newly framed family portrait of Lou, Shelly and Ricky that hangs on the wall. Lou had found it under some unpaid hospital bills. He dusted it off, hung it up, then beat her ass for not reminding him to pay the bills.

While Shelly gathers up her clothes and her memories, Smokey looks over Lou's ghetto-fabulous collection of wildly colored shirts and shoes. One of the first things to catch his eye is a pair of orange alligator shoes next to a pair of ice-gray Timberland boots. Closer inspection reveals a huge wad of one-hundred-dollar bills stuffed inside the Tims. He tosses the loot over to his daughter.

"What is that smell?" he asks, reaching into the closet. Smokey pulls out a sheer, hot-pink number that's at least three times larger than anything that would fit Shelly. He holds it up to his nose, sniffing it like a dog would an unfamiliar lamppost. He frowns, then tosses it as far away from him as he can throw it.

One thing you got to know about Smokey: he knows smells the way Coltrane knows jazz. And that damn sure wasn't Shelly he was smelling on that blouse. Or any other woman, for that matter.

"He said he was drunk when it happened," Shelly says, stuffing her favorite pair of gold hoop earrings into her bag. "But Ricky heard different. And told him so to his face."

"That's when Lou shot him."

Smokey's cell phone rings before he can comment on fathers who shoot their own flesh and blood. The call is from his other boy, Nate, who's parked outside Shelly's apartment in an old Ford pickup truck playing lookout. Most folks say Nate James looks a lot like NBA All-Star Kevin Garnett, the lean, bald-headed brother who plays center for the Minnesota Timber-wolves. But Nate's more wolf than Garnett will ever be.

"Lou's heading your way," Nate tells his father. "You want me to handle it?"

"No," Smokey says, low and dangerous. "Let him come."

Right on cue, Lou bangs on the apartment door. "Yo, it's me! Hurry up! I gotta pee!" he yells. Lou is too lazy to look for his keys. If it wasn't for his wife and kid, he'd spend most nights locked out.

"Just a minute!" Shelly shouts back in a familiar routine. Inside the bedroom she slides open the window to the fire escape. It's a getaway she's used plenty of times before to escape the monster she married, but this time she stops. Looks her father in the eye. Neither one says a word but both are thinking the same thing: *This is it.*

Lou bangs on the door again, that insistent, in-a-minute-I'm-going-to-pee-myself kind of bang. Shelly yells, "Coming!" but doesn't move. "Do it," she whispers to her father. Before Shelly can change her mind, her father has crossed the room and is rolling up the sleeve on her right arm. He wraps thick fingers around her bare arm. In seconds steam begins to rise from Shelly's soft, brown flesh. The pain is short but intense and even as it ends she can feel something forming beneath her skin. Something alien. Something alive. When Smokey lifts his broad palm, branded on her skin in perfect detail is a snarling wolf's head with glowing, red eyes. It is the same brand worn by Smokey. And Nate. And Quick.

Her father gently leads her to sit on the bed. Smokey then closes the window, draws the curtains, cuts off the light and they settle down in the darkness to wait.

Out in the hall, Lou's bladder forces him to find his own damn keys. *Damn bitch! She tried to lock me out!* He slams open the door and sprints to the bathroom. Over the sound of his piss hitting the water, he hears someone in the bedroom.

"Yo! What's wrong with you?" he yells. "Didn't you hear me banging out here? Shelly! Where the fuck you at?"

He zips up and steps into the living room, eyes darting back and forth, searching for even a hint of movement. Nothing. He notices the door to the bedroom is halfway open but he can't see inside.

From inside the bedroom, Shelly's voice purrs, "Come on in, baby! Momma's got a little surprise for you!"

"Oh, yeah? Well, I got one for you, too," Lou replies, rubbing his hand across one of the lumps Quick's nightstick left on his head. He pulls the gun from his waistband and adds a few more bullets.

Don't know if it was her or Mace done blabbed my shit, but ain't but one way to make sure I got the right one. Besides, drug dealing was hard enough without having niggas running around thinking you was soft.

He heads toward the bedroom, gun raised. *If I slap her head against the big pillow, no one will hear a thing.* He kicks open the bedroom door and comes face-to-face with pitch black. He can't see a thing. Out of that darkness comes Smokey's raspy voice: "Hello, Lou."

Oh, shit! That's okay though. Tonight I got a bullet for Daddy's ass, too.

Still aiming his gun at the darkness, Lou uses his free hand to fish for the light switch. "Smokey? That you? Big, bad Smokey. Hard rock motherfucker, hiding in the dark like a little bitch?" Lou's free hand flicks the switch.

And finds a man-size wolf snarling at him.

Quicker than a black cat can lick its ass, the creature's on top of Lou, pinning him to the floor. Each bite separating bone from flesh, each slash of its razor-sharp claws spray-painting the apartment's dingy, white walls with blood and human skin.

Later when telling the story, Nate would describe Lou's screams as similar to what you'd hear if a man got his testicles massaged by a weed whacker.

In response to the screams, several neighbors turn up the volume on their TV sets. A few get up to check that their doors are locked. As one brother tells his wife: "Whatever is out there, let it stay the fuck out there."

Smokey, carrying Shelly's overnight bag, exits the apartment building and walks toward the truck where Nate is waiting. Shelly is leaning against the side of the old Ford. She looks like she wants to vomit. Smokey hands the overnight bag to Nate, then turns to put an arm around Shelly as she loses the last of her dinner.

"Damn. You never told me it would be like that," Shelly accuses her father.

"You never asked," Smokey replies.

Just as she pulls the door open to climb into the truck, she twists around and throws up again. Nate watches his sister, on her hands and knees heaving her guts up, and he shakes his head slowly in a been-there-done-that nod of sympathy. "You'll be alright. Probably just something you ate," he jokes.

But the story doesn't end there. You don't get rid of monsters that easy.

Lou is covered in blood and looks like a well-chewed sparerib, but damn if he don't crawl on his belly out of that bedroom and into the hallway outside of his apartment. Just like a snake. So Lou is lying there, waiting on death or the tax man or both. But Lou always was too lazy to keep watch for long. That nigga nods off after a few minutes. To be fair, it might have been the blood loss that really knocked him out.

The first thing he dreams of is a fine, young, teenage girl. This sista turns into a mist just like a cloud or something. In the dream, that cool mist floats down and covers his bloody body, oozing in through the open wounds and feeling better than the best heroin high, the best cocaine hit he's ever had.

Lou opens his eyes. He ain't in the hallway no more. He's inside what looks like a jazz club decorated by somebody who never went to China but really wanted to go there bad. There are little Buddha statues and hanging red lanterns everywhere. Lou can even see a pit below where a live sumo wrestling match is taking place. The club is packed with people belly to butt. Lou is seated in a private booth with dark windows that allow him to look out but no one can look in. Seated across from him is the girl from his dream.

She's honey-brown, with a little girl's face and a grown woman's body. Lou's guessing she couldn't be any older than sixteen. But she's covered in diamonds and wearing an Armani suit, the skirt with a slit so high up her thighs he can almost see heaven. A Chinese dragon in black and red is tattooed on her neck.

"I'm Malika," she says with a throaty, British accent that makes his dick rock-hard. A James Bond fan, Lou's always had a secret thing for British babes.

"I'm here to make you an offer," she says, giving a long look to his crotch. A waitress drops off a round of drinks: beer for Lou and what looks like a Bloody Mary for Malika.

"No disrespect," Lou says, "but you look kinda young to be up in here."

"Looks can be deceiving," Malika purrs, the dragon on her neck moving as she speaks. "I got bit at seventeen, but I've walked the Earth for over three hundred years."

Lou gulps a beer and shakes his head. *Damn, she had looked so good. You just couldn't tell by looking who was crazy and who was not.*

"Well, you look good for your age," Lou says, thinking he better play along since she was crazy. That might make it easier for him to get a piece of that ass. The crazy ones were always the hottest.

He's looking out the glass at the crowd to see if there's anybody he knows and can hit up for some blow, when he sees Mace and Ugly Nikki. What the fuck! He knows for a fact he'd pumped enough bullets into that punk Mace to kill an elephant. And where the hell had Nikki come from? No one had seen him for weeks.

"You thought Mace was dead?" Malika says with a wild laugh. "Oh, he is. You shot him, didn't you, Lou? You killed Mace for telling your secret."

Lou reaches for his gun. He'd gotten good at that. But it's not there. Puzzled, he looks down. His hand is covered in the reddest, darkest blood he's ever seen. And he's seen a lot.

"You got a lot of blood on your hands, don't you, Lou?" says Malika, sipping her bloodred drink. The sight of that drink is making Lou sick. "Do you want to guess where you're at right now, Lou? I'll give you a hint: Jesus doesn't come down here too often. His office is upstairs, way upstairs!" Then she smiles. A big, wide, broad smile that shows all her teeth. All her vampire's fangs.

Lou jumps up to run, but he can't move. His ass is glued to that chair next to that crazy bitch. After a minute he stops stuggling to get up. He must be dead after all: "Are you . . . ? Is this . . . ?"

"No, I'm not and yes this is," answers Malika. "You could say I work for Satan. This is an outer ring of hell, sort of like a good suburb a few miles from the heart of the ghetto. Play your cards right, and your soul gets to stay here. Light work, good drinks. Mess up and your soul ends up in the barbecue section.

"The Boss likes your work," she adds, signaling the waitress for another round of drinks. "He wants to send you back to do more. Everybody here is a sinner but he likes to pick out the really sick fucks and make them vampires. It drives the other side crazy. The Trinity likes seeing sinners get punished, karma and all that. But vampires are like a supernatural loophole. Technically, you're being punished because your soul stays here. But you get to go back to the world with your memories intact and with the power to raise all kinds of hell. Sound good, so far?"

Lou nods slowly. Come to think of it, there were some asses he still wanted to kick. Starting with his wife's. But he wanted more.

"I can hear your thoughts and I can see why the Boss likes you." Malika laughs. "We have a few vampires who think they can be free agents. They don't want to listen. If they were ordinary humans, we would strip their souls from them and torture them. But as vampires, they've already turned over their souls, so we have to give them something extra. That's where you come in." She pulls out what looks like the drug Ecstasy and a vial of crack.

"Vampires do drugs?" Lou asks, holding both glass vials up to the light.

"Not exactly," Malika corrects. "It's more complicated than just sniffing coke up your nose or shooting up. The drugs have to be inside a living host. The vampire drinks the spiked blood of the host."

This was familiar stuff, thought Lou. Hustling was hustling whether in hell or in West Philly.

"Tell me what you sell. What do you specialize in?" Lou says.

"I'm a supplier. Ingredients, carriers, even premixed," she says, moving closer to Lou. "I do a lot of business with the Russians," Malika begins. "They have access to labs in the Netherlands and little lost girls from around the world. I got a Viking premix which features big-busted Polish chicks already loaded with X. I also sell Tropicals or what you'd call Latinas. And, of course, I provide Hot Chocolates."

"That sounds good, real good. What else you got for me?" Lou says huskily as he slides his hand into her lap and down between her legs. His fingers go searching. She's already wet. *Read these thoughts you little freak,* Lou thinks. When it comes to women, Lou's game plan is always the same: a little rubbing always leads to a lotta loving.

Malika reaches under the table and pulls out a thin folder. She lays it on the tabletop and photos spill out. Quick. Nate. Smokey.

"I've been watching them," Malika says. "Oh, yes. Right there, *mmmmm,* yes. I can get you inside . . . oh, yes, slower there, that's it, that's it . . . but it will cost you." She reaches under the table, unzips his pants and rubs up and down his shaft, feeling the blood running in his veins.

Lou's having a hard time staying focused. Somehow he manages to say the words, "Cost me?"

She's kissing him now. On the lips. On his neck. Hot tongue in his ear. "Your son."

He grabs her and hauls her close. Kissing her neck. Tongue in her mouth. Slipping a finger inside her thong. "You don't want him. That little punk can't do nothing for you that I can't do better," he breathes into her ear.

She laughs and pushes him back. "That's not what I want from him," she says.

Malika reaches under the table again. She pulls out a small envelope about the size of a quarter. Inside is a grainy, reddish-brown powder. She grabs Lou's penis with one hand and rubs a little of the powder on the tip of his dick. Then she goes down on him, her fangs adding a new sensation to an old pleasure.

At first Lou feels only the warmth of her mouth. But then intermingled with that comes an icy trickle that starts in his shaft and spreads down his legs. The room takes on a wild, fun house–mirror view. The walls spin like a carousel. Colors collide and mix, while strange animalistic sounds roar through his ears.

Lou has the most explosive orgasm of his life. He comes so hard that if he weren't already dead it would kill him.

"Oh, shit! What the . . . ?" Lou gasps as he drifts back. Malika is wiping her mouth. She pops in a mint, runs her tongue across her fangs and blows him a wet kiss.

"The bones of a virgin werewolf," she says, putting on a fresh coat of lipstick. "Ground into powder. The best high on the planet. And the one drug vampires can take direct. Very rare. And very, very expensive."

Lou reaches for the powder but Malika snatches it up in a move so quick his eyes blur.

"I'm working with some scientists to make a synthetic version of it," she continues. "But I need more of the real thing in order to run a few more tests.

"Tell me, how do you feel about your son?"

"Ricky? That punk ain't no werewolf," Lou scoffs. Down below he notices Mace and Ugly Nikki staring hungrily at a sumo wrestler wearing more rolls of fat than the Michelin Man. Ugly Nikki is making a beeline toward those fat rolls.

"Don't be so sure," Malika says, a twisted smile on her face. "Even if he hasn't had his first transformation, he's still got the gene. Activate the gene and you've got yourself a werewolf. All you have to do is bite him. His body will treat the vampire bite as a toxin and voilà—instant virgin werewolf."

Lou flashes back to the ass-whooping that landed him in hell. One thing he knows for sure: werewolves are no joke. Again, Malika picks up on his thoughts. "My associates and I have already designed werewolf-proof cages," she says. "Once the transformation is complete, we'll flood the room with a nerve gas that'll kill him almost instantly. Then we just skin him, debone him and grind the bones to dust."

Lou looks at Malika and sees she's ice cold and dead serious. He promises himself to tap that ice-cold ass. Soon. *But first I have to get paid.*

"So how much does a virgin werewolf sell for these days?" he asks, his mind on a new Ferrari. "Ain't no love lost between me and that little nigga. But he is my son. I owe it to that nigga to at least get a good price for his ass."

Malika reaches between Lou's legs and strokes with the touch of an expert. "I don't think you want money," she says, sliding her tongue in his mouth.

"No, you got that wrong," Lou says, pulling away. "I definitely wants my money."

"Then how about a trade?" Malika says. "You give me Ricky and I give you what you want most. I'll help you kill Nate, Quick and Smokey. I'll even deliver wifey to you still breathing so you can have a little fun."

Before Lou can answer, Mace and Ugly Nikki open the door, coming into the room with the sumo wrestler hanging drunkenly between them.

"Malika, you want some of this? The Boss says this one is due for a little extra punishment," Ugly Nikki says, still looking like a crazed Diana Ross in drag.

Mace glares at Lou. "Don't let me catch you by yourself," he growls.

Malika rises to leave, but pauses to grab Lou's penis and whisper in his ear: "Well, do we have a deal?"

Lou pulls out his wallet. Inside is a picture of his wife and son. If even half the shit Malika is saying about Ricky is true, he can definitely cut himself a better deal. *Getting payback or getting paid?*

He rips the photo in half. Half he hands to Malika. Half he keeps. "Deal," says the monster.

It's one month later. The screams are gone but not forgotten. The sun is shining on the Belmont Plateau, the city's most popular park, but Shelly is restless.

The violent dreams come more and more frequently. She doesn't know what they mean. Either she's becoming an insomniac or she's losing her mind. It might be the latter, because lately she can't shake the feeling she's being watched. Late at night. Every night. By Lou.

When he was alive he used to play head games by having his boys spy on her, secretly following her around the city. Lou got a sick thrill from telling her stuff she'd done while she'd thought she was alone.

She needs to talk to someone. Get her head straight. But who? Her brother Nate stays up all night watching ESPN. Her brother Quick stays out all night getting his freak on. Both still treat her like their baby sister instead of a grown woman who'd been married and has a kid. And that's what she craves most after years of abuse. To be treated like an adult. Like an equal.

She is left with only one choice: Smokey. He always makes her fears go away. Maybe because he doesn't have any. His faith in God keeps his world and his choices simple: you are either living right or living wrong. How he reconciles serving a God of love with his nightly role of supernatural vigilante was a puzzle she'd danced around but never tackled head-on. But she has the feeling that something bad is coming, something none of them will be able to dance around. And it just won't go away.

Smokey spots his daughter making her way through the park. It is summer and the place is packed with families, splitting their attention between southern barbecue and summer league basketball. But Smokey's keen nose can smell the fear on his baby girl.

He doesn't look at her as she cuts through the picnic tables to where he's manning a grill. The constant line at his grill makes getting Smokey's attention a little difficult. He cooks to please the nose as much as the mouth, and once those peppers and onions hitch a ride on a summer breeze, even vegetarians reach for a hamburger bun.

When Smokey tells the hungry crowd he needs a few minutes alone with his daughter, it is as if he has read her mind. Father and daughter walk off to a stand of trees, far enough to talk privately but close enough to keep track of the basketball game. A still-healing Ricky is playing point guard.

For a few moments, Shelly doesn't say anything and neither does Smokey. The music is loud in the park and seems to come at them from all directions, gulping down the silence. He knows what is riding her. But she has to say it out loud. It has to be her decision to talk. His baby girl is all grown up. He has to treat her like an adult.

"You sleeping okay?" Smokey asks. "You sounded kinda rough last night."

"How'd you—" Shelly starts to say and then stops.

Smokey softly taps the wolf's head brand on his arm. "I could hear your heart pounding," he says. "Smell the fear. You wanna talk about it?"

"You'll probably think I'm crazy," mumbles Shelly.

A few yards away, a young white man playfully tosses a Frisbee to his dog. The dog chases the spinning Frisbee over to where Smokey stands with Shelly. The animal stops in mid-stride, snapping his head around to gaze at Smokey. Smokey winks. The dog barks and winks back.

· Shelly takes a swig of her soda and begins: "Last night, I dreamed that I was talking with this guy with a wolf's head. He was dressed like an African prince or something. He was real muscular. Had to be at least seven foot. Crazy, right?"

"I know exactly who you mean. That's Yusef. Yusef the Destroyer. The first werewolf," says Smokey.

"Hey, put some of these burgers on a plate for me," he yells to the guy now at the grill. About two hundred yards away on the basketball court, the crowd roars as Nate slams home a quick pass from Ricky.

"Your son had the same dream," Smokey adds. "He joked about it with Nate. Of course, he don't know what you know."

"Thanks," Smokey tells the young boy who brings over the plate of burgers and hot dogs. Shelly uses her fork to spear a hot dog. "Okay, back to the dream. You want to know what it means?"

Shelly isn't sure now she really wants to know but she nods anyway. Smokey leans in, lowers his voice to a raspy whisper: "It means that someone in our family is gonna die."

A Jeep, recently reborn as a rolling boombox, vibrates past, blasting a reggae tune and shattering what's left of Shelly's nerves. She can barely get the question out: "Do you . . . do you know who's going to die?" *I hope it's me and, please God, not Ricky.*

"It's me," Smokey says calmly. "I have a brain tumor."

"Shelly! I've missed you, young lady," yells a woman's voice. Her thick accent screams Eastern Europe despite living through five American presidents.

This is Sylvia. She and her husband, Milton "Doc" Goldberg, an aging, short, bald-headed Jewish man with Coke bottle–thick glasses and a large belly, are longtime family friends. No, more than family friends. They are like blood. When Shelly's mom died while her daughter was still sleeping in a crib, Sylvia became the closest thing to a mother Shelly had.

"When are you going to come over and visit me?" Sylvia says. She is wearing a low-cut top in a loud color. This is her style. She calls it "Gypsy" and likes to joke that the clothes she wears show off her "womanhood." She looks silly. But nobody ever laughs.

Sylvia has a miniature Doberman pinscher on a leash. He's jumping all over Shelly, panting and begging to be petted. Shelly laughs and scoops him into her arms. In minutes, she's feeding him one of Smokey's famous hot dogs. "Soon, Miss Sylvia, I promise. I've just had a lot on my mind lately," she says.

"This is Mr. Big, my neighbor's dog," says Doc, watching the little dog take turns licking Shelly's face and eating the hot dog.

"He's sure likes you." Doc laughs. "He doesn't even like me that much! That's what I get for breaking my poor mother's heart and going to veterinary school instead of law school!"

Smokey laughs and passes Doc a hot dog. "Well, let's hope you're better at that than you are at being a vet," he teases.

"It's the big dogs that give me the most problems," Doc retorts. He and Smokey exchange a wink.

"Here. Go make yourself useful and flip a few burgers," says Smokey. He hands Doc his apron. "I'ma go grab the boys." Smokey nods for Shelly to follow him. They snatch an empty picnic table a few yards away from the basketball court and sit down.

"Doc did a few X-rays," Smokey begins. "Said I got something on my brain stem. According to him the brain stem controls all the basic life functions. Blood pressure. Heartbeat. Breathing. And I'm guessing it may also control the Wolf." He says it calmly, with neither fear nor remorse.

"How much time do you have?" Shelly asks. Her eyes are moist and she's trying not to cry.

Smokey looks out at the basketball court. His son and grand-son are so good they could start for the Sixers. The other players don't have a chance.

"Doc's not sure. I'm not all man and I'm not all wolf, so it's hard to read my test results. One thing's for certain, though, it hurts like hell every time I change." Shelly starts to cry, but Smokey hands her a napkin. "Stop that," he whispers. "The boys don't know. And I don't want them to know. You're the only one I've told."

Shouts and yells fill the air. The basketball game is over. Nate scored the winning shot. Smokey grins and waves. "I want you to run my business when I'm gone," he tells Shelly. "Not the barbershop. The other one. The real family business.

"Listen, I know what you're thinking. Why me? Why not Quick? Or Nate?" says Smokey. "I love my boys but neither one's right for the job. Look at that," he says, pointing toward the edge of the park.

His son Quick is leaning against his patrol car. In front of him, and swinging her ass in his face, is a well-endowed sista in a halter top. And booty shorts. And long blond hair. This is Tasty Boom-Boom, a stripper who can work the pole in more than one way.

Smokey continues, "Quick's the best fighter. But that boy's only interested in one thing . . ." As if on cue, Tasty walks over to Quick, turns her ample backside to him and bends over, pre-tending to tie her thigh-high boots. Her size 44-double-D breasts are a triumph of plastic surgery.

Smokey nudges Shelly to look over at the basketball court. "Then you got Nate. If Quick's Batman, then Nate's The Joker." The game is over but Nate is still holding court. His boys are laughing so hard they're in tears. "One day he might make a de-cent second-in-command." Smokey shrugs. "But he's got too much light in him to take the lead. To really lead, you gotta know darkness. It helps you live with the choices you have to make.

"You know darkness," he says, laying his hand on top of hers.

Shelly runs her finger along the brand on her arm. Even in daylight the wolf's eyes seem to look right through her. Smokey had told her, "I didn't burn it on you; it burned its way out of you." Her brothers both had the same identical brand. So did every man who shared Smokey's bloodline. Few women had worn the brand. Only the unlucky few who had known darkness. The unlucky ones who had faced monsters.

Shelly had faced a monster. But what had happened to Lou in their apartment had scared her more because every night she went to sleep hungry for more. Hungry to kill.

As Nate, Ricky and Quick walk over to the table, Shelly quickly whispers, "What makes you think they'll listen to me?"

Smokey leans in and kisses her on the cheek. "Because Yusef believes in you. And so do I."

Lou loves being a vampire. His sadistic ass gets a kick out of having teeth sharp enough to open cans. Or rip through flesh. Satan had been right: he was a natural monster. From her penthouse apartment in Society Hill, Malika had used a combination of musty old books on black magic and the Internet to give Lou a crash course in life as a member of the undead. He'd learned about vampires from around the globe: the Obayifo witches of the Ashanti, the Loogaroo of the West Indies, the Aswang *manananggal* of the Philippines, the Xiang-shi of China and the mullos of the Gypsies.

She also taught him how to hustle drugs to the undead. If he was going to be a successful pusher, he had to know which drugs were like crack for vampires and which ones were a waste of time. Take marijuana, for example. Weed was cheap and relatively plentiful, but you had too many players already in the game, so margins were low. Same thing with regular crack. And wasn't nothing harder to get rid of than a vampire crack ho.

That's why Malika only worked synthetic drugs, like Ecstasy. Vampires' senses were already fine-tuned. Ecstasy enhanced that. And made them horny as hell. Most vampires would fuck anything that moved because it made their victims' blood run hot. And anything that made the blood hot made a vampire horny. Most vampires spent their nights having sex with humans and their days having sex with other vampires.

Lou shared a coffin with Malika. They had sex. Often. But he still wanted something she didn't have. So he went back to old habits. He went back to meeting Ugly Nikki. Nikki was a man. But Nikki knew what he liked. When he was alive, Lou and Nikki would hook up while Shelly was at work and the kid was in school. That worked fine. Lou got what he wanted and no one ever knew. At least until the one day the kid decided to cut class and come home early. Ricky had caught Nikki and Lou buck naked, the neighborhood fairy on top of the thug gangster, and the thug gangster moaning with delight. Ricky had pulled a gun out of his book bag and threatened to shoot Lou, but as the father and son argued, Nikki was able to get to his own gun. Nikki was the one that shot Ricky, but Lou took the blame. Somehow word still got out, and Lou had decided to put a bullet in the heads of the two people doing the most talking: Nikki and Mace. Finding Mace had been easy. That new Navigator had stood out like a cat at a dog show. Tracking down Nikki had been harder. Now Lou knew why. He'd been turned into a vampire by Malika.

Now both Mace and Lou were dead. But Mace still wanted payback. Malika had slept with Mace a few times, using that tight ass to negotiate peace. But she couldn't guarantee how long it would last. Her advice to Lou: kill Mace before he kills you. Lou took that to heart, but Mace was number two on Lou's to-do list.

Number one was his wife.

* * *

It's sundown. Night is coming. One of the local radio stations is hosting a charity All-Star basketball game. Nate and Ricky have been invited to play with the radio station team. They are up against a collection of civic-minded pro football players. The recreation center where the game is being held has a near sell-out crowd lined up, waiting to get inside. Eager to see some b-ball.

"Being near all this food is making me hungry," Mace says. Lou had hoped to get someone else as backup, but everyone who had said yes had dropped out to raid a Baptist convention happening over in Camden. *Greedy motherfuckers!* Malika had promised to drop by after she finished going shopping with Nikki.

Mace makes eye contact with a full-figured sista with a Pocahontas-style weave dangling down to her waist, spandex skirt and fishnet stockings. He blows her a kiss, keeping his lips over his fangs. No use scaring off dinner. She blows him one back.

"Now that's what I'm talking about," Mace says. "Oh, I forgot. You don't like women. My bad."

Lou's face tightens but he ignores him. In Lou's pocket are silver-coated bullets. Folklore has it that silver can kill a werewolf and a vampire. For a split second Lou weighs the pros and cons of pumping a silver bullet into Mace's big ass. *Damn that nigga was hard to kill!*

"Whatever," says Lou. "I'm going to wait by the concession stand. Check the bleachers. Ricky's playing tonight and Shelly never misses watching him play, so if you see her, grab her."

Lou tosses Mace a dog whistle. "If you see her brothers or her father, blow that whistle as hard as you can. It'll slow them down long enough for me to come over and give you a hand."

Mace looks at the dog whistle as if it were a warm turd. "Nigga, please," Mace says, "like I'm gonna need your ass to help me." He throws it back to Lou. "I can handle mine. You worry about you." And on that happy note, the two enter the building, heading in two different directions.

Two minutes later Quick pulls up in his squad car. With him is Pete Escobar, a rookie who thinks he knows more than he does. Shelly is sitting in the backseat. Shelly hops out of the car and looks at the entrance. There are about ten people waiting in line.

"They're still letting folks in, so the game must not have started yet," she says. "Come on! Let's get some good seats."

Pete follows her, admiring her backside as she walks, after a quick peek back at his partner. But Quick's mind is clearly elsewhere. He's sniffing the air like he's smelling something foul.

"Hey, Partner," Pete calls. "You coming? Quick? Hey, you alright?"

But Quick has picked up a dangerous scent. Vampires. And they smell oddly familiar, like a word that's on the tip of your tongue but you just can't remember it.

"I'm straight," Quick says. "But I got a hunch something's about to go down. Watch your back, okay?"

The two men follow Shelly inside, Quick still scanning the crowd for that telltale scent he recognizes.

The two teams are warming up, stretching and shooting free throws. Ricky waves at a pretty girl walking to her seat. Malika looks as innocent as apple pie. But her tight jeans don't leave much to the imagination and her push-up bra looks illegal. She blows Ricky a kiss, drawing cheers from his watching teammates.

Nate glances over to the stands and sees the source of Ricky's distraction. He dribbles over and stage-whispers loud enough for the whole team to hear: "You could play the best game of your life and you still wouldn't get none of that!"

Ricky laughs at his uncle and shoves Nate away. He gives Malika one last smile and a wink, and goes back to practicing.

As Pete and Shelly find seats, Quick waves Nate over. "Yo,

you made it," Nate says. But the joke he's about to share dies on his lips. Quick has his nightstick out. He ain't playing: somebody's getting ready to get hurt. "Hope that ain't meant for me," Nate jokes, not wanting to ask questions while anyone can overhear.

"They're here," Quick says, eyes darting around the gym.

"Who?" asks Nate.

"Nigga! Don't you smell them?" Quick taps his nose. Nate inhales.

"Oh, shit, you're right," he says, the basketball clutched in his hands.

"Daddy in here?" Quick asks.

"No, he said he was going over to Doc's." On alert now, Nate scans the packed house. A vampire attack would likely cause a stampede that was sure to leave plenty of folks hurt, maybe even a few trampled to death. "What's the plan?" he asks Quick.

Quick points to the announcer at the scorer's table. "For now just keep an eye on Ricky," he says. "I got Pete helping me with Shelly. If you see anything or smell anything, I want you to grab that fool's mike and holla. Got it?"

Nate nods. Nightstick in hand, Quick heads off in the direction of the bleachers to look for Shelly and Pete. "Be safe," Nate hollers to his brother, then dribbles back over to where his team is huddled, waiting for the start of the game.

Quick works his way through the crowd. He finds Pete sitting alone. *Rookies! They never do what you tell them to do.*

"Where's Shelly?" Quick barks.

"Oh, she went to get some popcorn," Pete says casually, never looking up from the program guide. "She said she had to go now because once the game started she wasn't moving."

"Shit," Quick bites out. "If I'm not back in five minutes, find me." When Pete looks up, Quick is already gone. He sees his partner turn the corner, swimming against a tidal wave of cheering fans.

The scent of vampires is stronger with each frantic step Quick takes. He finally catches sight of his sister. She's standing in line at the concession stand, counting her change.

By Shelly's count, she has just enough for a hot dog and a drink. Now if only the damn line would move. She looks around. People slip into and out of the line. A man bumps into her. He doesn't say excuse me. Shelly thinks she sees a familiar face but it's hidden by the crowd. The two men blocking her view move, and the face is revealed. Lou.

Shelly drops her change. More people move. The crowd shifts. The face is gone. Still stunned, Shelly reaches the counter. She turns to place her order. Behind the counter she finds a monster.

"How may I help you?" Lou smiles. "Are you thirsty? Me, too." He grabs the concession girl and brutally slams his fangs into her. Those close enough to see run screaming in all directions. Lou tosses the dead girl away and walks toward his wife. Shelly is frozen. She's like a deer caught in a car's headlights. She sees the danger. She knows she has to get away. But she just can't move.

"I missed you, girl," Lou croons. "You miss me, baby? Come here. Give Daddy some."

Shelly feels her feet take a step toward Lou. She tries to scream. But nothing comes out. She takes another unwilling step.

Lou is concentrating on Shelly so hard he almost doesn't feel the tap on his shoulder. *That damn Mace! Before the night is over I'm going to shoot him for sure.* He turns with a snarl, and comes face-to-face with Quick's service revolver.

"Hey, Lou . . ." Quick says. "Catch."

The force of the shot knocks Lou backward. Quick rushes over to Shelly. He shakes her hard and gives one command: "Run!"

Lou is already back on his feet. And running after them. He's closing fast. He grabs Quick by the throat, lifting the big man off his feet. Quick lashes out with a roundhouse kick that would make Bruce Lee proud. Lou flinches but doesn't loosen his grip.

"My turn," Lou says, his powerful punch sending Quick sailing clear across the now-deserted room.

"Remember your vows, baby," he tells his wife. "For better or worse. For richer or poorer. Till death do us, well, we might have to work on that one."

Quick is laid out cold. Shelly frantically tries to revive him. *No! No! No! Smokey killed him. He's dead. This can't be happening!*

"He can't help you, baby." Lou laughs. He walks away from Shelly and heads back to the soda fountain.

"I know it's hard for you to believe right now, but I'm thinking we can start fresh, you know," Lou says, pouring a soda. "I'm gonna bite you. You'll be my slave. We won't ever fight again. Damn, you just gave me a new business idea: vampire marriage counseling. One bite and everything's alright!" He grins.

Pete runs in, gun drawn. He aims. Fires. Soda spills down Lou's leather, baby-blue, double-breasted suit. Even undead he dresses like a cheap pimp.

Lou grabs a paper towel and wipes off the dripping soda. Nice and slow. He's in no rush. He has all the time in the world. "I'm afraid I'm gonna have to fuck you up for that one, Officer," Lou says calmly.

He levitates over the counter and makes his way toward Pete, snarling to flash his fangs. Pete is frozen in shock. Lou reaches him, wraps a hand around Pete's throat and starts to squeeze the life out of him.

A blow from behind knocks Lou's hand away. The man-size wolf roars and slashes a ribbon of red across Lou's baby-blue suit. "Get Nate. Go!" yells the wolf in Quick's voice.

Lou grabs for Pete again, trying to get a stranglehold. Quick barrels into Lou's chest, knocking the rookie cop loose from the vampire's grip. Both vampire and werewolf regain their feet in a flash. They come together with a crash. Both know that one of them's going to die tonight.

Pete looks on in amazement, rubbing his abused throat. Gasping for air, he tries to make sense out of the snarling shadow attacking Lou. What had happened? And where was Quick? And how the hell was he going to explain this to head-quarters? Werewolves and vampires? They'd lock him up for sure.

Shelly hears a crash and a long, loud wolf's howl. A huge wolf appears beside her. It's Smokey.

"Shelly, you and Pete get out of here," Smokey says. "I got it covered." As Shelly and Pete run out, the wolf turns toward the still-grappling Lou and Quick. Quick is bleeding badly.

"Welcome back to the land of the living, Lou," Smokey says, "Hope you enjoyed your time in hell, 'cause I'm sending you right back."

Lou gives Quick a vicious blow. He looks up at Smokey and smiles. He reaches for his gun with the silver bullets, but before he can pull it out, Smokey rams into his chest, sending both of them careening across the room, smashing through chairs and tables. Lou is fast, but Smokey is faster. He has both age and ex-perience. The wolf lands on top, snarling and snapping for a lethal blow. Lou gets his feet under him and tosses Smokey off. But the wolf is back on the attack in an eye-blink. Quick rejoins the fight. The two wolves tag-team the vampire, hammering him down. The battle is coming to a close and Lou is losing. Badly.

Smokey smells her before she steps out of the shadows. Smokey stops. Sniffs. It has been thirty years, but he will never forget that scent. The smell of the creature that killed his wife. Malika.

She's holding a gun to his grandson Ricky's head.

Lou takes advantage of Smokey's distraction and hits him with a sucker punch. He tosses Quick off with a kick. Smokey lands against two soda machines, toppling the heavy metal machines to the floor. The older wolf tries to rise but falls back and reverts from wolf back to man, then doubles over and vomits.

"Not now, damn it! Not now!" he prays, trying to fight the effects of the brain tumor to force the change and failing.

Quick, still in wolf form, staggers to his feet. He is covered with blood. One eye is swollen shut like the loser in a fight with Mike Tyson.

"Daddy, what's wrong?" he calls, ignoring Lou.

Lou begins to move in for the kill, circling toward Smokey, but Malika pulls him back and shoves Ricky toward him. She wants this kill. She points her gun at Smokey. Aims.

"That's right. I killed your wife, Smokey," Malika purrs. "And a few minutes ago, I killed your son Nate. Silver bullet to the head. It was fast. Oh, yeah, then I slapped around your daughter and stuck my gun in her gut. And here's the best part. Later on tonight, I'm going to kill your grandson, grind up his bones and snort him up my nose."

"Buh-bye." She fires twice.

For Smokey, time seems to stretch out like molasses. Death always takes its time. He sees that both bullets are silver. He sees Quick, all four legs pumping, running toward those bullets and launching himself into the air. One well-timed paw swats away the first bullet. But by stretching for the first bullet, he puts his chest directly in front of the second bullet. Both father and son scream as the second bullet finds its target. Quick lands with a thud at his father's feet, a silver bullet through the heart. Quick reverts back to human. Smokey screams in anguish.

"Aw, don't cry, Smokey," says Malika. "I got love for ya. Silver bullet love."

"Hey!" Pete yells, running into the room. Both Malika and Lou turn. They recoil as one at the sight of the gold cross in his hands. The cross is shining, giving off a white glow, the bright light causing Malika to throw up her hands and drop her gun.

"Get out, you unholy bitch!" Pete screams. "And take that fucking tooth fairy with you."

"Oh, you got jokes now," Lou snarls, one arm shielding his eyes while his other is locked around Ricky's throat. He twists the boy's body so that it shields him from the direct glare of the cross. "You got jokes but I'm the one with the gun." Lou fires in the direction of Pete's voice. The young cop dives for cover behind the overturned soda machines.

The room grows quiet. After a few minutes, Pete ducks his head out. The two vampires are gone. Smokey is cradling the body of his dead son. His heart racing, he quickly scans the room again. The vampires have taken Ricky with them.

"This one's still alive!" The words ring through Smokey's head as he sits in the hospital waiting room. See, he's a man of faith. Strong faith. He knows his prayers will be answered. His daughter will make it through surgery. His grandson will be found. Born into a bloodline of supernatural beings, Smokey has never had any doubt that there is a heaven and a hell. He knows the tumor in his brain is terminal and he's willing to meet his maker and be judged. He just prays that before that final Judgment Day he can take a few vampires with him.

"You want sugar with that?" Pete asks as he hands Smokey a cup of coffee. Smokey declines with a silent shake of his head. The two men, bonded by tragedy, sit in the hard, straight-backed chairs, each not knowing what to say to the other. Pete breaks the silence.

"Whether she makes it or not, we gotta get back the kid," he says. "I just don't understand. Why do they want him so bad? He's just a kid."

"Something you need to know. But before I tell you, you got to promise me to keep all this to yourself," Smokey says.

"Deal," Pete answers. *No one's going to believe this shit anyway.* "What you got?"

"Red Snow," Smokey answers. "It's a drug that's made from the bones of a virgin werewolf. There was a time in the late twenties when a group of vampires camped out in Alaska. Alaska's got long winters. It's dark for months at a time. Legend has it that thirteen of the vampires were also witches. They worked out a deal with the Devil. If they could get him high, they'd win back their immortal souls. These vampires trapped werewolves, skinned them alive, drained their blood and ground up the bones into a fine powder. You get a man's bones and his blood and you pretty much got the essence of what he is," finishes Smokey.

"His soul?" Pete ventures, disbelief on his face.

"Pretty damn close," Smokey replies. "So close that not only did Satan get high, he got hooked. Back in the eighteen hundreds, about one out of every ten thousand men was a werewolf. Now you got maybe a hundred nationwide. Most got hunted down to feed the Devil's addiction. The survivors converted to Christianity and pledged their lives to working for the Lord by hunting down those who worked for the Devil. Vampires. It took ten years to do it, but the werewolves banded together and shut 'em down. But legend has it that one of the original thirteen got away."

"The teenage girl with the gun," Pete says.

"Yeah, she's the one," Smokey confirms. "When Shelly was just a baby, me and my sons got a false tip about where we might find her. While we were out looking for her she came to the house and killed my wife."

Smokey's not a man to cry easily. But tonight, his eyes burn with both anger and loss. Pete puts a hand on the old warrior's shoulder, offering silent strength.

"Why didn't she kill the baby?" he asks.

"That's a question I've asked myself over and over again," says Smokey. "My best guess, it was because of the birthmark on Shelly's neck. It's a cross."

"A cross? I never saw any cross on her neck," says Pete.

"I know. She got so many questions about it over the years, she started to hide it with makeup," Smokey says.

A doctor enters the room. The conversation stops. The doctor wearily pours a cup of coffee. He leaves the room after a few moments.

"If they gave Satan what he wanted, why are they still vampires? If he gave them their souls back, wouldn't that make them human again?" says Pete.

"The Devil's a liar and the truth ain't in him," says Smokey flatly. "I'm guessing that he didn't make good on his part of the deal. The only one who can win you back your soul is Jesus Christ and ain't no vampire looking to meet him. Satan probably offered the vampires something else in exchange for the drugs. Maybe power or special spells. Witches love secrets."

"And they recruited drug dealers to drum up more business?" Pete ventures. "Or maybe he's bringing in some competition to keep his current supplier on her toes."

Before Smokey can respond, the waiting room doors swing open. A surgeon pops his head in. "Which one of you is Smokey James?" he asks. Smokey stands and nods.

"Your daughter's going to be alright. She lost a lot of blood, but we got her in time. It's the damnedest thing, when the medic found her somehow the bullet she was shot with was in her hand. It's like she pulled the bullet out of herself."

A few miles away from the hospital, Smokey's best friend, Doc Goldberg, is getting a good laugh reading an *Idiot's Guide to Werewolves*. Flipping through the book, Doc mutters to himself, "Wrong, wrong, hmmmm . . . gonna have to ask Smoke about that one." He hears his wife yell. He hauls himself out of the chair and waddles out the room and up the stairs. Sylvia loves to watch TV late at night. She's probably scared herself again watching some silly horror movie. Or the *Jerry Springer* show.

"Sylvia!" Doc calls out. "You okay in there? Honey?" He notices that the bedroom door is ajar. *That's odd.* Sylvia is always complaining about the house being drafty. She always closes the door when she crawls into bed. Just as he reaches the door and puts a hand to the knob, it opens. He is snatched inside.

Doc sees his wife in Mace's grip (or rather in his one good arm, Nate having chewed off the other one). She is feebly struggling to break free even as Mace drains the last drops of blood out of her. He makes a slurping sound as he drinks.

"Losing your wife is fucked up, ain't it, Doc?" Lou teases, pinning the smaller man to the wall with one hand.

Doc watches helplessly as Mace tosses Sylvia to the floor. She lies there like an empty soda can. Drained and empty.

"Oh no. No!" Doc sobs. Mace grins at him. The fresh blood flowing through his veins regenerates his lost limb. In minutes the new limb is complete. Mace flexes it, twirling it like a pitcher doing a windup. Then belches, noisily. He smiles sheepishly, like a dinner guest with bad table manners.

"You monster!" Doc hisses at them. "She never hurt you! She never hurt anybody!"

"And you!" he spits at Lou. "She was a mother to your wife. Anything Shelly needed she gave her. Food, money, a ride to the hospital after you beat her—"

"Shut up!" Lou growls viciously.

"Monster!" Doc curses. "That's what you are. That's all you'll ever be."

Lou bares his fangs. The two men glare at each other. "You piece of shit," Doc says. "What are you gonna do now? Kill me, too? Get it over with then. I'm not afraid of death!"

Malika enters the room, Smokey's medical file in her hand. "Oh no," she says. "We've got plans for you, Doctor. Big plans." Mace grabs Sylvia's dead body and places it on top of the bed.

"Get your hands off her!" Doc yells, struggling wildly against Lou's iron grip.

"Ease up, bro," Mace teases. "She'll be back. Right around sunset. All hungry and shit. And thirsty. Definitely thirsty."

"Fat bastard!" Doc throws at him.

"Takes one to know one," Mace replies with a speaking look at Doc's belly bulging out over the waist of his pants.

"Quiet," Malika commands. She stands by Doc as she reads his notes on Smokey. "Let's see, brain tumor, huh? Intense pain whenever he changes. Powers may become unstable as pressure on brain increases. Aw, how sad."

Lou releases Doc and the fat, little man falls to the floor like a sack of potatoes. "You don't realize it yet," Lou says, "but your big ass just switched sides. You're working for us now."

Malika unbuttons Doc's shirt and then lifts up his undershirt. She holds up her right hand, the fingernails becoming huge claws. She slashes Doc across his stomach. He screams. Malika enjoys that. She whispers in his ear, "You won't remember any of this. You'll go back down the stairs, sit in your favorite chair and go to sleep with a book in your hand, just like you always do. Tomorrow morning you'll wake up. And you'll climb up the stairs to check on your wife. You'll find her just as we've left her and with these words written on the walls in her blood: 'This time everybody dies.'" She ends with a light kiss on the top of his balding head. "You will hate Smokey for getting you involved in this fight. A part of you will want payback. A part of you already does. Just remember this: he trusts you. Use that against him."

Malika's a bitch but she's hellishly good at what she does. The next morning, everything goes down exactly as she said it would. Several neighbors say they heard the wails that Doc gave when he walked in to find his wife dead and her blood decorating the walls. None of them could make out the curses he yelled, but they say it sounded like he wanted to kill somebody.

• • •

It's Smokey's cell phone that wakes them. Smokey and Officer Pete have spent the night in Shelly's hospital room debating their next moves. Doc's call and the bad news about Sylvia is painful to hear but not a surprise. Malika has a well-established pattern of destroying anything Smokey loves.

"It's just a distraction," Pete argues. "They want us to check in on Doc and while we're doing that, they'll do the kid."

Shelly struggles to pull herself upright. The effort leaves her a little dizzy. "We need someone to tell us where they've got my son," she says. "Who would know?"

Smokey stretches and walks over to the tray beside Shelly's bed and pours himself a cup of water. Sometime today he'll have to make funeral arrangements for his two dead sons. He's damned if he'll bury a grandson, too.

"I can think of three people who could tell us what we want to know," Smokey begins. "The one they serve: Satan. The one they've killed: Sylvia."

Pete rubs his tired eyes. "Wait a minute. How's someone they've killed gonna tell us anything?"

"Doc said they drained his wife dry right before his eyes," Smokey says. "That means that this evening Sylvia will come back as a vampire. Even if she wasn't bitten by the lead vampire, she's got a psychic link to that bitch. They're all branches off the same vine."

Shelly hobbles over to her father and puts her hand on his shoulder. "Daddy, you mentioned three people who could tell us something. That's only two. Who's the third?"

Smokey turns to her. The look on his face is one she's never seen before. For the first time in her life, Shelly can see fear in her father's eyes. "The third choice would be Yusef. Anyone who battles him can get any question they want answered."

"What happens if you battle Yusef and you lose?" Pete asks.

"Then he claims the soul of the person you love the most," answers Smokey.

In its heyday, the Windsor was one of the flashiest hotels in the city. Now it holds an odd mix of working folks, the poor and people who are part of what some called the "underground economy": drugs, stolen goods, prostitution. You can find just about anything in the Windsor. So the smart thing to do if you live here is to keep your doors locked and your mouth shut.

This is where Shelly and Lou lived. If you can call that living. And these are the neighbors who always heard Shelly getting beat but never called 911.

And down the hall is Ugly Nikki's apartment. Nikki has opened his home to his undead friends. Other than a high school picture commemorating him being selected by the newspaper sports section for All-City as a linebacker, Nikki's apartment is a pink paradise of femininity.

There's a lot of pink. The walls are pink. The sofa is pink. The thick fabric covering the windows is pink. And don't forget about the stuffed animals. There's a pink army of them.

Nikki had redecorated in anticipation of his "change." The one where he finally got to show the world his inner woman. Unfortunately, he was bitten by a vampire the night before he was scheduled to have his "elective surgery." The vampire that bit him has spoiled Nikki ever since, trying to make up for taking away his dream.

Today that vampire is seated on Nikki's sofa reading e-mail when Mace walks in, running his hand up and down his new arm.

"How's your arm?" Malika asks, not looking up from her laptop.

"It's alright," Mace says. "Just a little stiff, that's all. Kept me up all day."

"It'll be that way for a few nights," Malika says. "Just remember, you can grow back anything except your head."

From the other room Lou shouts, "Cool, he never uses that anyway."

Lou walks up behind Malika, yawning, then kisses her and sneaks a peek at her computer screen. It's full of e-mail in a variety of languages.

"I move around a lot," she explains. "Europe. Asia."

"What about Africa?" Lou asks. "They got vampires in the Motherland?"

"Of course," Malika replies. "The Ashanti called them *obayifo*. They were witches that fed on the blood of children."

"They went after little kids?" Mace says. "That's kinda foul."

"Few things demoralize an enemy faster than turning his family against him. Or make it easier for someone to switch sides." She looks up from her computer screen at Lou.

"That's why we needed your son," she says. "His death is more than just a victory in battle. Snatching him demoralizes the entire family."

Lou sits at a small, circular glass-top dining table. He's rolling a silver bullet in his palm. He's been dreaming about Shelly the last few days. Remembering the good times.

"How about his mother? Is she a werewolf?" Malika asks.

"Shelly?" Lou wonders aloud. "Wow, I never thought about that. I don't know."

"Naw, she ain't one," Mace says.

"How the hell would you know?" Lou snaps.

Mace turns on the TV and sits on the sofa next to Malika. "Think about it," he explains. "As much as you went upside that bitch's head, if she was one, you'd know by now. She woulda changed and beat your ass."

"That girl still loves me, man," Lou brags. "Know how I know? She almost let me bite her at the game."

"Wait a minute," Malika says. "You beat your wife?"

"Don't listen to that nigga," Lou says. "He's exaggerating and shit. I mean, we did some arguing and maybe sometimes things got a little physical, but that's what married couples do, you know?"

Malika shuts off her computer. "Let me take a guess. You abused this woman in your first life and you're hoping to make it better by turning her into a vampire and living happily ever after?"

"I don't know," Lou lies. "Maybe."

"Nigga, please," Mace says. "Even if you turn her, first chance she gets, you're outta here."

"Yo, I don't remember asking your punk ass for advice," Lou shouts.

"No, Lou. He's right," Malika says, sitting down at the table. "Do you really want to spend the rest of eternity having to sleep with one eye open?"

"Exactly." Mace smirks.

"I don't know. I'm thinking if we talked, maybe things could be different now. Hell, I'm different now," Lou argues.

"No, you're not," Malika says.

Lou gets up in a huff, ready to walk out of the room but Malika grabs him.

"The next time you see her I want you to kill her," Malika says.

"What?" Lou replies.

"You heard me," Malika says. "Drain every last drop out of her. She's food. Nothing more, nothing less."

Lou ponders a moment. "Shit ain't that simple, yo. She's my wife. I used to love her. Maybe I still do."

"No, Lou. She's your weakness. And that weakness could get you killed."

Lou pulls out of Malika's grip and walks into the other room.

"Think he'll do it?" Mace asks, toying with the idea of following Lou to tease him about Shelly some more. He loved to get a rise out of that nigga.

Mace suddenly notices Malika stripping off her top. She pulls Mace toward her and begins to undress him. "Lou doesn't want love," she says. "He wants control. That's what all men want."

She pushes Mace onto the floor, then shimmies out of her panties and straddles him, her lower lips singing to his manhood. Every time he reaches for her, she pushes his hands away. The sex is loud, hot and nasty. Hearing them, Lou walks back into the room. He watches. Malika has Mace pinned to the ground and sweating to the point of collapse. She turns to look back at Lou.

"Here's a little secret, boys: you don't control us," Malika says, tightening her pelvic muscles so that Mace moans on cue. "We control you. Now come here," she beckons to Lou. And he does.

Sundown. Doc's house. After the wild screams they heard last night, his neighbors are keeping their distance. But everybody is watching. And waiting.

As Smokey, Pete and Shelly climb out of Pete's squad car, Smokey pulls a spear the size of a man's arm out of the backseat and hands it to Shelly.

"What's this?" she asks.

"A gift from Yusef. A stabbing spear from our ancestors. It will make anyone it touches answer any question you ask. You might want to use it on Sylvia."

Shelly holds the spear in her hands, examining the symbols etched on it.

"So you already fought him once? And lived to talk about it," Pete says, clearly impressed. "What did you ask him?" Pete says, while unbuttoning his shirt to reveal his gold cross.

"I asked him if he would help me find the monster that murdered my wife," Smokey says. "Yusef held out the stabbing spear and said, 'When the child becomes a mother, darkness will flee the cross.'" Both men turn to look at Shelly. She starts to say something, but whatever the words are, they get swallowed in the sound of Doc's screams.

The chilling screams die away as they climb the front steps. "Spread out," Pete cautions. "And yell if you see anything." He heads into the living room. Smokey takes the stairs leading to the bedroom. Shelly walks to the rear of the house.

Both Smokey and Shelly race into the living room at Pete's yell. It's a horrible sight. They find what used to be Sylvia. This undead creature knocks away Pete's gun and sends him flying across the room and crashing into a wall-sized bookcase. She's bleeding from several bullet wounds. Smokey had prepped Pete with wooden bullets. The rookie cop fired them all. None of them struck her heart. They only pissed her off. Pete scrambles for a weapon as Sylvia moves in for the kill. He grabs a floor lamp and uses it to hold her at bay.

"Sylvia!" yells Smokey in a loud voice. She stops. A look of faint remembrance and intelligence crosses her vacant face. She recognizes her old friend. But the dark thirst is strong. And it doesn't have friends.

Smokey attempts to transform, straining, sweating and swearing.

Pete sees the old man's eyes shift from brown to bloodred, then back to their normal color.

"Damn it!" Smokey says. *Gonna have to do this shit the hard way.*

"On three, Pete! One. Two. Three." Smokey hurls himself at Sylvia, tackling her. Pete jumps on top. Sylvia easily throws off both men.

A sharp barking erupts behind her. "Mr. Big!" Sylvia gushes, her face lightening. "Come to Mommy, boy. Come to Mommy!" The little dog barks angrily, his teeth bared.

As Sylvia approaches the dog, she catches sight of herself in a wall mirror. She is shocked into stillness. Her body is human but her head is a fleshless skull crawling with maggots. She screams and tosses a book at the mirror, shattering it.

"Miss Sylvia," Shelly calls softly.

Sylvia turns and finds Shelly standing beside her. Shelly has Yusef's spear aimed at Sylvia's chest. Shelly drives the spear into the vampire's foot, pinning Sylvia to the floor. Pete and Smokey rise to their feet.

"Sylvia, tell me where my son is," demands Shelly. Sylvia trembles and thrashes against the power of the spear. But the magic is too strong.

"The Windsor," she grits out through clenched teeth. Shelly yanks the spear out of the vampire's foot and she collapses, moaning.

"Good-bye," Shelly whispers, choking back tears. She takes a firm grip on Yusef's spear, raises it high and brings it down quickly, slamming it deep into Sylvia's chest. The woman Shelly loves like a mother bursts into flame, then turns into dust.

Pete walks over to the carpet stain that used to be Sylvia. "Any sign of her husband?" Pete asks.

"Let me worry about that," Smokey says.

"We gotta go," Shelly says. "Sun's down. They may have already started on Ricky. We have to hurry!"

"Bitch, you ain't going nowhere," says a voice from behind Shelly. As she turns around, she's sucker-punched with an uppercut to the jaw. Shelly falls to the floor, dropping Yusef's spear. Shelly looks up at Ugly Nikki. He's dressed as Diana Ross in *Lady Sings the Blues,* with a gardenia coyly tucked behind one ear. Nikki kicks off his high heels and pops off his earrings.

"And once I'm through with you," Nikki yells, "I'm having them for dessert."

"Oh damn!" Pete says to Smokey. "Isn't that Ugly Nikki?"

"Oh no, you didn't!" Nikki says. "That was just out-and-out rude!"

Shelly reaches for the spear but Nikki beats her to the punch. "Sorry babe," he says with false sympathy. "But I ain't nobody's shish kebob!" Nikki kicks the spear across the room.

Mr. Big barks. Nikki turns and sees the little dog with one of his shoes in its mouth. "Now wait a minute, Rover," Nikki pleads. "Those are Manolo Blahniks! You don't know how much those cost . . ."

A growl comes from behind Nikki. It's not Mr. Big. Nikki glances back over his shoulder and sees a wolf in the same spot where he last saw Shelly. A big hairy wolf. With issues.

"It's bad enough my man was cheating on me," the wolf says. "But you could at least be cute."

"Well, if you were woman enough to address his needs . . ." Nikki throws back, hands on hips.

"What do you know about being a woman?" Shelly growls. "Look at your makeup!"

"Bitch!" Nikki yells, "I'll have you know that I am twice the woman your little furry ass could ever be!"

"What did you call me?" Shelly growls, padding closer.

The wolf grabs Nikki by the throat. The battle is on. The two fall to the floor, trading blows until Nikki kicks Shelly off him. She skids across the room, right next to Yusef's spear. She and Nikki both see it at the exact same time.

"You know you can't beat me without it," Nikki taunts. "Punk bitch."

Without grabbing the spear, Shelly jumps on top of Nikki and clamps her jaws on his wig. Her teeth bite down. Hard. And into Nikki's skull.

With one savage twist she completely rips Nikki's head off.

She trots over to the window and tosses the wig-covered head out the window and into the street. On the way down, it bursts into flames. The neighbors don't know what it is, but one little boy tells his class the next day that he saw fireworks.

"Good riddance, you ugly, bald-headed bitch," Shelly says, back in human form. "Those were some nice shoes, though."

The *Windsor is thick with vampires* as Shelly, Pete and Smokey fight their way inside. Both men fire guns with garlic-coated bullets, drawing attention away from Shelly.

Shelly heads for the stairs. It's seven flights up but the elevator's out of service. She has almost reached the entrance to the stairwell when Mace appears before her. He lands between her and the door. He towers above her, an evil blend of both muscle and menace.

"What's up, girl?" Mace says. "Where you think you going?"

He tackles her, pinning her to the ground. Mace laughs. This is too easy. He's still laughing when a wolf's claw razors through his neck, sending his head flying across the room.

That was too easy, thinks Shelly.

Shelly disappears into the stairwell. Her baby is somewhere up there. She isn't leaving without him.

Upstairs, Shelly follows the lead Sylvia gave them. Her intuition tells her that Lou will not have hidden him far. He is too lazy. Sure enough, she finds Ricky in her old apartment, tied hand and foot to a chair, Malika standing over him.

Ricky's tired face lights up at the sight of her. But falls again quickly. "Mom! Get out of here. Run! Run!" he yells.

"No, son," Shelly says. "No more running."

"Aww, how sweet. Has Mommy come to save her baby?" Malika taunts as she opens Ricky's shirt to expose his neck.

Behind her, Lou steps out of the shadows. "Hey, baby," he says to Shelly. "I been thinking about you."

"Yeah, right," Ricky says sarcastically, rolling his eyes in disgust.

"Shut up, nigga!" Lou yells. "This is grown folks talking." He walks over and stands behind Malika. The vampire begins kissing Ricky on the neck. The boy's blood rises, despite himself. And between his legs he can feel something else rising.

"Baby, I just want you to know that a part of me still loves you," Lou tells Shelly. He ignores his son completely.

"Let him go," Shelly pleads. "Let him go and I'll stay."

"Mom, no!" Ricky moans, enjoying Malika's touch and hating himself for it.

"Good times and bad, I loved you, girl," Lou says soulfully to his wife. His eyes are still locked on hers when he draws a wooden stake. He raises it in the air. And slams it into Malika's back so deep that it pierces all the way to her black heart. "But I got to do what's good for Lou, you know what I'm saying?" he whispers.

Malika screams. She falls to the ground, desperately trying to twist around to pull out the stake. In seconds all that's left is ashes.

Lou laughs. "That bitch thought 'cause she could read minds, she was always one step ahead of the game. But what I noticed was that the more I thought about you, the madder this bitch got. She played herself."

"So you'll let our son go?" Shelly asks. But she already knows the answer.

"I'm afraid I can't do that," Lou says. He takes a short step away from Ricky and back into the deep shadows.

A second later he tosses out the badly beaten but still-breathing bodies of Smokey and Pete. They land with a grunt at Shelly's feet.

"I got the Prince of Darkness himself jonesing for that kid. But you can have these two, if you want them."

Shelly helps her injured father over to the sagging sofa. He's been both beaten and shot. He looks like he's living on nothing more than force of will. The spirit is strong but the body is failing.

"Come on, Lou," Shelly says. "Let's deal. You got something I want and I got something you want. Let our son go and I'm yours, Lou. All yours."

"Oh really." Lou laughs. "You got something that I want? Ain't but one person got what I want, bitch. And he wants this!" And Lou buries his fangs into his son's neck. He drinks deep. Then he abruptly raises his head, spitting out the blood he's tasted.

"Oh shit," Lou says, looking at a laughing Ricky. "This nigga ain't no virgin!"

Ricky chuckles. "I got three words for you, Dad: Tasty Boom-Boom. My uncles chipped in on an early birthday present for my sweet sixteen. Thought you knew."

"Oh shit," Lou mutters. "That motherfucker knew. Satan played me." And with those words, the room fills with evil laughter.

Shelly notices Pete coming to and whispers to him quickly, "Get my father and son out of here."

"Alright. But what about you?"

Shelly pulls out Yusef's spear. "Me and my husband have a dinner date," she snarls.

As quick as lightning, Lou pulls out his silver-bullet gun, firing off a round at Shelly.

Still standing, Shelly smiles and opens her blouse. A bulletproof vest. It pays to have a brother in law enforcement.

"Ricky was right," Shelly chides. "You don't pay attention. See back in the apartment that night, it wasn't my father that ripped you to shreds. It was me. Didn't you notice that the claw ripping you apart was wearing a wedding band? The same cheap-ass gold band you bought me."

Damn her! Lou tosses a folding chair at Shelly. She ducks it easily. It clatters against the wall.

Shelly is moving so fast she's almost invisible. Lou doesn't even see her until she slashes her lying husband's face. Before he can lift a hand, she reappears in front of the door. Blood is running down Lou's face from the deep slash marks, blinding him. He blinks. Wipes away the blood. And Shelly is gone.

Lou points his gun at Ricky. "Where is she?" he shouts.

A wolf's claw emerges out of Lou's chest squeezing his still-beating heart. "Nobody fucks with my family," Shelly growls.

Lou looks down. There's a huge hole in his chest. But wait, that bitch he killed said he could grow back anything except a head. With that twisted thought, he points the gun at his son and squeezes the trigger.

Suddenly, a wavy blur comes between Ricky and the oncoming bullet. Smokey falls to the floor in human form, a bullet wound in his chest.

Lou laughs. He struggles to his feet, grabs Pete by his shirt, then heads for the hallway, dragging Pete behind him.

Ricky gets free and runs over to the fallen Smokey and cradles his head. He whispers in his ear, "Don't you die on me, Granddad. Come on, man!"

"Good-bye, Daddy," Shelly says. She kisses her father on the cheek. Ricky wails. She can still hear her son's anguish as she runs out of the room, Yusef's spear raised high.

In the hallway outside, Lou is dragging Pete inside an elevator. He feels light-headed from blood loss. He needs to feed. He pulls Pete close, prepared to drain every last drop of blood out of the cop when he feels something looking down on him. He looks up and sees . . .

Shelly. Standing upside down on the ceiling of the elevator. Shelly drives the spear through the center of Lou's forehead, pinning him to the back wall of the elevator. Lou jerks like a speared fish. His hands reach for the spear but don't have the strength to remove it. Then he sees Shelly coming back.

Shelly changes into a form that is part woman and part wolf. She raises her claws and rips. Lou's head remains pinned to the wall by the spear, but his body falls to the floor. Both parts erupt into flame, then turn to dust. There is a faint sound of demonic laughter but the joke's on Lou.

Shelly transforms back to human form and pulls Yusef's stabbing spear from the wall. "Consider that a divorce," she says.

She drops to the floor by Pete, and they enjoy their first kiss.

"Thank you," she says.

"Mom!" Ricky screams.

Shelly and Pete race back into the apartment. Inside they find Ricky still holding on to Smokey's corpse. He is now surrounded by the ghostly skeletons of werewolves. One stands on its hind legs and walks as a man over to Smokey, its body magically assuming full flesh and muscle until what stands in the room is a tall, African prince with the head of a wolf. Yusef.

Shelly recognizes him from her dreams. Yusef gently cradles Smokey's body in his arms as if he were a newborn babe. The wolf spirits begin to howl in unison. It's an unearthly and haunting sound. A bright light fills the room; then Smokey and Yusef disappear. The other ghosts fade away.

"Ow! It's burning!" yells Ricky, clutching his arm.

Shelly walks over and rips off the boy's right shirtsleeve. Underneath is the family brand, the wolf's head still steaming. It's a birthday present he'll never forget.

A day later, a few minutes before dawn, Shelly finds Doc sitting on a swing at the local playground. The vampire bite on his neck is still clearly visible.

"Pretty this time of day," Doc says. "Quiet. Like the world's thinking."

"Or praying," Shelly adds. "Daddy always prayed at sunrise."

"Your father was a good man, Shelly. I know you'll do him

proud. We'll be rooting for you," he adds. And then he turns to face the rising sun. And turns to dust.

Mr. Big shuffles over sadly. Shelly picks up the little dog and as they begin to walk home, she thinks about how blessed she is to have family. Both two-legged and four-legged.

'Cause there are monsters out there.

And, sometimes, you gotta fight back.